Hilda

A to

hope y.

Kelvin McMichael

COMING HOME
IN THE DARK

Born in Te Kuiti in 1941, Owen Marshall graduated with an MA (Hons) from the University of Canterbury and a Diploma in Teaching from Christchurch Teachers' College.

The author of seven short story collections and a novel, Owen Marshall has won many awards for his writing, including the PEN Lillian Ida Smith Award for Fiction in 1986 and 1988, the 1987 American Express Short Story Award and, in 1990, the Queen Elizabeth II Arts Council Award for Achievement. He held the University of Canterbury Literary Fellowship in 1981, the New Zealand Literary Fund Scholarship in Letters in 1988 and the Robert Burns Fellowship at Otago University in 1992.

Other books by the same author

Supper Waltz Wilson, Pegasus, 1979
The Master of Big Jingles, McIndoe, 1982
The Day Hemingway Died, McIndoe, 1984
The Lynx Hunter, McIndoe, 1987
The Divided World, McIndoe, 1989
Tomorrow We Save the Orphans, McIndoe, 1992
The Ace of Diamonds Gang, McIndoe, 1993
Burning Boats (editor), Longman Paul, 1994
Letter From Heaven (editor), Longman Paul, 1995
A Many Coated Man, Longacre, 1995

Owen Marshall

Coming Home
in the Dark

𝒱

VINTAGE

In memory of my Father

Random House New Zealand Ltd
(An imprint of the Random House Group)

18 Poland Road
Glenfield
Auckland 10
NEW ZEALAND

Sydney   New York   Toronto
London   Auckland   Johannesburg
and agencies throughout the world

First published 1995

© Owen Marshall 1995

Printed in Australia
ISBN 1 86941 266 4

All rights reserved. No part of this publication may be reproduced
or transmitted in any form or by any means, electronic or
mechanical, including photocopying, recording, storage in any
information retrieval system or otherwise, without the written
permission of the publisher.

CONTENTS

Acknowledgements

Some of the stories in this collection have been previously published or broadcast:

'Working Up North' (Radio New Zealand)
'The Occasion' (Radio New Zealand)
'Cometh the Hour' (*Listener*)
'Not a Visitor' (*Metro*, Radio New Zealand, *Sunday Star*)
'Recollections of MKD' (*Sport*)
'The Tank Boat' (*Crossing*, Australian/New Zealand anthology, Reed Australia)
'Pendragon' (Radio New Zealand)
'Prairie Nights' (Radio New Zealand)
'Peacock Funeral' (Radio New Zealand)
'Genesis' (Radio New Zealand)
'Cass Robbins' (*Quote Unquote*)
'Living at the Belle Monde' (Radio New Zealand)
'Goodbye, Stanley Tan' (*Landfall*)
'Flute and Chance' (Radio New Zealand)
'A Late Run' (Radio New Zealand)

WORKING UP NORTH

MY OLDER BROTHER arranged a job for me as a fish splitter in Nelson and I travelled up to Blenheim by train and then to Nelson by bus the next day. In the Rai Valley an old Bedford truck loaded with pumpkins had run off the road and lay overturned like a beetle amidst the pig fern, with the brilliant orange and yellow pumpkins scattered alongside.

We were the first to come across it and the bus driver posted people to warn traffic, then he and a thickset woman who said she was a physical education specialist decided to comfort the truck driver who had a broken wrist. The rest of us stood around to appreciate the novelty of it. The truck driver was quiet and self-reliant. I think that having a busload of gawpers at his mishap was the worst thing about it as far as he was concerned.

The pumpkin crash meant that we were late into Nelson and if there had been anyone to meet me, there wasn't any longer. I left my bag and walked down to Golden Seafoods on the waterfront. There was a blue sky, but also a strong wind that put grit in your face and stirred up the shallow water to make a dirty mix which slapped among the jetty piles and broke along the sea wall of the road to Tahunanui.

Golden Seafoods (1974 Ltd), it said on the wooden sign, and there was a picture newly glossed of a crab with its pincers up and what looked like a groper. I went past the small window of the direct to the public sales and further down to the large sliding door of the factory, where I got a good whiff of the fish, rubber and damp clothes that made the atmosphere of the place. A small man with blue gumboots and hair like a dunny brush was hosing out the place with such force that tides of water washed through the door and ruffled there in the wind. I stepped on a pallet to keep dry till he saw me. He raised a hand to show that he had, then finished off the job.

'Just having a good swill out for the day,' he said. 'This chop has meant there's not much coming in and gives me a chance to catch up. I guess you're another McGarry. You've got the look of your brother.' He spoke loudly into the wind, but the stiff, white crest of his hair moved not a bit with the force of it. 'Another soft-palmed varsity wallah is all we need,' he said with a grin as we went into the big shed of the factory. 'You fixed up for somewhere to stay?'

I knew this must be Mr Trubb, who was Golden Seafoods. I knew that he had five boats and the factory, three retail outlets, some big contracts, a stake in a helicopter safari business on the Coast, and that he expected all his employees to work hard and toiled more than any of them himself. 'I haven't got anything fixed up,' I said. 'I've just got in and my bag's still at the depot, but I don't want to be any trouble.'

Of course I was happy to have his help, so I ended up sitting in the factory to escape the wind, with the concrete floor a glistening shadow, while Mr Trubb finished his cleaning. All the factory staff had gone early, because there wasn't much catch in and he saw the opportunity to have a good dung out. When he'd finished with the water hose he did some of the plant with superheated steam. A nasty way to have an accident, it seemed to me. I did offer to help, but Mr Trubb said I'd have the chance soon enough. He shouted through the steam that my brother used to put in a fair day's work for a fair day's pay and I could see that some sort of bench mark was expected of me. There were stainless steel-rimmed tables, drip trays, trolleys, plastic and waxed boxes, a line of freezers and a rack of rubber aprons like new pelts. I guessed that it would all dwindle to the apparatus of monotony soon enough.

Mr Trubb had the build of a sixteen-year-old, and the full

head of hair, though grey, added to the impression of youthfulness at a distance. But not so nimble anymore and close up you saw how lined and worn was his dark skin and how the veins stood out over his arms and neck. He had a green 4.2 Jaguar and he said that he'd pick up my gear if I liked and take me to Chandler's where several of his casuals stayed. First he had three boxes of fillets to deliver to the Brightwater Hotel and as we drove he told me that he'd lived all his life in Nelson; left school at fourteen to begin nailing apple boxes and by eighteen had his own truck, which he drove between Nelson and Blenheim most of the day and night. You can't do that sort of thing now, he said.

As an ex-truck driver, Mr Trubb was interested in my story of the Bedford and the pumpkins in the Rai Valley. He thought probably a blowout caused the load to shift. There's a knack to loading a truck, just as there's a knack to building a haystack. Mr Trubb told me a good deal of the way he'd become established in the world. It didn't seem to be so much boastfulness as a wish to show the rest of us what hard slog leads to. He saw himself as no different from anyone else and wanted others to have the satisfaction of getting on through hard yakker. He seemed rather surprised when I told him that my brother had gone overseas for a spell.

At the Brightwater Hotel I helped carry in the big cartons. 'Duck under a load,' said Mr Trubb, 'rather than lifting it to your own height. It's a good lesson, that.' Mr Trubb was paid in cash and he shouted beer, which we drank inside because of the wind, and when he realised I hadn't had any lunch, he bought chips and pan-fried fish — his own, I guess. 'Go on, go on,' he said. 'We'll sweat it out of you tomorrow. One thing I've learnt is that you've got to eat well to work well. You ever done any real farm work? You can judge a farmer's savvy by the meals he gives his shearers and musterers.'

Mr Trubb had a packet of cheroots, thin and dark like himself, and he'd smoked two of them and eaten his food before I'd finished my fish. 'If you don't mind,' he said, 'we'll just drive a few miles up the Lee Valley. There's this hill property that I might be interested in, though not at the money that's being talked at the moment.'

It was lovely, quiet up the Lee. The river itself was small and clear in a rock bed, and the hills were being greened up with pine plantings. The no exit road wasn't much wider than the Jaguar and on the small river flats the wind showed itself as muted flurries in the long grass. Mr Trubb stopped the Jaguar in a paddock gateway that had a bit of height over the property he was interested in; quite steep country and some of it gorsed, but with the Lee Stream in a series of small cascades below. 'I reckon there's a different sort of tourism coming,' he told me. 'More people want to stay in the country, not city hotels.'

He had this idea for a lodge above the river and the whole farm around it for privacy — hundreds of hectares. He didn't want to let on to the owners about those plans, of course. 'Keep it under your hat,' said Mr Trubb with easy familiarity, as if I was someone he'd relied on for years. The late afternoon sun slanted down the valley and we went out into the wind and looked across to the terrace where Mr Trubb thought he'd build the lodge, long and single-storeyed to be in keeping. 'What do you think?' he said and I was close enough to see the veins standing out from his neck and the small skin cancers on his face and arms from years of sweat in the Nelson sun.

I appreciated being treated as an equal, as if I had already proved myself a toiler at Golden Seafoods, but I didn't want to presume. If he had to come into the factory in a day or two and give me a rocket over something then it would make it more embarrassing. 'The Asians,' said Mr Trubb, 'they jump at anything like this. We don't realise how lucky we are to live here. The best air and water in the world.' At the head of the valley was the sheen of old serpentine workings and there was a scattered mob of Hereford steers on the river flat. Among the green of the young pines on the far slope were the rust-coloured branches from the last pruning. There were briars close to us on the roadside and the berries had a summer burnish. Not one vehicle had passed us since we arrived, yet we must have been within half an hour of the city.

Mr Trubb walked back to the Jaguar and stood by the door for a moment. Then he leant forward and said something I didn't catch, before he slipped to his left along the flank of the car, which partly supported him. His body slid, taking the fine dust from the polished paintwork beneath. He lay in the grass by the car and when I knelt down I could hear his altered breathing, which was oddly similar to the noise that the wind was making in the wheel arch of the car. One of his eyelids was almost closed and a trouser leg snagged on a briar as I lifted him. The suddenness of it made me swear a good deal for relief.

There was a moment, with Mr Trubb belted in the front seat and the Jaguar's automatic roughly sorted out to get me to Brightwater, when I had a sudden, passing amazement that everything in the valley was just the same. The green and brown of the pines unaltered, the steers still filling their guts, the cascade of the Lee, the utterly indifferent whine and pulse of the wind.

A stroke rather than a heart attack, so I was told, and Mr Trubb died a few days afterwards, despite putting in some hard work to stay alive. I couldn't settle at Golden Seafoods and for the rest of the vacation dug potters' clay at Mapua and then did some fruit picking in the Upper Moutere. When the new term started I was lucky to get offered a ride from Nelson down through the Lewis and we passed the turn-off to the Lee Valley on the way. I had a glimpse of the Brightwater pub again. I'd been a couple of months in the Nelson district and yet afterwards I always associated the whole time with three things from that very first day — the pumpkin smash in the Rai Valley, Mr Trubb and his vision of the lodge, and that damn, persistent wind.

THE OCCASION

ON THEIR WAY to the North Island they had one night in the Astle Motels, Picton, before they were to cross over on the ferry. The motels were concrete block, painted cream both inside and out, so that several times that evening it took Mervyn a moment to recall if he'd come inside, or was still standing outside. There was a shower so confined that it felt like a coffin. 'Oh, it's only for one night, isn't it,' his wife said. 'One night won't kill you.'

The owners, the Perrits, had four units near the steep road, then their own home that looked as though it, too, was painted cream inside and out, then a long strip of lawn, with a faded trampoline to justify the phrase, children's play area, in the brochure. Right at the back, by a Japanese box hedge, was a tin garden shed with high windows.

Mervyn had these pills for what ailed him and after he'd taken a couple he couldn't settle to watch the game show on the television. Whoever was going to win the family sedan, the trip with spending money to Los Angeles, or be dismissed with just the sponsor's products, seemed a long way from the Astle Motels. Mervyn walked past units two, three and four, each resounding with the same game show host, past the Perrits' house. It was dark and the lights of the town glowed below with a spurious magnificence ending abruptly at the sea's edge.

He climbed on to the trampoline, gingerly lest it disintegrate beneath his weight. Much of the elasticity seemed weathered out of it. Rocking gently there, oddly reassured by the movement, he was high enough to see directly into the window of the lit garden shed, where Mrs Perrit was dancing among laundry powders, empty cartons, and heaped net curtains like Kleenex, which had long ago hung in all the units.

Mervyn had never been introduced to Mrs Perrit, had never heard her voice, knew nothing of her life beyond that day; had seen her just the once before, standing behind her husband and sucking her teeth as Mervyn signed in. Yet, oscillating four feet above the lawn in the summer night, Mervyn glimpsed her in some most private transport of euphoria, dancing by herself in the tin shed. She wore a sleeveless print dress, cut unkindly so that the puckered flesh and hair of her armpits were displayed when she raised her hands to place the palms together. She closed her eyes as she spun as if better to establish the consummate surroundings in which her dance was set. Mrs Perrit was a large, clumsy woman in Picton, who apparently wished to be set free. Her hair was lacklustre and her movements of absurd gentility.

The psychiatrist later was at pains to point out to Mervyn that of course everything at the Astle Motels was the occasion of his breakdown and not in any way the cause. He found it interesting and important to have Mervyn realise that the dancing, the trampoline, all of it, was merely a conjunction of phenomena. Mervyn had not been driven mad by Mrs Perrit's dancing in the back shed. No, there was a complex series of factors going way back that took a good deal of the psychiatrist's time, and a good deal of Mervyn's money, to identify.

Mervyn knew that his doctor was right, that the dancing Mrs Perrit wasn't to blame, but always afterwards when he thought of his illness, or when he felt very low in himself — how are you, in yourself, Mervyn, his wife would say — then he felt again suspended, oscillating in a summer night, while watching poor, desperate Mrs Perrit dancing in the hope of who knows what release. It was a parody that struck deep into Mervyn's heart.

He saw, as if the wind had turned suddenly, that the whole splendid ballet of life casts larger shadows, which are the jig of death.

Mervyn had crept down from the trampoline, walked back to his Ford Falcon by the concrete motel unit, and sat with the door open, reciting in sequence of purchase all the cars that he had ever owned. That's where his wife found him eventually. The first one, he told her gently, the very first, was a second-hand 1936 Morris Eight older than himself, and it was two-toned, black and a wonderful scarlet, and the doors were hinged behind the seat so that if they opened while you drove they could scoop in the whole world.

COMETH THE HOUR

THE SUN LAY stretched in the evening and summer sky, the weeping elms sighed and rustled in the cat's-paws of the easterly, and Crimmond's Alsatian, like a wine taster, raised its head to the promise of night. James Cumuth paused at the doorway of his wooden sleepout before going in at the end of his working day. Tall and spare he stood there, holding his left arm with his right hand in an odd posture of relaxation. In his urban backpack, as well as items from the Super-Doop store, were the latest copy of *International Creative Scientist*, his plastic lunchbox with the Gladwrap folded ready to reuse, and a piece of driftwood shaped rather less like a dolphin than he had first thought. In his jacket pocket was the half-size manila envelope that held his bonus from Palmer's Product Testing.

Cumuth wasn't insensible to the attractions of the natural world, though his was essentially a life of the mind. He registered the subsiding sun, the elms, his landlady's clumped irises, even the gleam of condition on the Alsatian's pelt as it cast an oblique glance to ensure that he hadn't ventured on to Crimmond property. It was all a banality, though, wasn't it? Cumuth still awaited some mission worthy of him: some palpable need that would justify the cool, implacable resolution he felt inside.

In the neatness of his one room he emptied the bag in a manner that did not lessen the order. It was the neatness of a man who puts no store on possessions: a travelling, on-the-road man who, by whim or principle, could pack in half an hour and blow, leaving nothing of himself behind. He took his one chair to the open door where he sat in the rectangle of amber sun and read from *International Creative Scientist* the Popoffvich article on salinity trends in large European catchment lakes.

Cumuth had not forgotten his bonus envelope, but it remained unopened. A cursory thing. He knew that he was not considered a valued employee and he knew from experience that Paul Bigelow was right when he said that the rich have a touching faith in the efficacy of small sums. At Palmer's Product Testing Cumuth's task that week was the deter-mination of epidermal resistal material in Paree Natural Parfume Creme after atmospheric exposure — in other words how thick a skin was likely to form on the top when the lid was left off. A man doesn't establish a personal creed on such things.

Cumuth had a BSc, but more than that he had a pioneer ancestry: lean men who had walked slow and tall through their time, proudly reticent men who could spit a double metre from the side of their mouth, without leaving a trace on their chin, when they heard a personal vanity spoken. Solitary men with a natural focus on mountain peaks, even the stars above them. Such men despise the even tenor of the life of the mass of citizenry and wait with a quiet half-smile for a challenge sufficiently cataclysmic to justify their acceptance. Their progeny are not numerous, for such pioneers are loath to spill their seed recklessly.

Cumuth himself told no one of such things of course, never consciously exalted himself. It was more a disposition, a detachment of view. He knew, however, that his paternal grandfather had done something in the war so special that no one spoke of it. So he sat in the open doorway of his sleepout, letting the dying sun copper his aquiline features and listening to the soughing of the elms.

Mrs Burmeister, his landlady, watched from the kitchen window and talked with her divorced daughter. I reckon he's a sandwich short of a picnic, she said. He's sunning himself with his mouth open. You could fart in his face and he'd still look at the mountains. Nadine gave her low, even laugh, full of knowing derision concerning men. A loser, she said. A loser with bells on. Neither mother nor daughter set much store by taciturn, frontier values.

He always seems to look past you, said Mrs Burmeister.

Always has an idiot half-smile, said Nadine.

James Cumuth was aware of them at the periphery of his line of sight, aware of the tilt of the Alsatian's muzzle also and the pulsation of the Harley Davidson, about two blocks away he reckoned. The magazine had fallen to the floor in the doorway and his hands were relaxed in the dying sun. The hands of a pianist, or a fighter pilot. When the hog was out of earshot it was quiet in the suburb, but not too quiet.

In the labs at Palmer's, Mrs Burmeister's opinion of James Cumuth was unknown, yet shared nevertheless. He was a loner all right. He was the cat that walked by himself. A one man band, that's for sure. Odd ball city, all right. He was a queer fish. He contributed little to the harmless gossip and advantageous obsequiousness of the staff cafeteria. He drank his coffee black, his bourbon neat and if he was looking out of the third floor lab window at the small people scurrying below when Errol Golightly PhD came around, then he made no pretence to be doing anything but that, watching the small people scurrying.

You can see that he wasn't one for cultivating the approval of other people and he had this habit of screwing up his eyes a bit and looking into the far distance as if to check for some menace there. One or two women at Palmer's, and one or two men, were initially attracted to his steady silence and his slender hands, but they found he meant no invitation by them. The personnel manager said that there was no reason for family pride; that Cumuth was brought up by an uncle who ran a video parlour and that he lived in a one-room sleepout over in Kodacks. No truth at all, he said, in the idea that Cumuth was part Easter Island chief on his mother's side. None at all.

And people don't like idiosyncrasy in a quiet person, whereas in a boisterous one they see it as being just hard case behaviour. Now that's the truth. Cumuth wore tan stock boots; always he wore them, when everyone knew that there wasn't any stock for miles and miles around. Even way out of the city what you got was crops, horticulture and stuff. Everyone knew that. Aaron Schoone came from the country. He'd survived out there for years and he said nobody wore stock boots. Glasshouses and orchards and nurseries and poultry farms were the things out there, Aaron told the cafeteria crowd at Palmer's Product Testing.

Once they had this full-day professional motivation course run by Clarence Best Associates and Cumuth came in a full twenty minutes late after lunch and never said as much as a word, but walked slowly to his chair and screwed up his eyes a little and put his left stock boot on his right knee — after he'd sat down of course.

On the fourteenth, Wesley Igor Drom, the notorious garrottist and entrail fetishist, broke out of the maximum security institution at Happy Glades with a body count of twelve. Some papers said more. Drom moved through the pigeon blue summer dusk like a kauri tree stump. He bit a man half to death at the motorway overbridge and even took flowers without paying from a little boutique next to the Bonafide Dance Academy and the waterbed shop. Blazing red roses, the boutique lady said and when the top psychiatrist being interviewed on television was told that, he said, ooh, red you say, ooh, now that's not a good sign by a long chalk.

The Enderby twins were roller skating at the Kodacks rink on the night of the fourteenth. Normally they'd be safe home, but it was Easter Mulheron's birthday and a whole bunch of them were skating before being picked up. Wesley Drom, irritated by the noise, crippled the gatekeeper with a twist of his left hand and took the Enderby twins as lightweight hostages. Tucked both of them under one arm, it was said, so that their blonde ringlets hung in the night. The armed offenders squads were all over, but no sign, and they had to be careful because of the twins.

To Mrs Drom, Wesley Igor was just her boy who took a wrong turning, I suppose: to the city he was the nation's galvanised degeneracy, and to James Cumuth he was manifest destiny.

Mrs Burmeister and Nadine were woken by the sound of Drom beating the Lewis-Smythes so that they would rustle up a breakfast for him in quick time. Dawn is a good time for screams to carry. Cumuth was at the door of the sleepout when his landlady came out on to the verandah and she told him all she knew about Drom and the breakout from television. Sweet Jesus, she said, that'll be him all right, murdering someone.

Oh God, he's at it. Right here and he's killing everybody, said Nadine. He's butchering people and there's nothing to be done. She stood in her pink, candlewick dressing gown and pressed both hands to her throat.

James Cumuth reached back into his sleepout for his boots and sat on the step to draw them on. There is a bleak, steely quality to the first dawn light and it seemed reflected in JC's eyes as he ran a hand through his hair before going over to the house of the Lewis-Smythes. You can't do anything there, said Nadine. You'll get torn to pieces. Jesus yes, but for the first time there was an uncertain note in her derision. Cumuth looked past her as ever and gave his half-smile redolent with a stoical serenity. He walked across the lawn belonging to the Crimmonds and the Alsatian bounded towards him with its ears back and lip up, but was checked by some emanation of the man's presence, and began fawning and dragging its head sideways on the grass. Attaboy, said Cumuth softly.

Wesley Igor Drom realised that it was almost the end of the line and was intent on taking a few more down with him. He still had the Enderby twins under one arm like bagpipes so that the sharpshooters wouldn't risk a shot at a distance. The breakfast can't have been to his liking for he gave both host and hostess their quietus head down in the full sink and when a brave unarmed combat expert made a rush through a skylight, thinking Drom had his hands full, Drom proved adept with a novelty bottle of peanut butter in the shape of Princess Di. It struck the expert's head with a sound like a greywacke stone on a rotten pumpkin.

A good many people formed a ring behind the police cordon as the light improved. Somehow JC got through both ring and cordon without so much as a word. People felt a need to step aside. They watched him stroll across the dewy grass and pause to trail his relaxed hand in a jasmine bush. He stopped on a nice piece of crazy paving between the back door and the barbecue area and stood balanced there with his hands relaxed by his side and his legs somewhat apart. The morning sun coppered his face in profile, glinted on his tan stock boots. The breeze made hush and not a bull horn sounded. Nellie Hambinder later swore that there was in the sky a cloud the exact shape of a tombstone. No mistaking it, she said.

How long am I going to be waiting here, Drom? said JC. His voice was even and dispassionate, coming from a long way inside the man.

Then Wesley Igor Drom stepped out of the door to face him and there was no shouting, no frothing. He saw the green grass, the elms, the summer flowers, the barbecue area, all in the light of a new day. He heard the uncaring birdsong and the water dripping from the overflowing Lewis-Smythes' sink. Tree trunk Wesley saw many of the police and gawpers who crouched at a distance and he saw as well the one man who stood before him and he dried his hands on the ringlets of the Enderby twins and gave the moment its due.

Put down the Enderbys, said JC, and for once his eyes were focused not on some distant thing, but on the man to whom he spoke. It was a match, you see. It was black and white, day and night, fire and water, it was the Greek guy and the Minotaur; it was the circle of the agonising grace of man's free will to face his destiny. For both of them.

Put down the Enderbys, said JC. And Wesley Drom put the twins aside as you put a pair of fire tongs aside and in the same movement drew a chromed sawn-off shotgun from beneath his coat and fired, and the police started firing, and when it was all over in slow motion and the birds had flown up from the elms in startled alarm, then the police came forward urgently to check the dead and Nadine said, he lived with us, in a voice of reverential exultation and Nellie Hambinder began to sing 'Rock of Ages' and Crimmond's Alsatian slunk away into history.

That's just as it happened and just how it's remembered. People still visit the place today.

A PART OF LIFE

ALL THAT SUMMER Polly was at the Shangri La Motels, Lake Tekapo. She and her daughter did the cleaning and were given free accommodation in an old, wooden bach that had no view of the lake and was close to the pine plantation. There were sixteen units at the Shangri La, including a new block of four, two up and two down, with sloping tiled bathroom floors set with chrome drainage grilles, which suited the Asian tourists. And they had air-conditioning and a balcony where you could sit and watch the water skiers and boaties.

The owners of the Shangri La had decided to go for top dollar, so they were very fastidious. When a party moved out everything had to be given a going over. The owners called all guests a party, no matter how many came. Polly and her daughter had to wash all the crockery, all the cutlery, wipe the microwaves, even if it was obvious that they had not been used. Mrs Beaumont gave the instance of stripping a bed that seemed immaculate, to find a pair of false teeth near the foot. 'We would prefer that you leave nothing to chance here, Polly.' She demonstrated the paper seal that was to be put on the lavatory after it had been cleaned. 'You know, Polly,' said Mrs Beaumont, 'the tourist standard has to be higher than their own homes, or ours.'

At the bach, Polly and Alice didn't waste a lot of time doing housework. After fronting up to it most of the day, neither wanted to be cleaning things off duty. 'A good scrub-up at the end, that's the ticket,' Polly told her daughter and she got no argument from Alice. An old, wooden place anyway, with only four rooms; you can only do so much with that.

Their day at the Shangri La depended a good deal on how many parties were checking in and out, because that was when most work had to be done. For other units it was mainly just the linen change and clearing the waste bags. On a good day they had time to talk to the longer stayers and take their time in the well-appointed laundry. 'Have the best of basics, Mr Beaumont always says,' said Mrs Beaumont. There were even times when Polly could let her daughter duck away to meet her new friends.

Polly was naturally sociable and would chat away to the longer stay guests. Mrs Beaumont encouraged it within reason as she had a shrewd understanding that, for travellers, some friendly words could be just as satisfying as a lake view. 'The personal touch, the little extra, Polly,' she said. 'That's the way to get return custom.' Mrs Beaumont knew that people away from their own locality develop a hunger for simple recognition; someone to greet them and to use their name; someone to provide a brief respite from the close company and predictable response of travelling companions, or from loneliness.

That's how Polly met Mr Sondeen. He was one of those very tall, short-haired Americans that you imagine having been on the college basketball team. His hair was still vigorous, although it had become grey, and his height still gave him a presence, although he was a little round-shouldered. He always wore very baggy, light-coloured slacks as though he were a fat man. He had lots of pairs, all with excellent creases. He had one of the new upstairs units for a month as part of a vacation he was giving his two older sisters — one who had never married and the other who had just lost her husband in a random killing in a diner on the southern outskirts of Kosciusko, Mississippi.

He told Polly all that and more within fifteen minutes of meeting her: told her how the weirdo in Kosciusko had kept shouting, 'Who's laughing now?' as he fired at the people eating, and his sister's husband just happened to be there because he was coming back from a blood test and hadn't been allowed a regular breakfast. 'He'd never set eyes on that diner before,' said Mr Sondeen. 'Just a sonofabitch chance, that's what it was.'

Mr Sondeen was a straightforward, candid man and told Polly that he had made a good deal of money in commercial dealership franchises, but at the cost of his wife who had left him to marry a high school principal in Gary, Indiana. 'Neither of my sisters can afford to cross the road,' said Mr Sondeen on another occasion. He was yarning in the laundry while Polly and Alice ironed sheets and pillow-slips. He had put his sisters on the stones of the lakefront for the morning and was set to go golfing as usual. 'I notice that in families. Either the women make the money, or the men do, but you don't get both sexes doing well; not in my experience you don't. Anyway, I've gotten into the shape to be able to show my sisters something of the world and so why not. Okay, so my wife's gone, but then again I could've been like Ben — dropping in to the wrong diner. There's cause for thought in something like that.'

On the Friday that began the second week of his stay at the Shangri La, Mr Sondeen sought Polly's help when she came with towels and another liner for the waste unit. It was very still and hot; the lake was a harsh blue. A party from number fourteen were assembling by their car below to go fishing at Alexandrina, but Mr Sondeen's voice barely dropped a decibel. 'Now I hope you won't take offence, 'cause none is intended, absolutely. I'm not entirely sure of your ways here, but I mentioned something of it to Mr Beau-mont and got no sense at all. The thing is I'm interested in womanly company, you understand, and I'm damned if I can find any such resource for a travelling man in this otherwise beautiful spot. Quite frankly put, I need to fire a round or two, you understand?'

'I can't help. I'm only here for a summer myself.' Polly just prevented herself from adding the usual courtesy that she was sorry that she was unable to help. It wasn't the sort of conversation she was used to.

'It's embarrassing, isn't it?' continued Mr Sondeen, yet without showing the slightest sign of it. 'Absolutely no offence intended. But at home, you see, there's a desk clerk, bell boy, or barman you can talk to man to man. Here no one seems to have a handle on it at all. Jesus, I mean Mr Beau-mont seemed to think I wanted to go courting and the guy at the lakeside hotel told me what a shame New Year was over. I've never known so little opportunity for a friendly transaction.'

'It's different here, I suppose,' said Polly and she thought that Mr Sondeen's tone was just the one that he had used when cloud prevented his sisters and him from taking the scenic flight over the Alps.

'Look Polly,' he said, 'it's not for a gentleman to go on about it. Let's just say that I've several hundred dollars for the local economy that isn't being taken advantage of.'

'Anyway,' said Polly, 'I'll just put in these new towels as well.'

'I see it as a perfectly natural inclination myself, but the last thing I want is to give offence as a visitor in another country.' Mr Sondeen yawned and spread his arms as if directing traffic, to show that he was done with the subject. The sliding door to the balcony had been pushed back and he stood in the gap looking out over the slope to the shingle beach, across the blue expanse of the lake towards the mountains.

'I tell you, Polly, this Kiwiland is something. I haven't had my eyes so drawn to landscape about me since I spent some time in Montana at the end of the seventies. Ever been to Montana, Polly? Now that's fetching country. Red Rock River and the Beaverhead Mountains, where they found gold in the sixties, about the time you did here so I'm told. Such beautiful, desolate country.'

Wednesday was the one day of the week that Polly and Alice had to themselves: it tended to be one of the quiet days for arrivals at the Shangri La and the policeman's wife used to come in and help Mrs Beaumont. For the first few Wednesdays Polly and Alice did those of the tourist things they could afford, but then Alice found that Ruby Corrigan, from the same netball team, was staying with friends in the camping ground. Polly didn't much enjoy being on the lakefront by herself. She had no husband for company and she was self-conscious about her white, middle-aged legs if she wore shorts.

She took to spending the day sitting in the open door of the old bach, which was shielded from the road and in which she could arrange herself to receive just that balance of shade and sun she wanted. She had lemonade and an economy cask of müller thurgau in the small fridge. She rationed her drinks, leant on a palliasse that smelled like the inside of an old biscuit tin and read, off and on, popular paperbacks about lissome, corporate bitches making it in a man's world. What she tended to think about, though, was how at forty-seven she had come to be in someone else's four-room bach at Tekapo and cleaning the Shangri La Motels for a living.

Looking back, she could see that the signs of such an outcome had been there all along, but, like the rest of us, she had taken her own experience, her own indecisions and opportunities, as something inaugural and not part of a normal population curve. It pained her enormously to be treated for what she was: to see people's attention slide away from her as she talked, to watch her pleasant, unremarkable face and plump legs in the windows of shops she passed, to have no skills or knowledge that were indispensable. She was aware, and Mrs Beaumont was aware, of the affable, egalitarian relationship between them — with certain tacit constraints. Your business is only as good as your staff, Mr Beaumont would remind his wife.

Polly told her daughter about Mr Sondeen's complaint. 'The dirty old devil,' said Alice with a laugh. She herself had begun a very fulfilling, but uncomplicated, relationship with a guy dumped by Ruby Corrigan and so was at peace with the world. 'An old geezer like that should stick to his golf and his memories,' she said.

'Right,' said Polly. She remembered when Alice's father would miss lunch and drive across most of Christchurch to spend twenty minutes making love to her in a flat above Sumner. He was very quiet, very intense and had one small patch of dark hair between the muscles of his chest. 'Do you know,' he would say, with his palms on her shoulders, 'how often I dream of this?'

Mr Sondeen liked to talk to Polly, but he didn't complain about his celibacy again. He was as cheerful and positive and loud as ever. Polly felt no particular physical attraction, but no aversion either. Mr Sondeen must have been sixty, but he was thin and very clean and his wealth and nationality seemed to give him a certain gloss. Most of all, there was that disconcerting frankness of which Americans are master and which is at once rebuked and envied by those more accustomed to modesty and deception.

Most days Polly passed at least a few words with Mr Sondeen and his elderly sisters. The sisters wished she could come sightseeing with them; Mr Sondeen gave her a four-pound rainbow trout he caught in Lake Alexandrina. She cooked it in foil the way Mrs Beaumont recommended. Almost every time she talked with Mr Sondeen Polly wondered whether he had found his opportunity for physical intimacy and what he was prepared to pay for it. She told herself it was more a natural curiosity on her part than an interest in sleeping with him.

It became Alice's practice not to come back to the bach several nights a week — staying over with Ruby she called it, but it wasn't Ruby who picked her up after work at the Shangri La, or dropped her off there in the morning. Polly felt neither anger, nor envy, just a sense of part of her own life being played out again in her daughter's easy, summer existence. Polly remembered the casual assurance that came from being young and desired, an assurance that assumed both immutable. Sometimes when she looked up from her work to see Alice's boyfriend waiting in his car — all brown forearms and light hair drawn back in a ponytail — she thought that he was waiting for her, as men had often done, but then she remembered that it was 1994 and that it was her daughter who would run over to the car and laugh and call goodbye.

No place is perfect, of course, even for those come only in a summer. On some days a fierce wind came right down the lake from the black and white mountains at its head; not cold so much as unpleasant and tiring. It chapped the face, blew back hair until it was painful at the roots, whipped words away so that conversation was a mockery. It scurried grit into the Shangri La Motels from the lakeshore, even into the bach further back among the pines, rattling the old door and window frames. On such a day, when the Japanese tourists preferred to regard the Church of the Good Shepherd from the glassed comfort of their buses rather than traipse around it, and Mrs Beaumont had been particularly vigilant in her inspection of the units, Polly thought that maybe she would let Mr Sondeen make love to her.

A considerable experience of very moderate success in life can create a defensive self-deceit, or be the cause of an altogether more detached and matter of fact view. Polly was inclined to be honest with herself. She watched the pines buck in the wind, heard their needles skating on the tin roof, as she made a sandwich of the last of her slightly fishy-smelling ham. By the end of March she would no longer be needed at the Shangri La and would have to go back to Christchurch for the winter. Five hundred dollars, say four then, could make quite a difference — the agent's fees, bond and rent in advance needed in getting a flat perhaps. Polly could have justified her train of thought by bringing in romance, but she didn't. No dream that wealthy Mr Sondeen might fall for her and offer marriage, a life in the United States. No, Polly was weighing up if the money would be worth the effort — the embarrassment of bringing up the matter with Mr Sondeen, the humiliation if he didn't want her, all the little auxiliary hassles such as shaving her legs and armpits, taking precautions, tackling any kinky stuff, worrying about her breath, her underclothes, her dimpled bum, whether he would want something to eat, where they would do it.

Polly watched the grit puffing in around the window frame with each gust of wind. The whole bach would have to be cleaned if they came there and it would have to be a time when Alice was away. She was surprised how much there was to it and told herself that the sums of money involved weren't that over the top after all. There was one big advantage if it didn't go well: Mr Sondeen and his sisters were leaving in less than two weeks. Polly didn't like the prospect of having to maintain the same terms with Mr Sondeen afterwards; bringing the towels and sheets, passing the time of day with his sisters, listening to Mr Sondeen explain his golf round, or the stop-off points on the day's sightseeing. Nor did she want too much opportunity for him to talk to the Beaumonts in the candid way he had about recent satisfactions he may have experienced, or any disappointments. And maybe he would insist she use his Christian name and maybe it would be Al, Myron, or Randy.

The wind blew itself out in the night and the next day was bright and still. From unit nine Polly saw Mr Sondeen putting his golf clubs in the rental station-wagon and she left her work in the kitchen of number nine and walked over to him.

'Lake's a picture, Polly,' he said. 'I aim to make the most of today.'

'It's beaut.' Polly wondered just how best to bring up the subject of the womanly company he had talked about. 'The wind's so tiring. Don't you find?' she said.

'Worse than rain,' said Mr Sondeen. 'You can fish in the rain. Sometimes it's even more likely that way.'

'I've been thinking about what you said — about a woman's company.'

'Absolutely,' said Mr Sondeen.

'Absolutely?'

'No change in the situation,' he said. 'I've just about given up on finding that particular recreation until we get to one of your cities. The last thing I want is to give offence. There's a civilised way with all of our needs.'

Mr Sondeen left the back of the station-wagon up, because it was creating a little shade for them both. The air was so still that they could hear people laughing up by the hotel and the swish of a car coming down to the little township along the lupin-fringed road from Burke's Pass. Blue, purple, pink, cream, less commonly white or apricot flowers on the bushes that never grew tall and were restricted to the roadsides where the sheep couldn't eat them. The road wasn't visible from the Shangri La but, hearing the car on the slope, Polly had the complete scene in her mind for a moment. Mr Sondeen had the grace to stand quietly, smoothing his eyebrows, so that Polly had the opportunity to think or speak. 'Maybe you'd like to be with me,' she said.

'Indeed I would,' said Mr Sondeen. It was Alice he usually watched when she and Polly were working around the motel, but he had a realistic view of his prospects and said nothing of that.

'Great, just great,' he said. 'How about I buy lunch at the hotel today and we can talk there. Say twelve thirty?'

'Better make it quarter to one.'

'That's really great, Polly. I look forward to that.' He was genuinely, unashamedly, pleased and so at ease with the situation that Polly felt it less unusual herself. His voice had retained the same volume he used for telling her of his golf rounds, or how the colour of Pukaki was milky green and not at all the deep blue of Tekapo.

She walked back to number nine to finish cleaning the kitchen. In some ways she was relieved that the details of actually doing it hadn't been talked about; in other ways she wished that such a discussion were already over. Mr Sondeen closed the back of the wagon and went up to fetch his sisters so that he could take them to the lake before he went on to play golf. When they were coming down the outside stairs of the new block, Polly could hear them praising the day.

One of the sisters said she couldn't believe that after the wind of the day before, it was possible for it to be so heavenly. 'You could just live in this place for ever.'

'Couldn't you though?' said Mr Sondeen.

Polly hadn't expected to be going to the hotel for lunch and she had no opportunity to go back to the bach to change. She wore a print frock and her flat working shoes, which needed a polish. At least she had been able to spend a while on her hair in unit eleven when she should have been vacuuming and as there was no wind at all, the walk to the hotel didn't muss it up. Mr Sondeen insisted they have the salmon and that he pay for it.

They sat on the terrace. Sondeen still wore his golf shoes and talked at first of other places that had some affinity with where he found himself, as those who travel a good deal tend to do. The link was often quite circumstantial — the salmon lunch, a guest speaking Italian, the wind of the day before. As he talked, Polly made a physical appraisal, so that there was nothing visible that she couldn't tolerate if he were to make love to her. She decided that, even as a young man, he hadn't been handsome at all, hadn't possessed any overwhelming charm, but the advantages he had then he retained; nothing of grossness had developed. He had a good head of hair; he was very tall and still so slim that the belt on his expensive, baggy trousers was a brief circumference and not an ounce of fat hung over it. He had a long, big-featured, plain face that was seamed rather than wrinkled. His mouth often hung open when he was listening, or thinking. He had a beautiful, gold watch that slipped very low on his wrist and his hands were large and clean, showing no other signs of wear except that from golf clubs. He was an ordinary man who, through hard work, or good fortune, had succeeded to a greater degree than other ordinary men and that success gave him assurance in his beliefs, his needs, his appearance, and it gave him good humour and tolerance as well.

'Now in Singapore,' Mr Sondeen was saying, 'it's different. Shoot, they run a tight ship there all right, I tell you. I've been there three times. The Chinese know what service is in Singapore. Mind you, you can't get privacy within a natural landscape there the way you can in this country of yours. That's what keeps reminding me of Red Rock River.'

Mr Sondeen talked so much of other countries that in the end the arrangements for their rendezvous had to be hurried through in his station-wagon as he drove Polly back just in time to start work again at the Shangri La. Polly would have liked to think it the result of a nervous anticipation on Mr Sondeen's part, but she recognised it rather as a true indication of his priorities. It was no big deal, after all, to bed a middle-aged cleaner at the Tekapo Shangri La Motels. She imagined there had been women in Montana too, but his recollection was of the mountains, the sagebrush, conifers, the high grasslands under snow that showed cougar tracks.

Polly spent much of her Wednesday cleaning the bach. She entertained herself with the ridiculous idea of the itemised account she could present to Mr Sondeen — preparation of venue, smoked cheese and a chardonnay, the forgoing of her normal relaxation, depilatory costs, loss of sleep. Prostitution was novel to her; she was surprised at the extra work and obligation involved even before anyone else arrived. Probably she wasn't casual enough, she decided, or sufficiently angry. Perhaps she should feel a righteous indignation that, as a woman, she had been forced by her society to obtain money in such a way to ensure her winter in Christchurch. What she did feel was disappointment that, after loving three men, she was left with just Alice dear to her — though very dear. There had been good reasons at the time, of course, for each break-up and optimism for better opportunities to come, but with hindsight she was able to see that each relationship was in fact a step to where she found herself — tidying an old bach in the pines at Tekapo for Mr Sondeen's visit.

In the slanted, evening sun Mr Sondeen came through the wooden gateway and up the dirt path to the bach. He had walked from the Shangri La Motels and wore his floppy golf hat to protect himself. He had tan shoes and a pair of his expensive, baggy slacks that Polly hadn't seen before — a very light powder blue. He carried a bottle of wine in a red striped paper bag from the Tekapo Hotel and in the other hand a purple lupin cob that he had picked from the roadside. 'Jeez,' he said to Polly, standing by the worn, wooden step, 'have these lupin things got a fair smell, or what!'

'They're not even native.'

'They're not?'

'I don't think they are.'

It was what Polly had feared — him arriving at the door and the awkwardness of talking about some such nonsense as the lupins, when they both knew he'd come to undress her and make love to her by arrangement. Almost as soon as the awkwardness was apparent, Mr Sondeen moved to dispel it with a direct matter of factness. He put both the wine and flower behind him on the bench with scarcely a glance. 'The thing is, Polly, you don't have to do anything. We can just drink this wine and talk if that's what you feel best with; if you've gone off the idea of bed for the two of us. The last thing I want is to give offence.'

'I don't mind,' said Polly.

'I've been looking forward to it ever since Thursday — after that damned wind when you mentioned it.'

'Would you like a drink of something?' Polly stopped herself adding the word, first. 'I've got cheese and fruit. It's difficult to bake much of anything here. The kitchen's not set up for it.'

Mr Sondeen didn't look around the small kitchen cum living room; he made no comment about it not being such a bad little shack, or anything like that. He kept his direct gaze on Polly. 'Now you can tell me I'm wrong here, Polly, but it seems to me that you're only going to feel embarrassed until we get to the loving, so the sooner the better. Afterwards, I'd say we have a damned good chance of relaxing. That's my best guess, anyway.'

And Polly knew that in his candid way he was right and she said so briefly and took him into the bedroom determined not to care about the smell of the palliasses, or the water stains on the ceiling panels, or the hangers of clothes on large nails hammered into the wall. She was far more comfortable with what she was doing than with trying to talk about it. She sat on the bed and watched Mr Sondeen take off his powder blue, baggy slacks and fold them on the floor to keep the creases.

'Let's see what we've got here,' he said kindly and he parted Polly's blouse, smiled and stroked her breasts firmly. Her nipples were small, pale and with almost no aureole. Mr Sondeen ran a circle around each with the longest finger of his right hand. 'Lovely skin, Polly,' he said. 'Lovely skin.' Her breasts were full and extended a good way down her chest. Her first lover had been able almost to contain them with two champagne glasses, but she must have told a good many lies since because they had continued to grow. Mr Sondeen tried to kiss them and did so clumsily because of his height and the stiffness of his joints. His head was very close; she could see his scalp beneath the grey, short hair and the sun-damaged skin on the tips of his ears. He smelled of anti-perspirant, a good aftershave and peppermint. 'How beautiful you are,' said Mr Sondeen cheerfully.

'I'm middle-aged.'

'You can't be forty yet.' He was delighted with his own flattery and showed white, even teeth when he laughed. All capped, Polly supposed, at vast expense; she felt a passing grievance that at his age he was able to have better teeth than her own. She had a soft wart on her right side above her hip and supposed that in time he'd see it. 'Ah, Polly,' he said, 'why didn't we think of this sooner?'

'And maybe regret it later,' she said.

Mr Sondeen slid his own clothes off so easily; everything was so loose on his thin body and he helped Polly out of hers with obvious enjoyment. He caressed her for a time. The loudest noise was the regular, rather loud rustle of his breathing. Then Mr Sondeen worked a little on himself, half turned away out of modesty. 'Hell, Polly,' he said, 'don't think that it's any lack of inclination; it's just age, you see. You get to be not so quick on the draw.' He was intent and just slightly impatient. She looked at the tendons in his neck, the fuzz of grey on his flat chest, the customary creases at his amazingly slim waist, the long, blue veins on the inside of his arms. When he first lay against her the slight mutual sweat before exertion was like an adhesive and their skin sealed, not altogether unpleasantly.

'Take a grip on it for a moment, sweetheart,' Mr Sondeen said.

Polly could see the pines through the one bedroom window. The sun was low and so bright still, that it shone almost parallel with the great branches and lit up, at random, patches of fissured bark, glittered on wept resin, singled out green needle clumps as if they were helmet plumes.

'That's it. Yes,' said Mr Sondeen loudly.

Alice's father was the third of the three men Polly had loved. She'd never seen any prospect for happiness in promiscuity. Each of her men had been a love for life until circumstances proved otherwise. Each of them had been a partner for several years. Alice's father had a breakdown because his personality proved incompatible with his job in local government. He longed to work outdoors, but his marketable skill was in computer software. After the hospital he went to northern Queensland and sent back just one letter, which didn't even enquire after Alice.

'Yes, upward and onward. That's it,' said Mr Sondeen. He meant nothing at all by it and his eyes rolled.

Polly had not expected to be sensually transported, and she

wasn't. Neither did she feel any aversion. Doing it was familiar despite a celibacy of several years. There was a surprising degree of localised pleasure. The circumstances did make her a little sad, however, bringing to mind the act when she had been passionately involved: sparking quick images of the ardent voices, bodies and hopes of the young men she had loved. Polly made the most of it; partly for Mr Sondeen, partly for her own gratification, mainly for the memories of other men in her arms.

'Home run,' said Mr Sondeen, his voice subdued for once. It was then she wished she had set the time rather later, when dusk was due. The light was still quite good in the bach; enough to show in unbecoming clarity the heavy droop of her breasts, the small, fleshy excrescence on her side, the mottled flush that she knew would be on her neck and breastbone. She pulled the sheet across her thighs. She could think of absolutely nothing to say. She watched the fly spots on the light fitting and listened to Mr Sondeen's heavy breathing. At such a time her second man had always kissed her stomach and said he was the luckiest guy in the world.

Mr Sondeen extended his arms behind and above him, arms so long that the hands hung over the wooden rail. They were crossed at the wrist as if he were tied in bondage and the long veins on the hairless, inner scope of his arms were drained of their blue blood. 'A man's a prisoner to it, Polly,' he said. His thin legs didn't share the sheet and Polly saw with some envy that his waist and legs had just narrow muscle and tendon shaped to the bone. His pubic hair retained much of the darkness that his head had lost. His cock had become subdued to a half-arch on his thigh. Sweat gleamed in the creases of his face and neck; there was a little white at the corners of his eyes.

'A prisoner?'

'Women are martyrs to their hormones, we're told. And I don't doubt a bit of it, not a bit of it. Shoot, I went through it with my wife for Christ's sake. But then a man is driven too,

Polly. Just think how many have been cock driven to humiliation and disaster, half knowing it, but unable to go any other way.'

'Is that supposed to make me feel good?' said Polly.

'This is by far the best thing of my holiday here. I just don't want you to think of me too much as a silly old bugger.'

Mr Sondeen brought his arms down and then sat on the bed side to put on his green boxer shorts. He stood up and took the few paces to the window. With his back to her he rubbed his face and his short, grey hair with his hands. 'Most of the pines here in Kiwiland come from America. The lot of them in fact, I've been told.' His voice became oddly high and distorted because he was yawning as he spoke. 'The species I'm talking about. I was in a foursome with a DOC guy in the weekend and he said that there wasn't a tree here before your settlers. The whole caboose was just snowgrass, he said, up to a man's waist.'

'When there's a strong wind at night here, the pines make a noise like the sea. It's uncanny.'

'Plenty of cones for winter,' said Mr Sondeen and then after a pause, 'You mind if I have a shower, Polly?'

'It's a bit Mickey Mouse,' she said.

'Shoot, I know what the plumbing's like in these huts.' The bathroom was next door to the bedroom and Mr Sondeen was almost through it when he turned back on impulse, leant forward with his hands on the end of the bed. 'That really did the trick for me, Polly. I feel good and easy.'

'I'm glad,' said Polly. While he had his shower she listened to the pipes gurgling; a muffled exclamation from Mr Sondeen as though the water was suddenly too hot, or he'd slipped on a soap remnant on the concrete base.

Polly decided that it hadn't been too bad. Not up to the best hopes that she'd had, but a good way from the worst fears. Everything was much the same, wasn't it? That was at once the most obviously reassuring response and, more subtly, the most worrying.

Polly had her shower after Mr Sondeen, not caring that by then the water was almost cold, and when she finished she found that he was dressed and back in the kitchen; that he had shown the initiative to open his wine and her cheese. 'It always does give you an appetite, don't you find?' he said. 'Sex and a mountain climate seem to do that. I imagine some really big eaters shacked up in your high country and in western Montana. Shoot, now there's magnificent country without question, Polly.'

'I guess so.' Polly liked to hear about places overseas, because she'd never been herself, except a seven-day Sydney package with her second partner. Mr Sondeen asked her about it and she enjoyed recalling the city. He knew it better than Polly, but he encouraged her to talk about her harbour cruise, the hotel by Elizabeth Bay, the trip to the Blue Mountains, and then he began on the interior of Australia, the Philippines, where he'd lived for two years while supervising the installation of plant for tanneries, and Mexico. Polly rather enjoyed hearing so much about his life, even though she knew there was no future in it for her.

'I must remember the money,' he said finally; the first sign that he was thinking of going. 'How much do you want?'

'You mean how much do I deserve — a fair rate.'

'No. How much do you want?' Mr Sondeen was interested in the attitude others took to money. He himself knew a lot about it and valued it, without at all being possessed by it.

'I've no idea. I told you it's all new to me. I don't want to haggle.'

'But you must have imagined some amount when you decided to let me come,' persisted Mr Sondeen. 'You had a target, that's for sure. Something you wanted and didn't have any other way of rustling up the bucks. This isn't your regular thing.'

'I was thinking that three hundred dollars would help me into a small Christchurch flat for the winter,' she said.

'Sure enough, Polly. That's a sensible way to go.' He took a bill-fold from his back pocket and put four hundred-dollar notes from it on the worn laminate of the bench top. 'Winter, eh? There's always something you've got to bear in mind, isn't there? Always a situation that's snuck up.' But Mr Sondeen was more concerned with looking into the mirror on the wall to inspect the side of his head. 'Goddamn shower. I hit my head a real one on the fitting in there. That sucker was just at head height. It must have been a bunch of small people who put up this place, Polly.'

Mr Sondeen put on his floppy hat again to shade himself from the setting sun as he left. 'Hell,' he said, 'we'll see each other at the motel anyway.' It undercut the need to deal with even a business-like farewell. He kissed her at the doorway where he smelled less of deodorant and slightly more of wine and cheese. 'Shoot, Polly,' he said, 'I just hope that I haven't given any offence. That's the thing.' He walked down the dirt track towards the road, the lupins, his two grateful sisters waiting at the Shangri La Motels.

NOT A VISITOR

SOMETIMES A BREAK in one routine sets off a collapse in others; a sort of non-political domino effect. You know? Perhaps a cyclone, an elephant amok at the circus, the discovery of a moa egg in a cave, or just a computer failure at work, the foreman falling and injuring his leg in the vehicle inspection bay, the mistaken delivery of a prefabricated garden shed.

On that very hot February day it was Marge Samuels fainting in her office. Checkletts and Mulveney has very modern offices, though the factory's the same vast barn. Almost all glass and you see through the walls, except Mr Mulveney's. Marge jarred her monitor against the glass side of her office with her shoulder as she went down and the rest of us heard the noise in time to see the last flurry of her hair on the carpet. Her knees flopped apart in a posture quite unnatural to her and were rearranged by Bette Haast from reception, who was the first to reach her.

Marge is a formal person and I knew she would be embarrassed by fainting even more than by those very few occasions when she was found wanting as the firm's accountant. 'It's nothing,' she said. 'It's just this appalling heat. All this glass and the dazzle and everything. Really, I feel fine now.' Her face was pale, highlighting for once the discreet make-up she used. She had small gold studs in her ears. Her tone was one of apology rather than concern at what had happened. She pressed her hair down with both hands. 'Absolutely fine,' she said.

Marge has a B Com and used to have her own business, but gave it up for family reasons and came in to do the more difficult stuff for us. A compact, competent woman in her forties and not inclined to be personal.

I've got to admit that Mr Mulveney played the concerned employer quite well over it all. He insisted that Marge take the rest of the day off and that she shouldn't drive herself home. That's where I came in — proffered as assistance by Mr Mulveney because I am the staff member whose services he can best dispense with, I suppose. 'Look,' I said, 'I'm only too happy to drive you, Marge. Take your time, just get what you want and then we'll quietly be on our way.'

'Well, it's just that Michael's in Christchurch all week,' she said.

'Maybe the computer came up with another nought on the company overdraft and it was too much for her,' whispered Danny Allen, 'or Reg flashed that great donger of his.'

Marge lived out past the racecourse on one of those lifestyle blocks that have eaten up the farms on the fringes of the town. The Samuels bought the original farmhouse so at least they had trees and some sort of garden and outbuildings, rather than a new home, toadstool fresh in a bare paddock. I drove up the track from the road gate and a little dust rose behind and drifted into the line of pines along one side. I parked by an old diesel tank on a frame stand, close to a pipe and netting gate that led to the house itself. 'There you go, Marge,' I said. 'You make sure that you rest up.'

I hadn't been to the place before. The staff at Checkletts and Mulveney didn't live in each other's pockets and when we had a do, it was on the premises, or we went to one of the places in town. Besides, Marge came in only in the afternoons. I knew, of course, that she and Michael had only one child and that he wasn't quite up to making a go of things for himself and so stayed at home and looked after chooks; enough to be almost on a commercial scale, someone said.

When Marge was still getting out of the car, her son stepped out of the shadow of the pines, over the rust dry carpet of old needles, and came round to my side and pointed at me. 'Just going, Eldon,' said Marge. 'Yes, what a pity, just going.' But Eldon gripped the frame of the open window and brought his face very close to mine. He smelled slightly of sacking, dust and chickens. His face was almost unlined, but his teeth surprisingly worn. His thin, fine hair didn't conceal all his scalp. 'Not a visitor, I'm afraid,' said his mother.

'Not a visitor,' said Eldon, each syllable a separate puff of sound. 'I'm Eldon,' he said.

'I'm Doug,' I said and I put my hand to the window to shake his, but Eldon didn't move his face back as he lifted his own hand and we ended shaking hands so close to him that the knuckles moved his soft hair and his eyes came and went.

'I want Doug to see my chicken houses,' said Eldon. Our hand shaking stopped after a fair while and I drew my hand back into the car.

'Doug didn't come visiting. He brought me home from work because I wasn't feeling well,' explained Marge.

'I want Doug to see my chicken houses.'

'Well then, you'll have to ask him yourself,' said Marge.

'I want you to see my chicken houses.'

I didn't mind staying long enough to see the chooks. It was all paid time after all and I thought that if I spent a while with Eldon, then his mother would have more of a chance for a spell. She told me not to feel that I had to look at everything, but that Eldon liked people to see his work and didn't get much company. 'Come in for a cold drink,' she said, 'before you head back,' and she looked at her son for a moment as if to be sure of his mood. 'Don't you be a nuisance now. Doug hasn't got all day to spend on chooks.'

Eldon stood so close that it was difficult to open the car door wide enough to get out, but when that was done he took me through the column of pines to his fowl sheds on the other side. There were three of them, all tin buildings with a run on the north side of each. I was given a tour: the perches, nest boxes, feeding trays, the water dispensers that he had rigged up with half-gallon jars. In a cubicle at the end of one of the sheds Eldon had a grinder for grit and bags of mash and wheat. There were a couple of savage-looking rat traps and some baits. Eldon pointed to the traps and said, 'Wham with the bastard,' and when I didn't rebuke him he said even louder and with greater enjoyment, 'Wham with the fucken bastard.'

The tin sheds were unlined and concentrated the heat cruelly, yet quite a few chooks were inside rather than in the runs. White Leghorns, said Eldon. He wore faded green shorts, a Stockmeel T-shirt and sneakers soiled to a uniform grey. He had a habit of shrugging his shoulders when he was about to speak. Every time he pointed to something he'd then turn quickly to see my reaction. He showed me around the tin sheds with all the pride of the curator of an orchid house.

'Well, you've got quite a set-up here. A fair few chooks, all right, and I suppose you do okay from the eggs.'

'I show you the bad hens,' said Eldon. He led the way to a low boxwood and netting run that could be pulled across the ground when fresh grass was needed. Useful for a clucky and her chickens, I suppose, but in it were just two hens.

'These'ns I caught eating eggs,' said Eldon. 'Once they start at it then they never give up. I had to wait for ages till I caught them.'

I imagined him sitting quietly, hugging his knees for whole afternoons at a time until he found the culprits. 'They're headed for the bloody pot now,' he said, then shrugged again. 'Straight for the pot.'

Eldon wanted to give me one for the pot, but I didn't fancy an old boiler. 'I'd better get back to work, or else the boss will pot me,' I said, and Eldon laughed a good deal louder than was justified.

'Wham, wham,' he cried and slapped his hands to his ears.

As we went back towards the pines, he made circles around me in our progress and flapped his arms at his side in support of entreaties to let him show me other things dear to him.

There was a goat with one horn, he said, and an old windmill in one of the paddocks.

We opened the house gate and went up to the large, comparatively cool kitchen that Marge and Michael had modernised, but in keeping with the impressive kauri farm table. Eldon told his mother of our tour and several times said wham very loudly without quite bringing himself to swear, because of Marge's steady eyes on his face. 'Doug is coming out every day now to help me and I'm going to give him half of the egg money.'

'Maybe he will come sometime,' said Marge.

'He is anyway; wham, wham.'

Marge brought a lager to the table for me and a Coke for Eldon, but as his mother and I talked about the heat in the offices at work, Eldon went off and brought back a lager for himself and reached for the opener that Marge put her hand over.

'You know you're not allowed it,' she said.

'Wham, bloody wham,' said Eldon and he whirled around on the spot like a dancer.

'It's the effect of the alcohol with your medication, Eldon. You know that. Otherwise of course we'd let you have a drink.'.

'He's having one,' said Eldon.

'Well of course he is, but that's different.'

'Wham, fucken wham, wham.' Eldon whirled again, arms half outstretched and his sneakers squeaking on the kitchen floor. Some flaky dust from the fowl houses spun in the air. Then he picked up his bottle and hurled it through the enlarged window of the renovated kitchen and the sound was a 'poomph' not a tinkle and for an instant the lager bottle and the shards of clear glass flashed and turned in the harsh sunlight.

It was all so quick that Marge and I were sitting in just the same way when it was quiet again. Eldon put his upper lip over his lower one in an odd face and began to cry. At the same time his nose began to bleed and the blood bubbled as he sobbed and ran his hands about his shorts and T-shirt in search of a handkerchief.

'Oh, Eldon, Eldon,' said Marge and she took a clean hand towel and dampened it under the cold tap and went to comfort him with a hug. 'He's got overexcited,' she told me.

Marge went with Eldon into the bathroom and I could hear her talking to him as she cleaned him up. Her voice was quiet, reassuring, and if he made any reply then it was too low for me to catch. Then the two of them went further into the house. Marge's voice became just a murmur and I was left alone in the kitchen with a few bright spots of Eldon's blood on the tiled floor and the shark's teeth glass around the window frame catching glints of the sun. I finished my drink and wondered if it would be best if I just slipped away. Through the window I could hear some of the hens pook-pooking beyond the pines, the cicadas in the shrubs around the house, a harvester at a distance. The offices of Checkletts and Mulveney seemed a long way off.

'He'll sleep now,' said Marge when she came back. 'He wants you to know he's sorry. He easily gets excited with people and sometimes it's all too much for him. Most of the time either Michael or I am around; one of us tries to work at home most days.'

'At least he's got the space for his fowls. Quite a little industry.'

'He's twenty-four now and won't ever be any better,' said Marge and there was no sign of bitterness in her voice. I wondered how you would become reconciled to something like that.

For me it was easy to leave the house for the first and last time, to go back to Checkletts and Mulveney and turn aside the idle questions there with a shrug.

Marge continued to come in the afternoons to do the books. She never fainted again that I can remember and when we talked in the course of the job I never asked about Eldon, or the chooks, and she never volunteered anything of them. The routine closed in reassuringly once more and I could pick the things I wanted to think about.

RECOLLECTIONS OF MKD

TREVOR LAYSTALL (B. 1939), for over fifteen years a sub-editor with the Christchurch *Press*, was an exact contemporary of M.K.D. Ash at Te Tarehi High School and kept in sporadic touch with the author until five or six years before the latter's death. Laystall saw this year's three-part television programme of Ash's life and works (*Phoenix From the Ash-es)* and considered it so little representative of the man he had known that he approached Ash's official biographer, Professor Forbes Kendaell, who recorded this interview for *Simulacre*. The interview took place at Mr Laystall's home in Spreydon, suburb of Christchurch, on the evening of 19 July 1994 and the transcript that appears here is a version modified slightly by subsequent correspondence.

FK: In utter predictability, which I will not pledge to maintain, I would like to begin by asking you when you first became aware of MKD.
TL: We came from different primary schools, but on our very first third form day at Te Tarehi High we juniors had to stay behind in hall after assembly to be sorted into classes. Old Bubber Greene, who was head of science, always used to do it. Anyway this day was wet, a typical drizzle from the sea, and Bubber couldn't do it outside. There was only one absolutely hopeless new teacher to help Bubber, who was losing his rag in the confusion and noise. Anyway, this tall, calm boy, almost beautiful, went into the wrong line —
FK: And this was MKD?

TL: No. Ash was the small, ratty kid who got under Bubber's feet when he charged forward to pull the tall boy out of line. That boy was Simon Oakes, the best winger the school ever produced. Should have been an All Black.

FK: But MKD?

TL: Bubber grabbed him and asked him his name and Ash said, 'Mulvey Kannaith Desmond Ash,' in that high faluting voice he had and Bubber mockingly repeated it several times and shook him till the tears came. Everyone gave Ash hell after that.

FK: So he was an extremely sensitive boy?

TL: Never happy with his peers certainly.

FK: In the course of my research for the biography, MKD: A Nation's Delineator, *I went into the schooldays. There was MKD's own memoir, of course,* Fallow Education, *the generally acknowledged autobiographical elements in the earlier novels, particularly* No New Bethlehem, *and the eponymous short fiction of the collection,* Marcel Proust and I. *I didn't know then of your own friendship, but I talked with other MKD acquaintances of school days, including Dr Errol Williams and your fellow journalist Jye Lee. I met Mr Norman Johnson, who had taught English there and retained very vivid and lively recollections of MKD. The picture that emerged in fact was that of something of an achiever. MKD himself in* Fallow Education *says that in his final year he would have been proxime accessit except that he refused to do any work in biology dissection on creatures killed for that purpose.*

TL: It's difficult to comment without appearing churlish, well, more disparaging perhaps. Snoz Johnson never even taught Ash and yet from that television programme you'd think that he had started it all, but was too modest to say. Errol Williams and Jye Lee were two of his chess club and photography club cobbers — anything to get out of sport. They were what the Americans now would call nerds.

FK: What, then, drew you to MKD initially? How was it that the two of you became friends? Were you a 'nerd'?

TL: With due respect I think you show just there that tendency to give Ash a retrospective significance: assuming that I was drawn to him rather than —

FK: I'm sorry.

TL: I realise that since those early days —

FK: Point taken, but what, then, did you find admirable in him as a boy? You were more than just classmates and you kept in touch for many years afterwards. Why was that?

TL: As to what I liked about him at first I'm rather hazy. I think more than anything else his willingness to entertain, his interest in your life because his own was so boring. He used to carry my first fifteen gear down to the lower ground and do his *Goon Show* impersonations as we went. About keeping in touch, I suppose because we were at the same university hall and he used to come along to my room and slaughter all the flies with a rolled up *Time* magazine. He kept asking me when my sisters were coming to visit: he'd caught a glimpse of Rebecca at a school prizegiving. I think he was very lonely at the hall and he knew there were often people in my room. I established an informal society called Quaffers.

FK: Do you know if he was writing at this time?

TL: At school, or university?

FK: Both.

TL: He always did have a knack with dirty limericks, I remember that. At Te Tarehi he wrote them on the wall of the fives court; at varsity he supplied the capping magazine. I don't recall anything else then. One of his best was about the young lady from Calcutta.

FK: I'm interested, surprised, that you didn't see any writing. His nickname was Dickens, wasn't it? That's well established. Surely there must have been some awareness that he was enthusiastic about literature, an aspiring author?

TL: That was a sort of sarcastic pun, you see. An undergraduate joke. Ash wasn't very well endowed and Dickens had an element of the diminutive as well. Simon Oakes gave him the name, I think, in the hall and so of course it stuck.

FK: If we could move on somewhat. There's the famous moral and intellectual crisis — *the nether vortex, he calls it in* Macrocarpa Bondsman — *which always recalls, for me, Shelley's line, 'a hell of death o'er the white water'. And MKD was totally unable to take his finals even though there was a general expectation that he'd get a first. There's his tremendously powerful description of waking in a cirrus mid-afternoon to the realisation that the Restoration drama exam is going on and he lies there cognisant of the vomit on the sheet and he sees on the wardrobe door the Ivy League shirt that his mother bought him but could ill afford and from some other room he hears that Roy Orbison song.*

TL: I don't think I know it.

FK: It's on the tip of my tongue.

TL: No, I mean I haven't read about his breakdown. I knew of course —

FK: Oh God, an epiphany of self-loathing. I read it in Vancouver where I was doing my PhD. I wrote on the flyleaf of the book — this has called me home!

TL: I don't remember his lead-up marks being that good actually. He could yap about anything, but I don't remember his grades being wonderful. He failed Philosophy II for example.

FK: A good many people recall him being very penetrative academically when he set his mind to it, though he could be dismissive about a proscribed course of study, about exams — in the way Housman was for instance. One of the sociology lecturers told me that MKD would quote Schopenhauer and Spengler.

TL: That sounds like him. You think that he really did have some sort of emotional crisis?

FK: Absolutely pivotal. Certainly he saw it that way: a final confrontation with the expectations that his father in particular had for him — Iapetus, MKD always called him, one of the Titans, but not to his face, of course. He fought it out within himself when barely twenty-two, the age-old dilemma for the artist between vision and a securely conventional life, between his own imperatives and the family expectations, yet something more deeply and innately contradictory in his case. It liberated him to go on to be the greatest of our writers, although at an immense psychic cost to MKD

personally. We lost one more graduate; we gained The Toby Jug
World, Cyclops' Second Eye, Journals of the New Te Rauparaha.
TL: At the time I thought he'd gone to pieces because of that
involvement with the Rawleigh's woman. Ash came round to
my flat a few times and lay on the verandah sacks telling me
about his sex life with this forty-seven-year-old woman. She'd
been going round door to door. Insatiable, he said. She had
three children and drew blood with her bite. He was finding it
impossible to get any work done. I think it was his first
experience and he'd talk, talk about it. Not a pretty story and
an unlikable trait to go on about it. I recognised a good deal of
it again in that book he wrote about the guy working in a bank.
FK: Cheque Me Out.

TL: Right.

*FK: There is this whole issue of the MKD libido, isn't there, and it's
been addressed best perhaps in John Cecil's articles in* Landfall *and*
Sport. *The rather strange essays on Zilpah, for example. Did you feel
that it was important to MKD? Do you feel so now?*

TL: Not as important as he would have liked it to be. I
remember him as essentially parasitic in regard to getting to
know women.

FK: Parasitic?

TL: Dickens — Ash — always depended on other people to
give him the opportunities to meet women. He always had his
ear open for a party, was always interested if a couple was
breaking up, but he usually just made an ass of himself. When
Simon Oakes had a party before going to Oxford to take up his
Rhodes Scholarship, Ash accosted his (Oakes's) girlfriend and
got his face slapped. He spent the rest of the night drinking in
the broom cupboard in case Simon had been told about it.

FK: You kept in touch after both of you had left the university?

TL: Susan and I married when I got a job at Hatherleys, which
was a firm of printers down by the station. This would be 1963,
or 1964, I suppose. We had a very small flat in Armagh Street;
the whole building's a women's refuge centre now. We have
some laughs about that.

FK: Yes.

TL: We were very poor, of course. Susan was still finishing her degree; I had no real idea what I wanted to do.

FK: And MKD was a friend to you in those somewhat difficult years?

TL: He was living in somebody's garage by Wilding Park, within walking distance unfortunately. He had this habit of coming in just before tea-time on a Friday after he'd been to the pub. He cottoned on to the fact that I got paid on Thursdays and that we ate rather better on Fridays than most of the week. Sometimes we tried to sit him out, a few times I threw him out, but Susan felt sorry for him initially.

FK: I imagine that for him these would have been the difficult years in which he was wrestling with No New Bethlehem *and* Room Between Sea and Sky. *Beckett's praise of what he termed the deanthropomorphisation of the artist comes to mind (laughs).*

TL: He certainly wasn't wrestling with any paying job. A few times, though, he brought a simple bunch of flowers, daffs, or —

FK: The considerate aspect of his nature so often overlooked.

TL: We thought it a nice touch, until our neighbour, Mrs Posswillow, burst in to complain that he'd stolen them from her garden on the way past. Ash pretended to be drunk, of course, and was still not sufficiently shamed to leave. We were having beef for the first time that month; he had a nose for such things.

FK: Did you see him in other circumstances during this period — an apprentice one for both of you perhaps? Did the two, or three, of you do things together?

TL: Once or twice we walked into the park. Ash always took a collection of stones and he would pelt the ducks viciously. He kept saying they were nature's bounty. And he would go on about his own wretched life; I don't recall him once asking about my job with Hatherleys. Later, when I was first with the *Press*, he became very interested, but it was only because he hoped I could get his stuff into the paper somehow. When he realised I wasn't able to do that he lost interest.

FK: Yes, I want to talk about those years too, but your comment about him going on about his life, extemporising from what must have been in many ways a painful experience. Did he talk about his work?

TL: Yes. He would still quote his smutty limericks from Te Tarehi and later, but he often talked about what he called his 'freefall novel', which he said would be the great Irish novel of New Zealand literature.

FK: *Hence the line many years later put into the mouth of Murphy Upshott — 'Amanuensis I to the almost totally blind.' His exegetes were slow to recognise the Irish debt that he acknowledged there so simply.*

TL: I was writing myself at the time — quite well received pieces about provincial rugby — and Simon Oakes was sending some poetry back from Oxford. Ash rarely made the pretence of interest, or attention. He had a very personal line of questioning which my wife found rather unpleasant.

FK: *Unpleasant?*

TL: I'd rather not go into it in detail.

FK: *You mean MKD intruded into your lives in search of material?*

TL: Well, one instance I remember clearly. In the height of summer Ash had bludged a meal and then wandered out of the kitchen in case a teatowel was thrust at him. I went through for something and found him standing in our bedroom. I remember the sun slanting across the room from the old sash windows on to his face and how his eyes were closed. When I asked him what the hell he was doing, he said he needed the smell of a married bedroom.

FK: *There's that remarkable scene in* No New Bethlehem, *isn't there, in which Lowell Knowell has returned from the maternity annexe knowing both wife and child are lost and he stands in the bedroom with sun stippling the unmade bed and he makes the first prayer of his life, yet aware during it of the residual physicality of the place. 'Marmalade, musk, mildew, moth dust and Maya.' Yes, an almost Orwellian concern with the olfactory.*

TL: He had a bit of pong about him himself.

FK: *Did you have any inkling then, when you were both young men and trying to find a place in the world to stand, that MKD would go on to become the greatest of all antipodean writers — one, as* Bungyjump *declared in a cover story, of the key figures perhaps this century?*

TL: I can't say I did.

FK: When did that perception occur to you?

TL: When I read about it in *Bungyjump* (laughs). No, I suppose in the mid-eighties when there was the publicity when *Bully For Me* came under such critical attack and Dickens started popping up on radio and television. That was when I could see that his writing was popular with the gurus.

FK: Were you still in contact with him at this time?

TL: Not so much. In about 1969, or maybe 1970, he shifted away to Wellington.

FK: April 1971, I believe.

TL: Could well be. It's fair to say that we didn't part on the best of terms.

FK: Would you like to talk about that?

TL: Simon Oakes had just been killed in England.

FK: The former companion of MKD and yourself?

TL: My friend. Simon considered Ash very much a second-rate mind and inconsequential as an athlete as well. Did I mention that it was Simon who gave Ash the nickname Dickens? Ash hated him for that.

FK: I think so.

TL: Simon died only a few weeks after receiving his PhD —

FK: His D Phil. You did say Oxford.

TL: What? Anyway, Simon was killed near a Shropshire village when he was leading the Federation Invitation Marathon. The well-known theatrical agent Hilton Fowlds had a heart attack and his Morgan V8 went out of control. Simon had no family here and his college sent all his papers to me. There were several boxes of his writing — a great deal of prose, which surprised me, for Simon had only ever shown me his poetry. Susan and I couldn't face reading it so soon after his death; we left the boxes virtually undisturbed and then on the Labour Weekend when we had gone to Susan's parents and left Ash in the flat because his garage had been flooded, all of Simon's papers were stolen. Ash must have left the flat unlocked at some time, though you'd wonder who would bother to steal typescripts. They did take my Dave Brubeck records as well.

FK: This was the cause of your rupture with MKD?

TL: I was very angry with him; furious, and so angry with myself for letting Simon down. None of that stuff ever turned up. Ash kept away and then I heard that he'd gone to Wellington, owing rent even on his garage.

FK: You did re-establish your friendship with him later, I understand, on his return from the capital. How did that come about?

TL: Actually, I did have a brief correspondence with him during his time in Wellington. He wrote asking if I would become a subscriber to a literary journal he was to start up there. He wanted me to find other subscribers in Canterbury as well — even sent me a list of people he considered possibilities.

FK: Have you kept the list? It might shed interesting light on who MKD considered were people of literary sensibility at the time.

TL: I didn't, I'm sorry. He also said that subscribers would receive what he termed 'positive editorial inclination', but although I sent three articles, none of them was published. Mind you, the whole thing didn't last long, did it?

FK: Mopsus had just the three issues, but is considered to have been prophetic of New Zealand literature, as befits its title.

TL: For years afterwards it kept sending out subscription forms. Ash must have found that a useful income.

FK: We have passed over two questions that I would like to return to now, if that's all right. The more recent concerned the picking up of your friendship with MKD after he returned here.

TL: Well, we're talking the late seventies now, aren't we. Susan and I were living in Sumner. I'd left Hatherleys and after a stint in the Social Welfare Department and then as a taxi driver, when I was writing a good deal, I got a job on the *Press*. Susan was teaching at Avonside Girls', I think — no, Papanui High School still, yes.

FK: And MKD?

TL: He had been taken up by the unmarried Devinne sisters who still lived in the family home in Merivale. They'd both known Charles Brasch quite well. Ash had convinced them his genius was worthy of support. They were almost gaga, of course. He would flirt and flatter to their faces and slander them at other times. He called them Gorgon and Gorgonzola.

FK: Did you ever meet Celia and Malisse Devinne?

TL: Yes.

FK: What were the circumstances?

TL: There was a sleepout by the shrubbery which was Ash's, but it wasn't big enough for his parties, so he persuaded the old dears to have a soirée in the big house from time to time. Gorgon and Gorgonzola were left tinkling at the piano while Ash and his friends boozed in the other rooms. It was quite sad, really; he demeaned their friendship and mocked their infirmity. There were even things stolen from the house. I stopped going.

FK: The suggestion is that MKD stole from his benefactors?

TL: I never saw him take anything, but I saw others remove ornaments — there was a Devinne jade collection that suffered. Finally there was a legal intervention by members of the wider family and the sisters were taken into care and Ash ordered to vacate his sleepout. I think in the end the whole place was bought by the Anglican church and became a diocesan retreat.

FK: Was it MKD's practice to read work at these soirées?

TL: Oh yes. He'd read on and on from what he termed 'work in progress' until he got too drunk and all his sycophantic friends would drink, chatter and applaud. By that time he had a sort of arty entourage of women with short black skirts and blue eyeliner, and one or two guys with pony-tails.

FK: The other question I wanted to come back to was that relating to the approaches that you say were made by MKD when he knew you were working for the Press. *You mentioned that your impression was that he cultivated you because he hoped for some advantage from that connection.*

TL: He was very interested in who decided on where books went for review, who did profile features, things like that. Bill Zimmerman did all that at the *Press* at that time. I introduced them shortly after Ash came back from Wellington. Bill told me later that the very next day Ash called at his office, saying that I was one of his closest friends and that he had been Simon Oakes' mentor in the year or so before his death. I had asked Bill to do a feature on Simon, but Ash persuaded him to concentrate on a living writer instead — Ash himself, of course. I tackled Dickens about that and I remember him saying, 'Let the dead bury the dead, Jinky old son. The inheritance is what matters.'

FK: You had by this time known him for nearly thirty years. You were familiar with his work.

TL: Certainly I'd read *No New Bethlehem, Marcel Proust and I* and *The Toby Jug World.*

FK: How did the consciousness you encountered there equate with the MKD you knew from day-to-day life? Could you hear Racine's wolves from the page?

TL: I've always been impressed by the intensity, by the absolute candidness, but it's just all his own life, isn't it — or rather experience and observation manipulated so that he has become the centre of it. It's a sort of regurgitation, but with his own bile become dominant. In *Bully For Me*, I think it is, he has seventeen pages about using the lavatory in the Lyttelton Domain.

FK: 'Sphincter Sphinx in crapt Crypt seated is the eye of I: retention is the name of the game, the pit and the sun's pendulum through the creak crack of the swings outside and the follicles of the salt gulls' cry.'

TL: It all goes on rather, for me.

FK: I have the impression that in the eighties, when MKD was increasingly gaining national attention, you and he were drifting apart. Would that be an accurate summation?

TL: Yes.

FK: In fact after the mid-eighties you lost contact? You didn't see him at all in the last years of his life?

TL: Susan and I had a sense that he couldn't be bothered with us once his prospects improved and, to be honest, I may have been somewhat envious of his success. The very week that *The Toby Jug World* won the big Commonwealth prize, I heard from Zeon Press that they had rejected the collection of my articles. But basically I feel that Ash wanted to kick off his earlier acquaintances, anyone who'd known him before he was important. That way he could create himself over again. The way he afterwards wrote about Te Tarehi High in *Fallow Education*, for example, and the accounts of his early years which became all excitement and bizarre experience and angst. I remember when he was in the garage behind Wilding Park he would spend hours catching blowflies with an old vacuum cleaner and he would stand in his duffle coat outside the window of Meehan's Electrical watching television for most of an evening.

FK: When was the very last time you saw MKD?

TL: I remember that it was the year of the big Canterbury floods; must have been '85, or '86. Bill and Heather Zimmerman were with Susan and me at the Bush Inn and Ash and his crowd came all dressed up from some mayoral thing; made a big entrance with their loud, affected voices. Dickens had been a small, ratty guy and I remember thinking that he'd become a small, puffy guy, like the old Sinatra. They came past us as they were leaving and Susan said hello to him. He stopped and stared for a few seconds then said, 'Bugger the proles' and laughed and went on out. I never saw him again. When he died, the editor asked me to attend the funeral on the paper's behalf and write an article, but I couldn't bring myself to do either. No one wanted to hear the truth about the man.

FK: I did a small piece for the overseas papers, I recall. MKD had insisted on having a Brubeck number in the Cathedral and a march past of the Ferrymead Fusiliers Dancing Team outside. Irony was everything to him. A tropism to be found throughout his mature work.

TL: Will his stuff last, do you think? Will people know *Journals of the New Te Rauparaha* and *The Toby Jug World* in fifty years?
FK: Absolutely.
TL: He wasn't likeable, you know; he used people, but all that's being changed now.
FK: How is it at the end of Gab's drowning in Bully For Me? — *'The evolution of the strongest lies is always towards truth.'*

THE AFTERMATH OF
MOLOCH'S HEAVEN

MOLOCH'S HEAVEN WAS published two years ago and you will no doubt remember the substantial and positive reviews that it received. Ecstatic and glowing were epithets applied by some of the more established literary commentators, though that's not for me to say, except that if you didn't read Wally Richmond in the *Eastern Southland Mah Jong and Cultural Gazette*, then you missed one of the man's most princely critiques. Issue twelve, and I believe that there are just a few back numbers available from Box 37, Wyndham.

But my point isn't to deprecate an adulatory approach to *Moloch's Heaven*, which is still prominent in several bookshops in Gore and available personally autographed from Box 38, Wyndham, but to apprise ordinary people of the obligations that accompany literary fame. It's not all cheerio lunches at the school library day, or reading to the womenfolk in the marquee during the possum-skinning contest at the AMP show.

Personally, I have always taken the responsibilities of celebrity status seriously, but I remain constantly amazed by the complacent assumption in other people of my goodwill. Nadine Undermeyer comes to mind as a case in point.

Nadine Undermeyer is a spinner–weaver who has four hectares of black sheep at Te Peka and once spent three weeks in the Salinas Valley studying with Choctaw moccasin maker and National Treasure, Shaking Snake Reilly. These three weeks equipped Undermeyer with the knowledge to be a self-appointed cultural messiah, and with a son whom the local policeman calls upon to track rustlers.

Nadine organised a station verse and rural poetry competition with a Yamaha 250 farm bike as first prize and drew 1,789 entries. She got the bike by having the gall to write directly to the national general manager of Yamaha, enclosing a photograph of herself and Shaking Snake Reilly welcoming Japanese tourists to his studio.

She came by my house with the 1,789 entries in a small woolpack and said that she and the rest of the committee were willing for me to judge them. Six prizewinners, she said, twenty highly commended and just a brief instructive comment for each of the remaining 1,763. There could be a crate of Speights in it, she said, and a bit of a do at which I would read out the winners and my judge's report. On the other hand, she said, if I was too busy with my own work then there was always the local primary headmaster, who was a whiz at impromptu portraits in jumbo crayons.

Celia Devinney was another I could use as an example. In the late 1860s the original lowly Devinney had been too drunk to find his way from Dunedin to the goldfields and ended up owning miles of swamp in Southland, which more sober descendants dried out with a sense of poetic justice and which proved firm enough on which to build a dynasty. It takes only two or three generations to develop an almost Jurassic sense of breeding and noblesse oblige. Old Celia has a face like a Cheviot ewe and a stable of trotters known from one end of the country to the other. She regards all non-landowners with an affronted expression, as if a fish in a jar has suddenly been held in front of her.

Until *Moloch's Heaven* I was a fish in a jar to Celia Devinney, but after my profile feature in the Gore paper I received a summons to the Broadlands homestead. She was choosing jodhpurs for a bob-haired, smooth-rumped granddaughter when I arrived, but graciously allowed me to carry some bags of potting mix into the glasshouse while I waited. She never considered the possibility of damage to my keyboard hand. Later she permitted me to come inside, provided I stood on a rug that caught any fallout of potting mix from my corduroys.

'The family want a first-rate Devinney history done,' she said, and I saw myself prefigured in the description, but she went on, 'so I've decided to do it myself. Who but a Devinney could do the Devinneys justice.' She gave a laugh that would make a huntaway proud. 'I've all the material; I've the gist of it,' she said, gesturing towards a vast, open chest of insemination reports, sepia photographs, diaries, paternity briefs and trophy rosettes. 'All I need is someone to pull it finally together. Would you like to pull it finally together?' She looked doubtfully at the fragments of potting mix that lay on the rug like a vanquished host of midges. 'Maybe there could be an acknowledgement in the preface,' she said. 'At any rate there'd be a few sides of hogget and if you wanted mushrooms in season perhaps you could ring the manager and the dogs would be tied.'

I'm sensitive to any gender imbalance in my illustrations of the demands made by the New Zealand community on its literary icons, so let's take Roy Rossiter as the next example. Roy runs the largest slink skin collection business in eastern Southland and when it snows in the spring he has a hard time keeping a gloomy face to match those of his fellows. I wouldn't say Roy Rossiter was an avid reader, not heavily into metafiction, for example, and he generally uses his index finger to help him through *Harness Tips*, but after he'd actually seen *Moloch's Heaven*, hefted it for the substance of its 447 pages, he was convinced that I knew everything. That's not quite true, but Roy has an overweening and hearty confidence in my infallibility. He will quiet a public bar to appeal to me as an oracle. 'Hey. Hey, listen up. Yow, yow, shut it, Maxie, Shakespeare will know the answer to this one, yeah, gofrit, Shakespeare.' And it will be some moot point about the moisture content of Nightcaps' coal, or why dogs get knotted. If I didn't know that Roy was thick, I might think that there was something else behind this sort of thing. The outcome is that I've found it easier to avoid the larger social gatherings with Roy present.

I read somewhere that the definition of a bore is the person who insists on telling his life story when you want to tell yours. There's an analogy there with literary fame. I often have two, even three, people a month wanting to talk to me about *Moloch's Heaven*. Trevor Jacke, for example, who lives in a room above the Mataura Post Office after returning from a course on existential graphics at the Dunedin Polytechnic. He rang me up at three o'clock one morning, moved to tears by Chapter Thirty in *Moloch's Heaven*, which depicts the angst of Arthur Pocock after the failure of his first exhibition. I'd have to say that Trevor seemed to have penetrated to the thematic crux of that section. He entreated me to come and talk with him about this monumental and universal novel — his words not mine — and I gave up a Sunday afternoon to pedal over and do so.

Trevor Jacke must be about six eight, but all slumped and folded and with a head like a Halloween pumpkin. No sooner had I sat down on a padded beer crate and begun to explain the genesis of *Moloch's Heaven*, than he pulled three asparagus tip cartons of manuscript from beneath his bed and began to read from it like a revivalist preacher. I escaped seven hours later by taking the louvres from the lavatory window downstairs and sneaking into a Mataura night redolent with scents of fennel and mutton fat. For weeks afterwards Trevor would ring in the small hours and rant, a practice that cost me the occasional companionship of Shelley Hambinder. If I didn't answer, he would come round in person.

Through all of this I have maintained my conviction of the salutary influence of the man of literature on his age, and have continued to give freely of myself, as Shelley Hambinder would testify. While waiting to hear from the Expedite Soft Cover Publishing Co. in Jackson, Mississippi concerning my second novel, *Flight of the Dodo*, I have held a creative syntax seminar for school leavers and, despite the inmates' malicious petition, remain available as a volunteer counsellor at the Croydon hospice.

You can see from all of this that I have accepted the demands and inconveniences which accompany artistic achievement, as well as the benefits which are more immediately obvious to the mass who merely aspire to fame. I expect such pressures to intensify once the international release of *Dodo* is negotiated. In fact I have serious doubts as to whether I will then be able to maintain my accessible and accommodating position within the community.

That, however, is in the future and I don't wish to make people downcast with the prospect. As I recently wrote in letters to John Updike, the replies to which seem persistently mislaid by New Zealand Post, he and I are, after all, bound to the total social consequentiality of our own genius.

THE LENNY FUDGE
BIBLIOGRAPHY

Lenny Fudge to the Rescue

Lenny Fudge and the Max Factor

Hark the Shadowed Moon: Lenny Fudge

The Lenny Fudge Primer of English Syntax

Toad Licking Deviancy Among Transients of the Californian Urban Ghettos: Len Fudge BA

Lenny Fudge Behind Bars and Other Hotel Stories

Effective Public Speaking: Fudge and Chickklegrubber

Lloyd George Almost Knew My Father: L. Dai Fudge

Mega Star Lenny Fudge

The Personal Lenny Fudge Scrapbook

My Struggle with Litotes: Lenny Fudge

Lenny Fudge on Religion

Lenny Fudge on Goddesses of the Silver Screen

The Fall of Communism in Words of One Syllable: Lenny Fudge

Come Back, Lenny Fudge

The Lenny Fudge Plain and Improved Shakespeare

The Future for Zion in the Hokianga: Fudge and Goldblum

Lenny Fudge and the Candy Man

A Libertine's View of Western Democracy: Lenny Fudge

Lenny Fudge Remembers

Arabic Made Easy: Lenny Fudge

Twenty Quick Feminist Hotpots: Lenny Fudge

Lenny Fudge in Concert

The Can Can — A Stutterers' Remedy: Lenny Fudge

Lenny Fudge As Seen by the Famous

Lenny Fudge: The Thirteenth Disciple

Reducing Overheads in the Demolition Industry: Lenny
    Fudge

Fudge Speaks Out — Again

The Lenny Fudge No Sugar Diet

Ten Years with the Tundra Bears: Lenny Fudge

An Open Letter to Prince Charles: Lenny Fudge

Lenny Fudge and the Planet Nemesis

The Best of Lenny Fudge

The Fudge Man Cometh

Growing Aspidistra for Beginners: Lenny Fudge

Living God Fudge of the Orinoco

Triple Agent Lenny Fudge

Oh List, the Takahe Calls: Lenny Fudge

Fudge's Centennial History of the Te Tarehi Dairy
    Co-operative

Lenny Fudge: A Critical Reassessment

Arabic Made Even Easier: Lenny Fudge

Fudge's Illustrated Purchase Garden Supply and Coupon
    Book

Fudge Becomes a Sugar Daddy

All Time Mystery Grates in the Fudge Fireside Series

Levitation Among the Arctic Hare: Lenny Fudge

The Return of Lenny Fudge

Lenny Fudge Goes for Broke

The Sociological Implications of the Rise of Dry Cleaning in the Twentieth Century: Len Fudge BA

Lenny Fudge's Churchill Letters

A Probing Research Report of Nymphomania: Lenny Fudge

Feeding Your Pets on Less: Lenny Fudge

Great Potting Mixtures Through the Ages: Lenny Fudge

Fudge Twenty Years On

Fudge's Freudian Primer

Write Great Lyric Poetry the Fudge Way

Victorian Devotional Catechisms Revived: Gladstone and Fudge

Alas the Fife and Drum: Lenny Fudge

Fudge in Trouble Again

Where Are You, Lenny Fudge?

The Great Lenny Fudge Pontius Pilate Debate

Carrion as Usual: Lenny Fudge

Lenny Fudge Remembers: Volume 7 — The Years 1952–53

Abyss of Fatal Desire: Lenny Fudge

Rage Against the Night: Tantrumm and Fudge

Alzheimer Meets Lenny Who?

A Confectioner Looks Back: Lenny Fudge

Lord Lenny of Fudge

Safari Hints and Tropical Remedies: Bwana Fudge

Winning Handball the Fudge Way

Lenny Fudge and the Fat Lady in Concert

On Blossom Hath Thou Fed: Lenny Fudge

Table d'Hôte and Other Inflatuations: Lenny Fudge

Fudge: Legend of Our Times

Bonny Braes and Bras of Otago: Lenny Fudge

Benisons for Denizens: Lenny Fudge

Lenny Fudge Strikes Back

The Unabridged Fudge Tourist Guide to Taihape

Lloyd George Knew My Mother: L. Dai Fudge

A Senior Administrator's Memoir of the British Raj: Lenny
    Fudge

A Guide to Better Posture: Fudge and Quasimodo

Unfinished Timpani: Lenny Fudge

Of Course You Can Write: Lenny Fudge

The Fudge Book of Ubiquitous Quiz Questions

Sacro-guilt Symbolism in J.K. Baxter's Poetry of the Jerusalem
    Period: Len Fudge BA

Four Thousand Selected Lady Di Photographs from New
    Zealand Magazines in June: Lenny Fudge

Learn Mah Jong From a Champion: Lenny Fudge

Lenny Fudge Nudge Wink Wink

Living with Fame: Lenny Fudge

Fudging the Issues with Lenny

My Desert Island Book Choices: Lenny Fudge

Fudge in Darkest Eketahuna

Crowned Heads I Have Known: Lenny Fudge

One Hundred and One Fudge High Country Mutton Recipes

The Fudge Handbook of Political Rhetoric and Stock Denials

Conspiracy Against Genius: The Fudge Story

Rugby Leit Motifs in New Zealand Prose Fiction: Len
Fudge BA

Fudge's Indoor Cacti and Succulents for Pleasure and Ozone

Fudge Without Peer

Fudge in the Footsteps of Jesus

The Lenny Fudge Almanac of Low Cholesterol Foods
Grouped According to Star Signs

The Post-humorous Works of Lenny Fudge

Baton in My Knapsack: The Fudge War Recollections

Lenny Fudge Lends a Hand

Send for Lenny Fudge

Lenny Fudge at Charterhouse

The Rake's Progress — An Examination of Technical Advance
in Agricultural Machinery: Len Fudge BA

My Years with Michael Joseph Savage: Lenny Fudge

How Leave I My Country?: Lenny Fudge

Stinking Rich with Fudge

The Family Fudge: A Celtic Genealogy

Significant Prorogations of Early British Parliamentary
History: Len Fudge BA

Aloe Again: Fudge on Purgative Drugs

A Life Among the Ngai Tahu: Lenny 'Waka' Fudge

A Definitive Guide to Naturally Occurring Orchid Additives:
Lenny Fudge

Caliban to Calabash and Back: Great Routes of the East in the Fudge World Travel Series

Doltish Games of the Hanoverian Court: Lenny Fudge

Fudge to the Rescue

Fudge to the Fore

Fudge's Sweet Revenge

A Thousand Famous Death Bed Utterances: G. Reaper and L. Fudge

Open Water Snipe Shooting with Lenny Fudge

Lenny Fudge Remembers Grub Street

Another Thousand Vegetarian Fondue Recipes: Lenny Fudge

All You Ever Wanted to Know About Computers But Couldn't Find the Key to Ask: Lenny Fudge

Fudge on Plate Tectonics

Dost Rata Twine?: Lenny Fudge

The Quintessential Fudge

Olda Growum Alonga Me: The Lenny Fudge Pidgin English Retirement Guide

THE TANK BOAT

FIRE AND WATER were the fascinations of my boyhood. I understand the adult anger when I read of yet another school, or pine plantation, burnt down, yet see a simulacrum of my former self dance before the flames. When I pass a group of kids heading into the mangrove swamps, or biking the side road to the shingled river, I experience a familiar, powerful inclination to follow.

Cog was my best friend in Form Four, even though I accidentally shot him with a home-made spear gun. What sort of a friend is that, his mother asked mine. Her judgement was based more on consequence than intent. Cog knew our town's river intimately, noticing every change, whether the cause was slow evolution, or sudden flood.

On a day so windy that the poplars heeled and we were buffeted on our bikes, he took me to the tall, tin fence of Cram Light Engineering. We leant the bikes on the fence and stood on the seats, gripped the sharp tin top, to look into the yard. The compacted ground behind the workshop was uneven, unsealed, the rust and oil and chemicals kept any weeds from springing up among the hulks, the piled plough blades, stacks of iron reinforcing for the concrete people, galvanised sheeting, old railway wheels and curved silo segments.

'So what,' I said. The fence moved in the wind and Cog's long, almost yellow hair was flung back from his face. 'What's so special?' I said.

'Look over by the riverbank,' said Cog. On the far side, lying by itself next to the frame elephant that Cram

Engineering had built for the children's playground at the gardens, was a large oval tank, grey-green with black lettered markings. 'It's a fuel tank from a plane,' Cog said. 'I checked it out last night.'

I knew at once that he meant to steal it. My own inclination was just the same, even though at first I couldn't think what use it would be.

'A boat. A boat, of course,' said Cog. 'D'arcy McDonald had one at the estuary and he'd cut out part of the top and put some wooden slats in. Absolutely watertight. A bottler.'

'Yeah,' I said. In my mind's eye I saw Cog and myself in it with the alterations already done. We were slipping beneath the town bridge with a lot of the other guys watching wistfully from the bank. Maybe we had some sort of a sail up so that we didn't have to paddle, and the smooth, blunt front of the tank made a slight bow wave on the quiet water. 'Yeah, Jesus,' I said. 'A boat.' I saw the tank transformed into a launch and myself inviting an alluring Susan Wedderburn to come aboard. The same Susan Wedderburn who had refused to be my partner at the junior dance, who had a slow, easy voice, who trailed through the school grounds like Cleopatra.

I reckoned the fuel tank must have been at least three metres long and it was shaped rather like my father's hip flask. Stealing it was going to be one thing; finding somewhere to hide a sucker that big was another. Cog and I got down from the fence and went and sat behind the old water tower in the railway yards where we could be out of the wind and think.

Cog remembered about the derelict milking shed on the Watsons' farm. It was left from the time that the Watsons had run a house-cow and before the town had grown out that way and brought a milk delivery with it. The shed was small and run down, it had only a dirt floor, but it was close to the riverbank and we could keep the tank there out of sight. 'No one would give a toss,' said Cog. 'Maybe when we've made it into a boat then we'll ask them if they mind us keeping it there. We could do a few hours work, or something. Who'd mind that?'

It took only that possibility of an approach to assure us that the cowshed was legitimately ours to use as we saw fit. 'We could fix it up a bit for them,' I said. Surely we were doing the Watsons a favour by taking responsibility for the shed.

'When it's done,' said Cog, 'we can take the tent and supplies and go downstream to the estuary for the weekend. There's this metal table base we've got in the basement which would do for an anchor.' I saw it clearly: the tank boat expanded and buoyant while Cog and I were eeling, and torching for flounder, in the estuary.

At dusk, Cog and I met on the other side of the river from the engineering workshop. We sat under a birch tree and peeled pale wafers from its bark as the light faded. There was an aviary closer to the town centre on the same side and peacocks and parakeets were screeching. Cog and I wore shorts and sneakers with no socks so that we could wade across the river to the yard when it was dark enough. I had the tow rope that my father kept in the car boot for emergencies. Cog had one of his father's thin, dark cigarillos and we lit half each, drawing in breath slowly and bracing not to cough when the smoke caught suddenly in our lungs. There was rough grass extending from the birches towards the river and rushes and some clumps of arum lilies along the bank. The slow water surface of the river grew darker and more polished; the vegetation was losing its separate colours, apart from the strangely disembodied luminosity of the white bog lily flowers. 'The only thing is, getting that big sucker over the netting fence on this side,' said Cog. He had only a stub left and held it carefully so as not to burn his fingers as he gave a drag that lit up his hand and cheeks.

We pushed through the lilies into the small river, working our way across to find the shallow parts so that the water came no higher than our waists. The water was cool, but not unpleasant in the summer night and the cries from the aviary had ceased. The far bank wasn't under the park's care and the few upward sloping metres before the high fence of Cram's yard had soft lupins, but also cutty grass and boxthorn. Cog and I stood and looked through the netting fence at the fuel tank. Its colour was almost lost in the limited light, but it bore faint stripes cast by the frame elephant and a far streetlight. Cog pulled speculatively at the bottom of the heavy netting. He worked enough slack for us to wriggle beneath, but there was no way the tank would fit under there. It was a good deal bigger close up and had several awkward bits sticking out that we hadn't seen from the street.

What a beaut it was, though — so strong, sleek and obviously watertight. Cog and I sat down quite hidden behind it to gloat and figure out how to move it to the river. Cog struck it secretly with a stone and sniggered at the start I gave at the sudden clang. 'If you could've seen yourself,' he said. He made a sucking sound with one of his wet sneakers by moving his toes, as he thought about the logistical problem we faced.

'Quit arsing around,' I said, 'or we'll get caught.'

'There's no way this'll go under the fence and we've got nothing to cut it. Maybe we can get the road gate open and take it that way.'

I didn't think so and, besides, who wanted to be carrying the thing around the streets. Cog seemed quite happy to spin out our crime, to camp and fool there in the premises of Cram Light Engineering, but my fear gave clarity to my thinking. I realised that the way to free the tank was over the back of the elephant, which stood higher than the fence. 'Hey, yeah,' said Cog. 'With the rope that could work.' We tied the rope to the tank and threw the other end over the elephant and the top of the fence. With our combined strength we managed to hoist the tank, smooth side down, on to the tubular back of the elephant. The noise of metal on metal was enormous, but we had abandoned stealth in favour of speed. I then climbed back under the fence and took up the rope while Cog sat with the tank, ready to push as I pulled.

'Don't let the bloody thing come down on you,' hissed Cog, without telling me how to avoid that very fate. At the end of a countdown Cog pushed and I pulled, the tank slid on to the top wire, teetered and then fell into the lupins and thorns of the riverbank. I had sprung to the side along the fenceline and caught my bare arm on a twisted tie of number eight. From there I rebounded into the thorns. Cog wriggled under the wire, but then just lay there laughing, unable to get up. I knew he was having one of his laughing jags and that it had to run its course; not even the arrival of the police would have had an effect. Once he'd started laughing in the headmaster's office and despite Batman saying, 'Coughlan, you will stop laughing this instant. Do you hear me? This instant,' Cog hadn't.

I began pushing the tank down the few metres towards the water. It wasn't all that easy. Bits stuck out, where the fuel lines had been I suppose, and they snagged on anything to hand. I was getting the wind up, not just because all the noise was bound to bring someone soon, but also because I could feel a good deal of slippery blood on my forearm. Cog stopped laughing when I launched the tank and he came down as it floated free and I paid out the rope.

'If you could've seen yourself,' he said. 'Jesus.'

'That's all very bloody well for you,' I said. 'I'm pig stuck here and you're laughing.'

Cog dipped my arm into the water and then put his face close so that he could judge the cut and the amount of the blood flow, dark in the limited light of the moon. 'Tie your handkerchief round it. It's not so bad.'

'Yeah, but then we've still got to get this thing to Watsons' shed.'

'That's easy,' said Cog. 'The hard work's done now, Denny. I can float her down quietly to Watsons and leave her in the willows and tomorrow night we'll go down there.'

Cog made sure I didn't feel that I was piking out halfway through. One of the things I liked about him was that, although he was often in trouble, there was no personal malice in him. 'It's just about on my way home,' he said. 'Look, look,' and he climbed on to the tank, which rode high in the water, and lay down in a pose of exaggerated ease. So I tied the handkerchief around my arm, waded across the river and through the arum lilies to the park side. 'Hey,' called Cog quietly. 'Is this boat going to be something, or what!' I had a last shadowy glimpse of him, balancing on the tank, drifting and turning with it away into the darkness.

The next evening we went down to Watsons' farm and furtively carried the tank from the willows to the unused shed. There was no door, but room enough to prop the tank against the single cow bail. The tin roof was just about shot and let in bright shafts of the westward sun, which fell on the rough, dirt floor, a part of the bail worn smooth by cows, the matt, grey-green surface of the fuel tank. Cog had brought a flat carpenter's pencil, a hammer and tin-snips. We began to plan the outline of the cockpit. Cog wanted to cut much of the top away, but I was more cautious. I told him that we could always take more off afterwards, but nothing could be replaced if we overdid things the first time. Cog could see the logic in this, though in fact the cutting proved so difficult that we never got round to making any modifications.

I had imagined straight sides to the cockpit with the edges neatly turned under, but the metal was surprisingly thick and until we'd opened up a good deal of it, there was no space for leverage. There were some partitions inside as well. It took us most of the next Saturday to finish. We developed a rough and ready technique of holding the tin-snips in place and belting them with the hammer. The level of our workmanship deteriorated as our enthusiasm lessened and our hands got knocked about.

When the cockpit was finished it showed some very nasty edges, despite our attempts to burr them with the hammer, but Cog's optimism returned once the job was done and the tank almost ready to launch. 'Look,' he said, 'we can get some sacks and stuff and pad round the edges and the inside. Later we'll line the thing with wood. She'll be okay. You wait. I bet she'll be sweet on the water.'

'Tight as a bloody drum,' I said.

'Bloody right,' said Cog.

Cog had to visit his grandparents the next day — all of the family were going — and with school and everything it wasn't until Thursday that we both went back to the cowshed, walk-ing up the river line through the willows as usual so that we wouldn't be noticed. The tank boat was just as we'd left it, except that birds had shat on it. I'd brought some coal sacks and Cog had a torn bedspread. We put them into the tank and carried it over the short, summer grass of the paddock to the riverbank.

The tank was a totally different thing once in the water. It became animated, skittish even, bobbing and swerving as we lined it with the sacks and the bedspread. I clambered in while Cog held the rope to the bank and then he came aboard. What had seemed a large enough space when we were cutting it in the cowshed was now shown to be inadequate, as Cog had thought, but neither of us made any mention of it. After all we'd done to be floating in the tank boat, after all the times I had imagined how it would be, the reality at last was disappointing. My legs were cramped inside the tank and instead of the boat moving easily in the direction of our choice, it persisted in turning as it went, which made both steering and paddling difficult. We spiralled out on to the smooth river and went mainly downstream, despite using our plank paddles against the flow.

Cog paused for a rest, breathing heavily. 'The thing is, there's no rudder yet. We should've thought of that. Once we get some sort of rudder attached she'll be beaut. With a rudder she'll hold her line and paddling will be a breeze.' The flailing of the paddles had beaten a good deal of coal dust from the sacks, and water had streaked it over Cog's face and arms. I must have looked much the same.

We made a last effort and brought the tank pitching clumsily up river a bit so that we could land a fair way down from the cowshed. 'It'll be much easier when we get the hang of it,' panted Cog.

'Sod of a thing's got a mind of its own, I reckon.'

'A rudder'll make a hell of a difference. Don't you worry.'

'Yeah,' I said, but my doubts were growing.

We decided to leave the tank in the willows and gorse that night, turning it over so that there'd be no problem if it rained. We had a wash-up to remove the worst of the coal dust and then walked along the riverbank towards the town. Magpies were coming in for the night to the stand of pines behind the dairy factory, and higher, noiselessly, gulls were making their way to the coast. One or two dogs were barking on the outskirts of the town, but without conviction. Cog was full of ideas about how we could fit a rudder and get some decent paddles. The river was very smooth, with the current disguised, and the sun lit a fire behind the hills as it went down.

Two days later the paper had the story of Nelson Miller's death; how he had drowned with his legs caught in a home-made boat made out of a fuel tank. Nelson and Peter Wiremu had found it along the riverbank. The police wanted to talk to any kids who had used the boat, anyone who might know the owner. Mrs Miller normally took her son to cricket practice herself, she said, but that night she had visitors from her home town of Feilding and let Nelson go to the river with Peter Wiremu. What was the reason for things like that, she asked the reporter?

Cog and I had a talk about it at school that day during break. We sat at the edge of the playing field by the sycamores and flicked their one-winged seeds in the air. 'I don't reckon it's our boat,' said Cog. 'Tons of people have got tank boats like that. D'arcy McDonald says he's seen hundreds, and anyway it's your own fault taking a boat that doesn't belong to you, isn't it?'

'Even though it's some other boat all right,' I said, 'I don't reckon we should go out there again. The coppers will be doing a check. They'll have found it and worked out it was pinched from the yard.'

'Yeah, okay. That's fair enough, but next summer we'll go

back and get her all set up, rudder and all.' There was a false vehemence in Cog's determination.

'That's for sure,' I said.

Next summer was a long way off and by then Cog and I had sort of drifted apart. I never went back to that stretch of the river. I started playing a lot of tennis with Buster Kerrigan and David Posswillow, and I decided to take my subjects a lot more seriously in the fifth form because of School Certificate at the end of it. After all, you have to look ahead in life.

GROWING PAINS

When I was fourteen I began suffering cruelly from lovesickness. It was a debilitating and socially unacceptable disease which so ravaged me that I survived it only at the cost of much of my emotional capability. Infatuation, which is simply the imagination uninformed, was torn out of me by merciless experience.

My first coveted love was the wife of the golf professional at Prippen Lea where I used to caddy and search for balls. Mrs Lassiter. She must have been all of twenty-three and had a toddler around whose soft throat I imagined my hands. Mrs Lassiter liked me: she said I had a cheeky face. With a thrilling freedom of language, she said bugger and shit. There were wisps of pale hair at her neck and she looked at me sideways when she laughed. You men, she said indulgently when her husband joked with me about the girls' team he was coaching — you men. She smelt of silver paper and fabrics dried in the sun. On the occasions when she and the golf professional took me home in their Volkswagen I imagined him having a collapse at the wheel and myself taking decisive command. I couldn't understand how he could bear to go to work at the golf club and be parted from her. He was a generous man with a quick wit, but I never took to him.

I played football in the seconds with Jeremy Annis who was a Christian and he invited me to go to a Bible class camp at Kaikoura. I met Ruth Rossons, who lived there, and, after playing charades in the youth hall, I experienced sharp pains in my left side and decided that I must marry her. She was very meek and when discomforted in playing out charades, put her hands to her face. The inside of her knees took my breath away and I thought that I wouldn't live long. In the boldness of this desperation I arranged to pick her up at her place on the Sunday and walk with her to church. On that morning I walked the several blocks to her house and it began to rain: something that I had made no plans for. Wet and wretched, I hung about outside her gate and then went and sheltered in a phone box a little way down the street. I had so little understanding of courtship that it didn't occur to me to walk up their path in a manly fashion and introduce myself. I imagined that Ruth's parents would be aware of my intentions towards their daughter as plainly as I was myself. So I hid. They went to church in a dark blue Morris Oxford and Ruth gave one long, backward look through the rain to the phone box in which I stood in abject humiliation with hair plastered on my forehead. I've never seen her since and couldn't bear to do so.

My friend Alun, the one with his right-hand little finger as long as all the others, had a brother in the navy. Sometimes when he was home on leave he would deign to answer our questions. These questions were so unimportant to him that he answered them only when he was also occupying his time with more worthwhile pursuits, such as polishing the chisel toes of his immaculate black Italian shoes, or shaving carefully down to the dark hair at the base of his neck. 'What's it like?' he answered. 'Well, it's like a flock of sparrows flying off your arse.' Alun told me that his brother in the navy had more fucks than hot dinners. It's like that there, he said. More than anything else in the world, I wanted to be part of a profession that had more fucks than hot dinners. A good many have shared that ambition, I imagine, and only grudgingly become reconciled to being brain surgeons, solicitors, software millionaires, physicists and silversmiths of international repute.

Amelia Bennie had the best tits at the girls' school. On her way in the mornings she pedalled past the lower entrance to our school and often we would wait there just to have the pleasant sight of her passing. There was no mockery, no shouts, just an admiring and respectful regard as she went by; rather as dockworkers stop work a while to watch a ship of grand armament glide past them in the channel. After seeing Amelia Bennie, even a double period of mathematics with Bodger could be borne and the bullies by the cafeteria stood up to because of a surfeit of testosterone. I wonder if she was ever aware of the hundred phantom hands upon her in the course of a day.

Travelling up to a family holiday in Nelson I fell in love with the motelier's daughter in Blenheim when we stopped for one night there. Jasmine Courts. I never knew her name, but she smiled twice at me in the little cabin of a motel office and I lay awake most of the night in case she came to tap on my window. She must have been able to restrain herself, but for weeks the random recollection of the blonde pony-tail against the tan of her shoulders would cause an ache of despair and loss in my heart.

Albie Joseph's good-looking sister was three years older than us and heavily into narcissism, although then I didn't recognise it as such. Normally she was almost as contempt-uous of me as she was of her brother, and surrounded by a galaxy of moth-like friends of both sexes. One very windy autumn Sunday I went round to the Josephs' two-storeyed brick and roughcast house above the park and found Melissa there alone. She held the door ajar and said nothing when I asked for Albie; she looked hopefully beyond me for a better class of company. 'Oh, come and help me for a minute then,' she said. Her bedroom seemed full of round, soft mats, frilled cushions and mirrors. 'I'm sorting out sets of things for the week,' she said. 'Ensembles.'

She stood, self-consciously unself-conscious, before the largest mirror in bra and pants and held frocks, tops and skirts to herself from time to time. 'Ideally your legs should be longer than your head and torso combined,' she said. 'I'm lucky there. Feel how smooth my skin is.' She moved my hand to her ribs and watched my face intently, but only so that she could see the wonder of herself reflected in my expression. 'It's hopeless in a town like this, no matter how beautiful you are. I've sent a folio of photos to a modelling school in Sydney and had acknowledgement of receipt already.'

Only her feet spoilt it a bit: quite large feet with several deep creases above the heel of the fashion shoes she tried on. Her feet were asexual, common, rather like my own in their very practical configuration. Her feet lacked those attributes of gender possessed by the features to which I was naturally drawn — the heavy hair as a frame for her face, the flare of her hips, the slight pout of her belly above the waistband of her knickers.

Melissa tired of my few, feeble compliments. Even as a makeshift audience I was unsatisfactory. 'You'd better go now,' she said as the wind blew the small branches of the silver birch against the bedroom window where they tapped and scrambled like the antennae of lascivious lobsters. I never told anyone of my privileged session, because of my shame at her complete dominance, her sure knowledge that I was utterly without masculine threat.

Towards the end of my fifth form year I had a notable success with Pamela Burridge, who was friends with Samantha Chesterfield, whose older sister, known as Stunner, was so beautiful that Nobby Allidger, halfback for the Firsts, drowned himself in the Rangitata when she dumped him. Albie Joseph and I met Pamela and Samantha at the skating rink one Sunday evening. I didn't dare ask Samantha out, so instead I asked Pamela if she'd go to the end of term rage with me. Afterwards, I heard that the main reason she agreed was that she was taken with the Ivy League shirt I was wearing. It was my brother's and I'd snaffled it while he was in hospital with blood poisoning. What made Pamela's agreement particularly sweet was that Albie aimed too high, asked Samantha, and got refused.

Only later did I realise that the date with Pamela posed something of a difficulty regarding wheels. I had been a licensed driver for seven weeks and knew that my father wouldn't let me have the car at night. It always seems to be that way with young love — the practicalities almost overwhelm the benefit. To admit to Pamela that I wouldn't have a car, to scrounge a ride with someone else, was unthinkable. What has to be done for love, has to be done. It was necessary to steal the family car for the night. Late on the Saturday afternoon of the rage I told my father that I'd wash the Humber Hawk and put it away, as he wouldn't be using it — would he? I cleaned it zealously, particularly the back seat where I imagined Pamela recumbent, but at dusk I crept out and pushed the car from the drive and partway down the block, where I came to it later when I had dressed for the dance.

All manner of things could have gone wrong, of course, but for once the whole thing was a triumph of dangerous deceit. The adrenalin rush sustained me most of the night and even assisted me to maintain something of a conversation with Pamela. Although I was a poor dancer she allowed me afterwards to kiss her in the back seat and I squeezed her so tightly into the corner that she was almost melded into the upholstered junction. I think I could have gone out with her again if I'd shown more interest in her suggestion to take her ice skating at Lake Tekapo the next day, but even theft from one's family has its limits.

As an adolescent, my life within my family was completely apart from my life outside it. More than that. I was a different person in each context; different principles and beliefs, contrary motivations and emotional responses. I think for my brothers and sisters it was just that way too. If I came across them socially, at the dance hall, the beach, or movie theatre, there was only bare recognition between us. This was perhaps the reason for my failure with Prue Golightley, who was my doubles partner when we won the under seventeen title at the

Sinjohn Tennis Club. She had coloured pom-poms on the heels of her sports shoes and a very solid forehand volley: in a long game her sweat would slick some of her dark hair to her forehead and neck. Sometimes, after watching her play, I had difficulty walking. What completely stumped me was how to bridge the gap from discussing service actions and school friends to a request for her to take off her clothes. What possible form of intermediary communication was there? Often I feared that the tension of it all would send me into a swoon.

One evening when I had been particularly impressive at the net and we were alone in the trophy room, I interrupted her talk of Monty Finchley's ringworm by reaching forward and putting my playing hand down the front of her blouse. It was a madness that I was helpless to contain. Prue and I both waited for a few moments, almost as if we expected some explosion, or some external admonition. Her bra was very confidential and easily defeated me. I think she, too, was disappointed with the experience: she removed my hand. 'Don't ever do that again,' she said. 'If we weren't playing in the final tomorrow, I'd tell your mother.'

I played like a man possessed in the final, hoping that a brilliant victory would save me from a charge of carnal knowledge in the High Court. Prue's mother and mine were friends. Two weeks later my mother came into my room and asked me if I ever wanted to talk any things over with her. 'No,' I said, 'not that I can think of.' She told me that Prue Golightley told her mother everything and not to hesitate if I wanted to talk. Was I sure that there was nothing? I was sure. There was nothing, I said, nothing that I could think of.

In the seventh form, when I was nearly eighteen, I was put out of my misery. I met Sandra Browning, who came down in a Diocesan team to the National Secondary Schools' Netball Tournament. A group of us seniors from Boys' High were invited to the dance at tournament's end in the gardens' hall and Alun's sister introduced Sandra and me. Sandra was tall and strong, with a bandaged graze on her wrist from the semi-final and a straight, dark blue dress. 'Are you much at sport?' she asked me, and as she had little access to the truth I enlarged my reputation somewhat. All's fair after all. She had a very long face, well chinned, which wasn't unattractive, and she could stand a pause in conversation without uneasiness as we danced. 'I'm going to try for phys. ed. school,' she told me.

Towards the end of the dance she came with me from the hall and into the gardens. It was a cold time of the year, but someone had left the door to the hothouse unlocked and we went into that warm and heavy atmosphere, the narrow path between banks of ferns and orchids, the hanging baskets of tropical and fragrant achimenes, the sinuous hoses lying discarded and barely visible in the moonlight through the glass. We avoided the pain of conversation. Like Adam and Eve, we climbed into the rich natural profusion of the hothouse gardens and lay down, wasteful of the flowers crushed beneath us. Her breasts were sweeter and more full beneath her dress than I had guessed. The act itself was so explosive that I expected to be bleeding from the ears, but the only wound was a deep cut on my left ankle from a ponga trunk. I had been in such transport that the pain had failed to register.

It never occurred to me that Sandra might be in need of some reassurance. She wept freely on my almost hairless, adolescent chest and then was suddenly cheerful and began to organise our life together. Distantly I could hear the thudding of the band in the hall and was amazed that the world had gone on, that any continuity could have survived what we had experienced. All the world was winter and only Sandra Browning and I lay together in a perpetual summer, or so then it seemed.

REBECCA

MAYBE THE VERY worst thing that a woman says to a man is that she feels towards him like a sister, and almost as bad is to want to talk about Our Relationship, as though it's one of a set of abridged novels.

'I need to know where I am,' says Rebecca. She is sitting on the sill of the window in our flat above Montgomery's Kitchen Showroom in Madras Street. Full summer and the warm air brings scents from the park, intimations from the Chinese takeaway, as well as fumes from the traffic. She seems settled, prepared to give time and attention to what it is that explains our presence together here. The late sun glints on the hairs of her tanned forearms, two large top teeth rest on her lower lip, but such things are inadmissible as evidence. She taps a stainless steel table knife on the grey, worn wood of the window sill.

'Don't you have any ambition whatsoever?' she says.

'To get you back into bed,' I say. In a sense this is true.

'Don't you have any long-term plan,' she says, 'and see yourself in five, ten years' time, in the phases of its achievement?'

Rebecca wishes to be a television frontperson. She is quite open about this career and already has a post-graduate journalism diploma and a part-time reporter's job with Peninsula Radio. She acquired professional training in front of the cameras and practises the techniques before our mirror. She can retain a direct gaze and small natural smile indefinitely as a fadeout. It had been remarked on, she once told me, that she had no tendency to rictus.

'I've always thought I'll die young,' I say.

'Why's that?'

'I just do. Whenever I try to imagine myself twenty years on, or whatever, there's just a fog there, grey and damp and dense.'

'That's weakness,' says Rebecca. 'You're this sort of drifter who never imposes himself on life.'

So much is interpretation, isn't it? The emotional climate in which we experience things. Nine months ago, when Rebecca and I began living together, she thought my drifting a positive thing: a refusal to be hog-tied by the conventional. She would lie bare-breasted beside me in the midday sun and eat hard-boiled eggs. Small pieces of yolk, their outer surface gun metal blue, shimmied on her warm skin. Now she has her arms tight about her knees and she rocks impatiently on the window sill above the kitchen showroom. Even her smile has a slight constraint of impatience. 'Anyway,' she says.

We have spent a good deal of the night on it — Our Relationship — and in that exposition I have realised how unsatisfactory she considers it to be. Most of her grievances cut so deep that I've no reply, but I offer to do something about not having a car. 'I could buy one,' I tell her. 'I could get together the deposit. I think Richie Tomlinson is wanting to sell the veedub.'

'It's not just that, although I'm sick of not having a decent set of wheels. This flat here, four rooms stuck above the shops and still with the cruddy student furniture. A toilet cistern which won't flush properly, yet never stops running.'

What we're talking about hasn't anything to do with cars, or sofas, or the warm scents from the Chinese takeaway, nothing to do with red diamonds worn from the lino around the stove, or the ice cream pottle substituting for the missing bottom louvre. What we're talking about is the failure of our infatuation with each other. Ambition is a loveless thing. As long as Rebecca was in love she was content to lie eternally naked in the sun and eat boiled eggs; a concern for her future as a television frontperson signalled a change of heart. As soon as she let me go then she saw that I was drifting.

'We can still see each other around,' she says. Everything about this woman is admirable, except her opinion of me. Her big front teeth, the muscles of her shoulders, the faintest stubble of her armpits, are part of the wonder. 'No reason at all we can't still see each other around,' Rebecca says. There is an advertising blimp floating behind her in the blue sky above the city. DOOLEY'S TOYOTA. The moment is there for me to say something that will undercut triviality and strike her soul like an arrow.

'You're right. We're bound to still see each other around.'

I feel hard done by, that's the truth of it. I have established the pleasures of my life on her without thought for any future and now she wishes to be free. What is the use of talking of the north wind when the southerly is blowing?

Rebecca sits in the frame of the window and, although we continue to talk, I can see so clearly that there is a past now, and a future, in her conception. We have separated, she and I, as the holistic present has divided.

'Don't think that I regret any of it, though,' she says.

'Nor I.'

As we talk we are separate and there is the past, the present and the future once again. A consciousness of those divisions is with us when we are out of love, so that in a sensible fashion we order things in the hope of consequences to our benefit.

'I just have to give more time to my work,' she says. 'I've got to get ahead.' What she has to get ahead of is lying in bed until the afternoon sun is in our eyes, not answering the phone because we know we've done nothing deserving of good news, spending the rent money on a Hello Dolly Masquerade Ball.

'Do you remember the Hello Dolly Masquerade Ball?' I ask her.

'So what?'

They had a terrace at the ballroom, just like in the movies

and Rebecca and I went out and looked over a carpark, but also, in the moonlight, a line of concrete tubs with ornamental conifers. The cooler air made me realise that my shirt was wet with sweat and Rebecca's hair had started to come down. She was one of the best-looking women there, by anyone's assessment. An older woman who had argued with her partner came out and fell over the small balustrade into the carpark. She broke her collar bone and was in the papers. It happened after Rebecca and I had been standing together with the breeze on our flushed faces, but because I was only a few minutes from being there and have seen the photograph, it has become part of my experience — this heavy woman with puffed sleeves and tears on her cheeks, the thud of her on the asphalt.

'Look,' says Rebecca. 'If it's better for you I can stay for another day or two. I want you to feel that we've talked it through, not just that I'm walking out or something.' The blimp bobs as if in agreement with such counsel. Every time I kissed her I was excited by the smooth, white keys of those two front teeth. 'People are changing, growing all the time.' All such generalisations are perfectly true, but I see no connection between them and what is happening to us. Rebecca drums with the knife on the window sill, holding it loosely in her fingers so that it can reverberate.

'I'd rather not draw it out,' I say.

Less than a year ago I first met her at the final of theatresports in the old town hall. She had a love-bite on her neck and neither of us made any mention of it then, or since. She told me that she'd been invited to apply for the Drama School in Wellington, but wanted to go into journalism. As she goes down the stairs, what we have between us is drawn tight for the last time and then parts. We will indeed see each other around, as she says; will see each other here as she comes for her things. Nothing will be the same. From the window I see her walk past the display of whiteware, microwaves, dual sinks and cupboard units that we live above. We have talked a great deal over two days and the more intimate the discussion, the more certain was the outcome. When a glance, a kiss, a hand on the shoulder, an old joke half told, can't do the job, then recourse to analysis is bound to fail.

Rebecca doesn't look up and I see, in contrast to a Chinese girl she passes, that her hair isn't black after all, but very dark brown. Maybe in a long time I will find myself, clear of fog, in Dooley's to select a car from the gleaming new models there and I will get an odd snag in my breathing, unaccountable, as I see the Dooley's sign. Maybe I will sign a contract and think of boiled egg crumbs on her warm skin, her slightly buck teeth, whole glamorous kitchens beneath us as we slept.

PENDRAGON

Pendragon's left shoe squeaked as he walked. The shoes were not new and had never squeaked hitherto. They were of finest shagreen, yet the left one began its complaint as he passed over the mosaics of lapis lazuli and between the courtiers towards the duke. The sound increased in intensity as his awareness of it grew and with his awareness came cognisance to all those about him. These are the immutable laws that govern such things. The lords and ladies allowed their lips to lift in supercilious scorn, the coxcombs simpered, the motleyed fool capered, e'en retainers bent their heads to smirk and keak at rank as they carried roasted barnacle and widgeon to the tables.

Pendragon intended to laugh lightly to dispel tension as he approached the dais, but his laughter had a despairing, thudding sound like a howlet beating its wings on the moonlit edge of the glebe; marry, like the second cock at the passing of the primrose way.

'Thy dexter shoe abominates in sound, sirrah,' cried the duke.

'Actually 'tis the left, my liege, but from where you're sitting looking back down the hall it — '

'Shut your face,' said the duke. He had something of a reputation for succinctness and, as temporal ruler of all within ten days' ride, he was able to indulge what reputation he pleased. From a proffered salver he took some peacocks' tongues, open sesame and caraway. From another he took ground boars' tusk and, with genteel and summary negligence, sprinkled it over a line of seely aristocrats shuffling past behind his chair. Pendragon was left to wait before him.

'My lord,' said the duke's seneschal, 'the minstrels are without.'

'Choice,' cried the duke, ruler by divine right and by the possession of the best pikemen in Europe. 'The duchess loves to hear the sons of Jubal and so do all the poplollies of the court. Lady Volupt, I hear tell, delights in a jig, eh Pendragon?'

'The Mistress of the Mirkins knows refrain from a round-elay I dare say, my lord, and apportions more the former as is seemly and meet in such a chaste dame,' said Pendragon, who was wary of the duke's mood.

But the eleventh of the line seemed almost jocund as well as rotund in his cups. He fell to quaffing goblets of malmsey and stuffing his cake-hole with suckling pig in a sauce of panache and ossian. Occasionally he paused to break wind, or pick his teeth with a bare bodkin; occasionally he tossed a bone of barnacle, or swine, to the brach, lyms and water rugs that growled and fawned on the floors of the banquet hall.

The seneschal was so bold as to remind the duke again of the players and the duke was delighted at it. 'We have forgot the minstrels indeed, sirrah, ergo you do well to remind us. Pray, what is the variety of sound and instrument they please us with?'

'Several rebecks, my lord, a number of hautboys, lutes and sackbuts, neshtwangers, tabors and a mameluke who leaps prodigiously and strikes his shins together in mid-air to render the sound of contesting stags. The last sent to you with utmost deference by the castilian of your fortress at Tunn.'

'We love a prodigy,' replied the duke. 'And what is the course of the music? What nature has it?'

'Indeed, a paean, my lord, to your own self.' The sene-schal's words caused the court physician to awake with a start and an interruption.

'Paean, my lord? Where is't? Forsooth, I have physic enough to forestall the most fell of bodily corruption.'

'What ails me sits in thy place. You are a calf and a mountebank not fit to carry out the stales of punks. Avaunt, to your low-caverned and airless slumbers once again.'

So the court physician had to pretend to sleep once more, though he was the focus of the gibes and shrieks of the dining hall and of the bones, crusts and maw-wallop tossed upon his pate. He was a man of the streets and contented himself therefore with a few guttural asides that went unremarked.

Pendragon was not loath to find the duke's interest blowing to another quarter, but knew his own case was only as far from the duke's mind as the jesses allow the hawk from the falconer. The duke raised his hand, on which glinted a great kernel of ruby and adamant; the seneschal lifted his staff (a dwarf from Tarragon); the musicians entered to the sound of their own goodly accompaniment. 'Bonzer,' said the duke.

'Most entertaining,' endorsed the duchess and wiped demurely a touch of strawberry syllabub from her lips with her gown of sarcenet and ermine.

'But we must consider in our wassail our vassal Pendragon, cousin to ourselves from misty Merlin's rampart. 'You stand accused,' said the duke insouciantly, 'of using Sir Boef's beaver.'

'My liege,' expostulated Pendragon, 'I know not his mistress!'

'His helm, you pretty varlet, you dullard, you scullion of language.'

'I handled not his rudder.'

'Dost bandy words with us?' exclaimed the great chevalier and he wiped his hands upon the fair hair of a page boy lest he require fair purchase on his broadsword. His voice assumed a shrillness that subdued the nobility ensconced within his favour. 'His helmet, I say, Bart Boef's helmet. Are you not privy to our language, sirrah?'

'Fain would I not be that receptacle,' said Pendragon boldly and marked the faint smile that moved the damask of Lady Volupt's cheek.

'Always the smart-arse,' said the duke. 'And we too have married at your sallies. But nevertheless, do membrance in your tune that here I pay the piper; that the moon's fair light depends yet on the greater sun unseen.'

The duke waved on his musicians, gambollers and balladeers, and mulled on the wine in his goblet. 'Is this the bustard from Spain?' he said.

'All who jolly nigh are native born, my lord,' replied the seneschal, 'although which side of the blanket I know not.'

'Give our Lord Pendragon a cup,' said the duke. 'Even though he is the butt of our Boef's claim, on the field ere this he has served well.'

'My liege remembers the spicy breath of Saracens when he was knocked from his percheron and how I too did dismount to jostle with them.'

'I do wot. You slit one brute from guggle to zatch. Yet all that was but your duty and that day my palfrey paltry.'

'I rejoice, my lord, that you survive to so chastise me,' said Pendragon, whose family had always been undone by pride.

'Get knotted,' replied the duke and he nodded, not in affirmation, but as a sign to the axeman who faced him behind Pendragon. The Cambrian head parted like a melon and the last duplicate vision from Pendragon's separate eyes was of the start of tears to my Lady Volupt's own. The duke was delighted with the nicety of it and the tables at a roar.

'So to the tomboys and trulls of the other side, Pendragon,' he cried. 'A leman of the devil with the other name.'

'Good one,' said the duchess, who was peevish only when bored.

'Well, he had it coming, didn't he?' said the duke. 'Always up himself because of his lineage and his couthly ways.'

He leant across to Lady Volupt and seized her braided hair in purchase that brought his whisper close despite herself.

'What say you to the lady of my bedchamber, my lord?' said his wife.

'Marry, I advise her to chew her food well,' quoth the duke.

PRAIRIE NIGHTS

SOME PEOPLE, SO I'm told, dream always of the sea, an endless flux and an exhilaration that is part liberation and part threat. The year I worked at the agency in Auckland and still had some residue of imagination, I dreamt of endless prairie under a cheesy moon. Nothing but flowing grasses between the earth and the sky and the unrestricted wind of the night.

Sure, it was an escape. I could even feel it coming on when I was talking with clients about extrusion plumbing fittings, or listening to Simone Proctor giving her staff ra-ra sessions. I would drift away from myself until I stood knee-deep in all that endless, moonlit prairie grass. Sometimes the passing wind bore snatches of Simone's inanities, or my own.

Never neglect the enduring small client base.

There's a useful angle in that your grandfather founded the firm.

Animals, for example, are big, very big, at the moment.

Doco footage can be a sweet thing.

A very exciting prospect, Mr Whirler.

When the Spaniards first pushed northwards from Mexico they were at a loss as to how to navigate in so vast a sea of grass.

I had a three-roomed flat in Mount Eden. The house was an old one on the slope of the volcano. In some small caves in the scoria beneath the garden bluff the owner's father had discovered Maori relics and refused to give them up, although there was nothing impressive, or particularly valuable.

How happily we enter our own tombs. I can still remember my joy when the agency took me on and the mixture of envy and congratulation with which I was received by my fellow graduates. Broglioli's was the best restaurant in Palmerston North. I invited my friends to a farewell dinner and a good many came, although they had to pay for themselves. I had been the editor of the varsity magazine and in my speech said that I expected to bring a new thrust to advertising. Blow winds beneath a cheesy moon.

What I lacked was a conceptualisation of product. Simone Proctor pointed that out to me after I'd been with the agency six months. I knew on that occasion even before she spoke that she'd given up on me, because she stayed behind her desk rather than moving around to take a chair on my side. You've done the management courses yourself. Conceptualisation of product was her jargon, of course, but it was quite true. There wasn't anybody in that office who could manage alliteration, cadence, associative imagery, assonance, the way that I could, but increasingly I just couldn't relate them to almond moisture crème, or long-run colour-baked roofing iron. She said that my talent had an inward orientation and lacked market coupling points. Maybe I had something of a knack for brochures, she said. Not even a wolf moves across the albino grasses of the prairie night.

It's clear to me now how predictable was my response to comparative failure. I became the office hard case; all the best laughs and an inventory of weekend successes to disparage anything between Monday and Friday. If I had little to say at Simone's brain-storming sessions on Tuesday and Thursday, then I made up for it in the wine bar on Friday after work. Who wants the indignity of taking such a job seriously and still not being able to do it? Mike Dermott won a national award for his mime ad for Zeus Acoustics. It was funny and novel and I knew that I would never have come up with it.

In October I resigned from the agency to take up a position with Statsfact Polling Agency as a survey question writer. I told the people in the agency office that the new job paid more, that I was suited to it, that I'd been invited by management to apply. The first two were correct, the third an excusable lie in the circumstances. In a material sense I've never looked back, though question writing was only the first step. That first failure, that first painful inadequacy, became the goad for a conventional success. Think of a night on the old prairie, not a tree beneath the moon. Have you any idea of the sound the wind makes over a thousand miles of natural grassland?

I invited the others to come to the wine bar after my last day at the agency. Mike Dermott had a special client briefing to attend with Simone Proctor but he made a point of wishing me well during the afternoon and Simone left a bon voyage card on my desk. Of the rest, David Lymes and Estelle Hargreaves came. They were an item and later almost married. With such a modest number at my staff farewell I felt able to shout and we had three bottles of a good Gisborne chardonnay. I had the item in stitches on several occasions over recollections of my meetings with more unusual clients and professional differences with Simone, but after I was held up at the bar by Bernie Kinsman, who wanted to talk about varsity days, I got back to the table to find that David and Estelle had gone.

From the Mount Eden bus I could see a grey and white sky and although the traffic had worn shower water from the roads, the trees, the grass, the flowers and weeds of October had a fresh glisten to them in the evening.

A very exciting prospect, Mr Whirler.

I thought of climbing the mountain at dusk — just a hill really — and looking at the grassy crater again, at the remains of the old kumara pits along the rim. It would have been quiet at that time of the day, but Miss Hoddie, who had the better flat downstairs, invited me in for a drink. It was, I suppose, the eighth or ninth time I had spoken to her in as many months. She was very sharply black and white, and the white of her skin was just beginning to infiltrate the black of her hair.

'I've resigned too,' she said, 'and I'll be in Europe by Christmas.' Miss Hoddie taught French at a boys' school and was tired of their muscular dim-wittedness. She must have been almost thirty years older than me, yet had been no more successful in gathering close friends to celebrate such an important decision. 'I haven't heard a decent French accent in years,' she said. Appropriately enough, she opened French brandy and even from her lower flat we could see over a great many houses towards Herne Bay. Hoddie was thin, wiry. She even looked French, though the language was the only connection she had. 'It's mainly a lack of courage,' she said, 'that makes us put up with lives other than those we wish for ourselves.'

Her decision seemed so much more dramatic than my own. After all, I wasn't changing countries, cities, tongues, not even flats perhaps; just moving away from my inability to conceptualise product. But how the moon and clouds and wind combine to send dark vessels sweeping and dipping across the infinite prairie, and how the pelt of the world flows on for ever.

'Did you get a good degree?' Hoddie asked me, as we drank brandy on the window seat. 'It's so much more difficult to be reconciled to mediocrity if you've got a good degree.' Good degree or not, she had the wiry forearms of a French seamstress and the dark hairs lay all the same way on the pale skin. I would like to use her first name for I remember that she offered it, but it has succumbed to time, along with my imagination. 'No one gives a damn for excellence,' she said with a fine emphatic flourish. It occurred to me that maybe I had given up on advertising one chance too soon, that I could make something of Hoddie's black and white tautness, her given damn for excellence, that would double brandy sales in the land of the long white cloud.

'The problem with my generation of women was that it couldn't be selfish enough,' she said. 'You recognise too late that there isn't anyone else worth pleasing.' It was dark outside Miss Hoddie's bay window and the houses, gardens, streets below us, all of sensible and calculable dimension, had been replaced by a shimmer of lights.

Hoddie didn't become drunk in any way that led to a loss of composure, but after a time she spoke only in French and I couldn't respond, so I thanked her and went up to my own three rooms. We were both making something of a bolt for it, Hoddie and I. From my flat I could look down into hers and see her still on the window seat, talking, although the words were now inaudible as well as unintelligible.

Think of the effortless power of the wind across the land of grasses and wildflowers, the gliding shadows and the cool linen of the moon over the dips and long upward sweeps of the high plains. Think of the tremors you might feel from the ground as, far out of sight, the vast herds of bison rush through the night with the white wolves of the moon in silent pursuit.

PEACOCK FUNERAL

A RETURN TO the place made Hammond think of life, you see, and death, which is necessary at least to highlight life. And the cry of the peacocks across the grass courts from the gardens, and the small children's cases, almost phosphorescent green, or pink, bobbing like marshmallows to keep the cars away. The hospital on the hill where Hammond had worked, the perfumed gardens between it and the town; enduring trees with name tags to introduce themselves to passing generations, a clearing, too, with Humpty on a wall to supervise the swings and regard with an eternal smile the great plaster bum of the elephant slide. The peacocks strode through the paths; tails rich and dark swept in the leaves, but the cries had always an empty truculence.

The mood was self-imposed, of course. Despite having given no warning, Hammond was well received at the hospital. The one departmental colleague who still recalled him made time to greet him, to reminisce, to introduce him to the head of the unit, with whom they had herbal tea. Ginny had been fond of such drinks. She had small packs of them, each with a name more wondrously aromatic than the contents could hope to be, and there were always a few small, discarded bags clustered at the plughole of the sink. His mother once told him that the only thing from her childhood which could still move her was the recollection of the blue sky seen through the branches of a yellow plum tree in Motueka.

An offer was made to accompany him around the place, but Hammond knew the pressures of their work, how much of a nuisance the passer by can be in a busy day. The colleague had become intensely interested in the hospital grounds as an unofficial extension of the gardens; the unit chief, on the other hand, was curious, he said, as to how funding was controlled in Hammond's existing job. There were condolences as well.

Structurally there had been little change; it wasn't large as hospitals go. A new ambulance put-down bay at casualty admission, an internal décor of lighter pastels, a lot more signs outside informing people of possible destinations. It had all seemed common sense before. There were still the rose plots before the main block and still they seemed in half bloom, unable to provide a full show at any time of the year. The grass was stiff with drought, the garden clods ash grey. Hammond could see the third-floor window from which Mr Neilson, with good reason, did a header to the carpark. A wind from the sea was persistent on the hill, bowling in from a horizon always flat and far and sad.

Hammond followed the exact way he had always taken to the house in Liebers Street. Some of the mundane landmarks were still there. A plaster lighthouse on the Seddon Street corner; the paua shell porch further on; the home of a woman who was once the mistress of an ex-mayor. At the Bidewell Boarding House there was no old garage any more with a hole cut so that the door could be closed and just the front bumper stick out like a moustache at the other end. The dairy had become gaudy and its produce spilled out into makeshift displays on the footpath. Hammond caught a glimpse of the high counter where his children would wait to hear Mrs Lee say, 'Hokey-pokey, or plain?'

He had been filled with confidence then, believing that, having achieved the qualifications for a professional career, he had passed the greatest test and everything else would come naturally. That experience proved it almost true was the greatest danger.

The house was too far from the gardens for the peacocks to be heard except in the still of night. Then, when the children were asleep and Hammond and his wife lay together, sometimes they had heard those urgent calls. At first Hammond thought them exotic, but as his own life soured the notes became more discordant. Why, after all, should a creature's beauty be any indication at all of benevolence?

The brick house was part of the archaeology of his life and even without going in, he could see things as significantly and trivially vital as the ossifications, shards and simple beads in site strata. The cracks in the roughcast beneath the main ridge facing he had twice filled with sealant, and once fallen from to lie painfully winded in the hydrangeas. The golden elm that shook leaves into the gutterings, he had heeled in and sequestered with sacking. There was a false bolt hole in the letter box that perpetuated one of his lesser mistakes, and the concrete lip to the basement garage was never quite enough to prevent water running in during the worst rains of winter.

The things he recognised were overlaid by the habitation of other people and as he stood on the sunny footpath the house was both painfully intimate and painfully strange to him and he had a slight taste of copper at the back of his throat. In one year, inspired by some neighbour since forgotten, they'd had a street party — well, a sort of their end of the street party. Trestles, barbecues, lights strung in the trees and the access denied to vehicles by coloured ropes that depended on toleration for obedience. Ginny had been one of the prime movers responsible for a great success, and people had eaten, laughed and talked in the street well into the night. Everyone was filled with neighbourly bonhomie and vowed to do it again.

And it was never done again.

Hammond walked on back to the church where he had left his car. At the service there had been several invitations to visit people before he left, but the hospital and the house were all he wanted to meet. At the crematorium Michael and Rae had rested their hands on his shoulder to show they understood that not every father was able to make a success of marriage, but they told him little about their own lives and he was too proud to ask. The three of them had perhaps become accustomed to the detachment of correspondence. Lynley Grath had glanced at Hammond coldly at the crematorium. She had been Ginny's friend and he'd fucked her just once from behind at a midwinter party in the Tilbury Rooms. He remembered the sharp moon like a searchlight and the sharp pleasure. Lynley had remained a loyal friend to Ginny and sent Hammond a letter of contempt after the divorce.

Despite all that, the crematorium meant the least to him of all the things of the day. It was a new place with much stained glass and blond wood. It overlooked some sloping paddocks that must have been close to the farm on which Bruce Mulherron fell from his tractor and had his legs so badly injured in the discs. Bruce told him that as he lay there at first, in the shock before the pain, he was aware how sweet the fresh soil smelled. After the rare rains towards the end of summer the mushrooms would come, especially around the gateways and the tops of mounds. Hammond and Ginny often went to Mulherrons' and other farms to gather them. Real mushrooms, not the designer ones sold in the supermarkets. Large and quickly black on the underside: sudden of growth and strong and dank and black and white. The kids wouldn't eat them. Ginny would bake them with bacon and onion in a pastry shell and Hammond would bring up a bottle of pinot noir. The plots at the crematorium were mainly roses. They seemed to do better there than on the high ground of the hospital.

The cost of life is everything you have. Hammond was glad that Michael and Rae were making their way independently north. He looked forward to their company for a day or two. More than he could express, he looked forward to having them with him, but for the moment, driving away from the church, driving past the peacock gardens, the associations and reproaches of the small city, he wanted only his own admonitions.

Maybe at last you can be happy, Ginny had once said. I

truly believe that you meant the best for us all, but you weren't willing to forgo anything yourself to make sure it happened. At the time he had assumed that it was requitable malice in the guise of reasonableness. Later he had admitted it as honesty. Thinking of it again after the peacocks and the crematorium, he decided it was truth. How does one find out all the heartfelt emotions that masquerade as love?

How many couples had held each other in the summer nights, in the arbours and ardours of the ratepayers' gardens, and thought the peacocks cried just for them.

Hammond's face itched. He found it necessary to draw the flat of his hand down his face again and again. The sun, still powerful, was at an unkind angle and made him sneeze. Sometimes in the summer, after a big blow, the kelp would lie in caramel heaps, rotting on the stones, and the stench would drift into the town centre. Hammond thought he had a whiff of it as he drove north. Sometimes his wife had read Larkin to him while he ate a late supper on return from the hospital.

Had Hammond stayed until dusk he would have heard the empty truculence of the peacocks although they had been taken from the perfumed gardens years before. Their phantom cries were exactly as the pain a man feels in an amputated leg.

THE ORCHID HOUSE

IN WHAT IS euphemistically termed middle age, Paul Amiss was becoming accustomed to his life using earlier settings for later experience. A sensible, psychological economy and the natural consequence perhaps of returning to live in the city of his youth, rather than continuing a geographic movement that has a comforting illusion of progress. He sat again in the college assembly hall, on parent-teacher evenings, to support his son, half expecting Bomber to come striding to the stage with his verdigris gown flapping. Every weekday he passed the museum shrubbery on the leafy floor of which he had lain with Lucy Ogg one far and warm New Year's Eve; no temperature since had exceeded it. From the modest boardroom of Glidden, Buckle and Browne, where he sat twice a month with his agenda papers, he looked down on the very yard where, as a vacation job, he had scoured old coppers with steel wool and dilute nitric acid. Shapscott's Light Engineering had taken its trash and gone; the yard was cobbled and had seats and umbrellas as an extension of the Brindisi Café.

The public baths in Victoria Avenue had bided their time in just the same way. Paul's long-standing squash partner, Raf McIntyre, moved to Wellington and then Paul's doctor advised him not to go on jogging because of the stress on his knees. 'Swimming's the thing,' said the doctor. 'The body is sup-ported while it flexes, but it's easy on the load-bearing joints. There's some evidence of therapeutic value as well.' Probably the doctor was a swimmer himself; his hair went sleekly back from his forehead as if he had just surfaced at the end of a stroke and his hands smelled faintly of chlorine.

The Victoria Pool was on the south side of the Victoria Park and when he went there, just to make enquiries, it was the park that sparked first recollections. He could pick no change at all. A small, single-block park with not one tree, not one flower bed, not one concrete toilet to break the rectangle of green grass marked out for sports fields. The college was close by and on dull, winter afternoons they had walked down to the park for soccer practices, had kicked and shouted aimlessly until Mr Madigan came and the irascible Scottish vet who volunteered to help coach because he had it in for rugby.

When Paul reached the pool at the south end, higher than the rest of the park on a sort of terrace, and went into the new, glassed foyer, he could still clearly see the marked soccer fields and the goals. There was just a thin man with a beret and a King Charles spaniel, for it was the middle of a Thursday afternoon. Roddy Pike had vaulted the fence one winter practice and run out into the avenue after the ball. He had his pelvis shattered by a truck carrying pig-slops from the hotels and the stench was sickening as they stood waiting for an ambulance.

Unlike the park, the pool had undergone considerable development. It used to be open air, unheated, used only in the summer when they spread out towels around the sides to sunbathe, or honey-potted from the high board. It had become fully enclosed, heated, all year, all weather; somehow muted and subterranean and with no diving boards at all. It had its own artificial and humid climate, like an orchid house. The smell of chemicals was a heavy pollen in the nose. Swimmers moved purposefully up and down the lanes.

You could have a concession ticket, or a season ticket, Paul was told. If you were going to be regular, then the best of all was the year's subscription, but you'd be shrewd to wait until December for that and in the meantime have a concession ticket. The custodian was a large man with the deceptively smooth body that real swimmers have and freckles on his shoulders congealed into caramel patches. He was hosing under the seats with a strong jet of water and wore only shorts and jandals in his own domain, even though it was winter outside. His face seemed familiar and his manner assumed it would be familiar: Paul supposed he had won in his time some fame as a swimmer and probably appeared frequently in the paper as a coach. 'Have you done much in the pool?' he asked.

'I haven't swum for years,' said Paul, patting his stomach. 'I just want to maintain a basic fitness, keep the weight down.'

The custodian smiled. He didn't deny that the activity was needed for the purpose stated.

Paul chose to come in the early session, six to eight in the morning, which was reserved for adults and a few top juniors in serious training. He figured this would be less disruptive to his day, though whether he could maintain the motivation to be at the pool by seven in the mornings, time would tell.

He carried his new togs into a long changing room that seemed remarkably original except for three warm showers by the door. There was still the sluiced, abattoir-like floor, the long slatted forms, the battery of cubby holes for clothes. Two boys followed him in to get dressed. The water beaded and ran from the sheen of their smooth stomachs, while Paul was conscious of his greying chest hair, his thin legs.

'Old Mackie'll want our assignments in this morning,' said one.

'Choice,' said the other.

A slight fug-mist seemed to hang over the pool so that the light from the windows was a dissipated aura and the girders of the great roof were indistinct. Three signs on stands were placed across the width of the pool on the concrete of the near end — slow, medium and fast. Only the fast lanes had much activity, for there a group of teenagers were doing their lengths under the casual eye of their coach — not the custodian, but a smaller man, darker, who yawned a lot and tilted his head far back on his shoulders as an exercise of weariness. Paul slipped into the slow side and began a length of breaststroke. In the low and medium lanes there was only a handful of adults: a couple who swam on and on inexorably, a couple who spent a comfortingly long time standing at one end, or the other, between lengths.

Paul found that he lacked a natural buoyancy and that it was more difficult to remain horizontal than he remembered from his youth. His legs tended to sink despite his frog-like kick and his breathing was not well co-ordinated. He tried overarm, but that was less successful again, although a little faster. He swallowed some water, had trouble seeing beneath the surface and misjudged the rail so that he was left grasping at air a metre short. He rested more, knowing that he was in it for the long haul, that it might be weeks, months even, before he could swim easily for thirty or forty minutes with only occasional stops. It wasn't as if he had a level of achievement to recapture, for he had never been much more than a recreational swimmer. Soccer had been the big thing with him when at college and then university.

One thing he noticed was that almost all the swimmers had goggles and he resolved to get some himself. In the time he remained resting, or swimming, only two other people came. Both were men and both had some difficulty in walking; one swam expertly. Paul wondered if that was the reason for many of the regular winter swimmers — people with temporary, or permanent, handicaps who needed the supported flexing of limbs that his doctor recommended. It was a pleasure to watch the teenagers instead; the girls had well-muscled thighs and small, high breasts.

So it became a pattern for most weekdays, though he wasn't a zealot about it and sometimes he stilled the alarm without any great guilt. As summer came it was easier to be up early, to anticipate the short drive, the walk along the terrace at the end of the park and entering the orchid house. What had seemed cavernous and strange and complex, became finite and reduced. Paul and the custodian, and Margery who was often his rostered replacement, were on first name terms; even the dark, yawning coach would sometimes nod.

Armin Sheere came at much the same time in the morning session as Paul. Often they talked a while in the stalag-like changing room, or more briefly while at the end of one of the lanes surrounded by the misted light, the high timing clocks, the voices of the teenagers training, the slop of the water against the wall beside them, the flat percussion of arms upon the surface. Armin was one of the two handicapped men Paul had seen on his first day, the one who swam expertly. He was part Lebanese, which gave him a good tan, and he was recovering from a serious stroke that particularly affected his left side and had put his medical practice in abeyance. Armin was an expert swimmer not in an absolute sense, but in the way he made the most of his resources. He swam an easy sidestroke, the small, blue rubber goggles gleaming at the water line, his mouth taking air exactly in the turbulent water hollow formed by his head. When he rested, standing at the end of the pool, he would put his elbows back on the tiles and his long hands would droop from his wrists.

He allowed no self-pity to show, but the sardonic openness of his conversation was proof that the realisation of what he had come to was a bitter cup. 'I can swim now better than ever before,' he said, 'and walk and talk less effectively than at any time since I was a four-year-old. A good many of my former patients see my condition as evidence that everything I professed, and prescribed for them, was fraudulent.' Armin had a high, skittish laugh, often at odds with what he said.

At the beginning of December, Christine Flowerday returned from her sabbatical in California and began swimming in the mornings again. She was a geomorphologist at the university, not a very public figure, but, oddly enough, known to both Paul and Armin. Armin said later that she and his wife had been bridge partners. Paul knew her because they were both on the Museum Advisory Board; also she lived next door to his sister in an inner city wayfarers' hostel that had been converted into art deco apartments.

Armin saw her first, backstroking majestically in a medium lane, but had no reason to remark on it to Paul. Paul failed to recognise her for some time: his goggles tended to fog, so increasing the mist through which he saw things for much of his time in the pool. Only when he was rinsing them did he happen to see Christine surging in at his own end. She was one of those people whose personality was constantly being refuted by her appearance. A woman of astringent, clear reason, she had a soft, overflowing body that brought to mind opera singers and scarlet boudoir cushions. Her navy costume cut into the white expanse of her legs and shoulders. Her face was pretty and fatuous.

'So you've decided to get fit at last,' she said to Paul.

'Or kill myself in the attempt,' he said.

'Well, one could almost embalm oneself in this water. I think there are more chemicals than H_2O. My colleagues tell me that I have the most distinctive and persistent perfume within the department.' And she was away again, her body high in the water, her white arms slapping amid the ripples and the confusion of reverberating sounds in the high raftered building.

Once she spoke — clear, well-enunciated and quietly confident words — the impression of her appearance was diminished and Paul could remember the forceful views at the Museum Board and imagine her at the podium for the plenary session of the Los Angeles conference on glacial topographies.

'Yes,' said Armin later, when they had established that she was known to both of them, 'at the bridge tournaments those pairs who don't know her smile to see such a softie and then find themselves well taken to the cleaners.'

Armin, Paul and Christine remained three of the early morning regulars, greeting each other, as well as old Gilbert, Roger Mains, Alice Gough, who had hands but no forearms, Margery in the booth, or the custodian. They passed remarks between lengths, disparaging each other's performance in the cheerful way acquaintances do, they commented on the weather outside the pool, on the good they were doing themselves, on the grace, speed and enviable youth of the youngsters who were trained by the dark, yawning coach, and Paul may have had no greater insight, except that, on the twenty-first day of the new year, during the early session, there was an accident in Victoria Avenue in just about the same place where Roddy Pike had been hit all those years ago. Not a pig-slop truck and a schoolboy, though, but a motorcyclist and a Commodore wagon.

The world of the pool was a noisy one in its way, an insulated one, and most people had water in their ears. No one heard the crash; no one knew anything of it until the Commodore driver came running in to get help. The custodian, knowing that Armin was a doctor, went to the pool edge and shouted and gesticulated as Armin slid by in a medium lane. Armin Sheere was still dripping water as he walked awkwardly to the avenue and his blue rubber goggles hung on his chest. Paul followed to see if he could help and Christine, who was fully dressed, showed typical presence of mind by collecting the towels from the women's changing room and bringing them in a bundle in her arms.

The motorbike rider had injuries to his face and arms. Armin took immediate charge. Rapid treatment was the thing, he said, no problem with moving him. So Paul drove to the hospital and Armin and Christine were in the back with the rider. The young man leant on Christine's breast and never attempted to shift, or speak. His head was swaddled in towels red with blood and only his eyes moved alertly, making inventory of each of those who helped him. Out of his vision, behind the car, the custodian ran back to the orchid house to phone the hospital. The golden helmet swung forgotten from the strap in his hand. The Commodore driver and passers by were dragging the motorbike to the side of the avenue.

At the hospital, Christine and Paul watched the staff going with the injured man down the long corridor of casualty. The motorcyclist, supported on each side, walked very well and it was Armin who stumbled and bobbed to keep up. The veins stood out on his thin, brown legs, his hair was still slicked from the pool, the blue goggles hung as a necklace. He was briefing the staff as best he could while the group hurried on. Paul felt an unexpected and powerful affection for Armin Sheere; admiration for the professional persistence despite his stroke and the disregard for the odd figure he made, although he must have been aware of it and was a man very sensitive to ignominy.

'I suppose his life is limited a good deal now and just at an age when he would have been enjoying the very best return on all the years he spent developing his career,' said Paul. He and Christine talked while they were waiting in his car. He had soaked one of the towels in the fountain by the main entrance and swabbed the blood stains on the charcoal grey fabric of the back seat.

'In the drama of emergency no one thinks of the necessary contributions by people caught up in it by chance and it's insensitive to mention them,' said Christine. 'The blood on your seats and my blouse, the towels taken without permission from the changing room, someone late for an appointment because they were helping to clear the road, Armin cold and almost naked in casualty.'

The morning sun warmed the car, but Paul had the tartan rug from the boot across his shoulders and with the rough comb of his fingers he arranged his hair. His togs had wet the seat beneath him unpleasantly. 'You know him quite well?' he asked.

'It was his ex-wife I knew first, but as I grew to like her less, I came to think more of him.'

'Were they very unhappy then?'

'No, not very. He was very busy, of course; she was a social climber and gadabout. In the end they just didn't have patience for each other. He was a part-time respiratory specialist at Ethel Gray. Did you know that? He was offered a position at the Harlow Centre in Sussex, a personal invitation after one of their professors had been out here for a year.'

Christine was matter-of-factly working on the blood stains on her blouse as she spoke. The eight o'clock traffic began to build on the street beside the hospital carpark.

'God, how he was looking forward to going over there, and I'd half decided to go with him when he had the first of his strokes at forty-seven. He won't let anyone close to him now. You'll have realised that. All that he had, and the extra just within grasp . . . Then his life work played him false and so he retrenched on everything because of so much pride. It's his pride keeps everything at arm's length.'

Armin Sheere came out of the main entrance and stood, searching for the car. He looked an old man. Someone had given him a white, orderly's coat, but he still had his goggles around his neck and bare feet. The coat was too short: his wrists and legs were thin and dark. He favoured his left side markedly. More than anything else, he looked like an inmate making a poorly planned run for it. 'Don't you tell him I've been talking about us,' said Christine Flowerday.

Paul opened his door. 'Armin,' he called, 'over here.'

All three of them continued to have their early morning swim at the orchid house, to greet Margery, or the custodian, to pass a few words, to develop an increasingly easy style that enabled them to muse and observe a misty reality as they swam and, when finished, to go their own way alone as they had come. Sometimes Armin Sheere wasn't there for a few days and would then reappear with his face more lined and his words more slurred. As the youngsters porpoised in the fast lanes, as the big face stop-watches ticked on, as the visible humidity rolled beneath the rafters and before the spangled windows, as the orchid house echoed to splash, to voices and whining pumps, Paul wondered sometimes how Armin reconciled the life he had with what was given up — his full health and wealth, the appointment at the Harlow Centre in Sussex, the caress of Christine's great diva's breast against his brown skin. He thought perhaps disappointment, like failure, was an adder's bite: the wound must be sucked free of poison.

GENESIS

IT WAS ONE of those long centuries at the Creations Bureau, during which the front office staff had so little to do, and such small hope of promotion, that they sat open mouthed in a number of suns, or gossiped with enervated malice concerning the goings on at the last Seraphim executive training conference.

There were some magnificent and imaginative projects on the go in other areas of Heavenly Administration: Resources had a plan to harness the para-kinetic energy of time if it could be bent into a full circle and Onus and Obligation proposed a voluntary depletion of personal vanity in all choirs below Cherubim.

In Creations, though, things were rather ho-hum and ho-hum wasn't good enough in Heaven. G.O.D.'s foremost corporate slogan consisted of the Three Vees — Vision, Vigour and Versatility. Archangel Lucifer was Creations Chief, however, and for longer than most heavenly memories he had received the trust and confidence of G.O.D. Creations was the senior executive portfolio below G.O.D. — well, equal with Resources anyway. Many in Heaven thought Lucifer the obvious angel for the top job in due course. A brilliant mind, absolutely, even if he was resting on his laurels somewhat. Who else could have originated the expanding universes concept and overseen the immense detailed planning required for implementation? Who but Lucifer could come up with a plan of such imaginative symmetry as a standardised set of wave velocities — light, sound, thought, matter. Oh, you could hear the comments about austerity and pride, about ruthless efficiency, but no one denied Lucifer's ability.

Gabriel was pretty bright too. He had been a senior echelon executive in the Creations Bureau and pushing for all six wings. His flair was for personnel and PR, but he'd found himself increasingly out of sympathy with Archangel Lucifer's management style and policy direction for Creations. So Gabriel resigned, devoted all his time to his best idea and then presented it directly to G.O.D., whom he knew quite well socially and through a common interest in metaphysics.

G.O.D. told Lucifer that he thought the project should be considered and the Creations Chief said that he didn't want to and that he resented Gabriel not going through channels. G.O.D. insisted.

How do such things happen? In even the best run and most successful corporations, tremendous consequences can result from nuances of personality. Perhaps Gabriel was too ambitious and presumptuous; perhaps Lucifer was too proud; maybe old G.O. still felt the necessity to demonstrate his power from time to time.

Gabriel received a curt request for a full documentation of his proposal, but no invitation to make a personal presentation on it before the Chief of Creations. Lucifer and his 2IC, the great Baal, read it separately and then met in Lucifer's domed office with the distinctive ornamental flames casting images into reflection.

Lucifer drew the heavy documentation towards him on the desk. 'Another world,' he said contemptuously. 'Always another world.'

'Earth, this time,' said Baal. His face was heavy and yellow.

'Since G.O.D. made the first one — how many applications for worlds!' continued Lucifer. A good idea flogged to death. They're so limiting, so concrete. And you and I know that if G.O.D.'s best idea had been synchronous entities then not many people would be bothering with world projects.'

'Does one more matter then? One more world. Is it worth a

stink?' said Baal loyally. 'Is it worth jeopardising your position with G.O.D.?'

Lucifer understood the value of the point; every successful administrator has to be something of a politician as well. Yet he considered that there were principles at stake concerning both standards of project excellence and the proper channels for submission.

'It's a bad project, a badly realised world. Isn't it?' asked Lucifer. Baal nodded. 'Then we must say so. I can't believe that G.O.D. will go for it. Not when all the defects are pointed out to him in an objective way. G.O. and I go way back.'

Lucifer and Baal, a pair who respected each other's abilities and were renowned as a team, began to prepare their critical report. There was the provision for free will, for example. It made Lucifer very angry. Gabriel knew quite well that intrinsic loyalty to revelatory guidance was a prime ordinance of the Creations Manual. And allowing the highest beings of Earth a knowledge of their own mortality when it was so obviously beyond their emotional capacity to bear! It must become a cause of melancholia and unhappiness. Even the science sections were faulty. The basic instability of the gaseous spectrum, for instance, so that within a few million years atmospheric breakdown was highly likely. 'Oh, there's so much that doesn't hang together in so many ways,' said Lucifer testily. 'A continuous creation period of seven days! I ask you. Imagine the lower Choirs Guild's reaction to that.'

'Then there's all that about instincts,' said Baal.

'Instincts?'

'The whole section about instincts and logical intelligence is muddled. There's no clear established dominance for either mode of behaviour. The wretched folk proposed here wouldn't know if they were Arthur or Martha. Gabriel's always been indecisive on that sort of thing.'

'Exactly. He's a generalities man, but he doesn't think things right through and isn't scrupulous about the practical details. The anatomical visuals, for example; apart from the bizarre gender division, which is sheer gimmickry, even at a quick glance I picked up that he'd placed the defecatory and procreative organs side by side. It's a small enough thing, but so typically slipshod.'

Baal was pleased that Lucifer had mentioned the visuals of the proposed beings. He brought them up in greater definition and colour on the display screen. He made them rotate. 'Look at them closely,' he said. 'Of Whom do they remind you?' Archangel Lucifer leant over the desk. There was something, yes.

'Gabriel's made them look somewhat like G.O.D.,' said Baal softly.

'The cheeky, ingratiating little bastard!' Lucifer very rarely laughed, yet both he and Baal did so. It was so Gabriel, so calculatingly PR. Of course it only hardened their resolve to oppose the creation of Earth.

G.O.D. set a time for both parties to make their submissions to him personally. The project of Earth, minor in itself, was becoming an arena for powerful political forces in Heaven. Lucifer and Baal waited outside G.O.D.'s office and Gabriel and Raphael sat just a squab away. When the time came for them all to be ushered into the haloed room, Lucifer went and stood beside Gabriel for a moment. 'Reconsider,' he said genuinely. 'You won't win and think how divisive such an argument could be.'

But Gabriel, of course, saw Earth as his best shot.

CASS ROBBINS

ANGIE BRUIN WAS used to people coming down from the North Island looking for cheap accommodation. It had become a trend over several years. After all, if you had no work to go to and a fixed welfare benefit irrespective of location, then why not have a better house at least and not such a distance to walk to the shops. The populations of places like Oamaru and Waimate and Palmerston were becoming used to such people, even if they weren't sure whether they wanted them.

Cass Robbins, though, was a bit different right from the start: a single and middle-aged guy who said in his letter to the agency that he didn't much care about the size, condition or location of the place as long as it was cheap and had a view of the sea. He was buried somewhere in a boarding house in Hamilton. Angie Bruin was in the rural real estate side of Kelly and Tarrowe, but in practice that included fringes and clusters of settlement: one-garage towns on the main south road, fishing huts at the estuaries, the obsolete hydro village, old baches and farmhouses hidden about the headlands. If he wasn't fussy about mod cons and appearances other than a view, then she had plenty to show him.

Cass couldn't afford to take a trip just to look; when Angie wrote to him with some examples, he just packed his two cardboard suitcases and took a bus down to the ferry. On board he was candid enough to strike up acquaintance with a group of stilt walkers and clowns who were doing a tour of the South Island in a van and so he came to Angie Bruin's office only a day or two after he'd said to expect him. Angie was out

negotiating an irrigated block for a switch to dairy use so Cass
left his two old cases in the office and wandered about the
main street putting up stilt and clown posters. 'What a great
place this is,' he told the Kelly and Tarrowe receptionist after
being in town for eleven minutes. 'You know, I really believe
there's something in the air down here we don't get north of
the strait.'

'This is the place to be all right.' The receptionist was
regularly applying for secretarial jobs in Wellington where
there was some night life, for God's sake.

'People here have the courtesy to look at you when you're
speaking with them,' said Cass, 'and there are still animals to
be seen going about their own business rather than ours.'

It was on five when Angie got back, but Cass Robbins had
been waiting contentedly at the office. He remarked cheerfully
on the shimmer of the late afternoon sun on the poplar tree
behind the town hall. But he was keen to see the real estate
she'd picked out for him and at that time of year there were
still hours of daylight. 'I mean I could come back in an hour
when you've had a chance to eat,' said Cass. 'Don't let me push
you. I guess you get sick of houses just as a teacher gets fed up
with kids and a driver loses the thrill of the road.' He took his
cases with him to Angie's car, because he had nowhere else to
leave them. He said it was deplorable the way people would
nick your stuff given half a chance.

Cass decided on the very first place Angie Bruin showed
him: an old farm cottage on clay cliffs between Kakanui and
Moeraki. There was a vast, half burnt out macrocarpa hedge
on the south side and across the gravel road some crouching
boxthorns worn into green riffles and tunnels by the sea
wind. Not another place in sight; just the rolling, close
cropped paddocks of dry summer grass on the one side and
the cliff and the ocean on the other. Some of the weatherboards were off and the timbers showed beneath, and
clumps of bird nest straw. The road and the hedge formed
two rough boundaries and there was a solitary waratah with

a splash of blue paint at its head to mark the junction of the other two. The sheep had found the unlocked laundry for shade and shelter and the pebbles of their shit were thick on the floor.

'Marvellous,' said Cass. 'There's not one window broken. Do you notice that?'

'Some of them might be a bit stiff, mind,' said Angie, which in agent speak meant they were nailed up.

'I reckon that old table's totara.'

'You realise the power isn't on, not even connected now any further than Jamiesons' at the corner.' Angie was slightly disconcerted by the reversal of the usual roles. Cass enthused about everything he saw, while she felt obliged to make the realistic comment. However, the change was almost liberating after a while.

'A whole acre you say. One acre.'

'The macrocarpa must cover half of that,' said Angie.

'Ah, what a sweet smelling tree it is, despite its ordinary appearance.'

She watched him cross the road and stand in a gap among the boxthorn on the cliff top. His brown trousers looked as if they might once have been the bottom of a suit and he wore a tartan shirt with the sleeves rolled up on arms surprisingly muscular for a short, pale man. 'Listen to the stones going up and down the beach with the swell, Mrs Bruin,' he said.

'Be careful there. The cliff gets undermined and comes down every so often.'

'I'll bet you could sit in the kitchen and see all of the horizon if a bit of this thorn was knocked back.'

They stood in the kitchen for, despite the farm table, there were no chairs and they could see the broken line of the ocean horizon through the boxthorn.

'I'll take it,' said Cass Robbins. 'Twelve thousand dollars for the freehold to a house with an acre of good land and a view of the sea. It makes you wonder, doesn't it? You know in the city you could hardly put a deposit on a section with that.'

'Cash,' said Angie. 'The Jamiesons were clear about that. And everything as is, where is.'

'I always feel,' he said, 'that the coast is alive in a special way. Anywhere that's a meeting of the land and the air and the sea.'

Cass didn't want to go back to town for the paperwork. He decided that he wanted to take possession that night and cheerfully opposed anything that Angie said to the contrary. He handed over five hundred dollars as a sign of good intent and said he would appreciate it a great deal if she could bring out the papers the next day. 'I don't mind what time,' he said. 'I'll be making a start tidying here and getting a list together.' He turned on one of the taps above the yellowed sink and was overjoyed when, after some spluttering, the water began to run reasonably clean. He got down on his hands and knees outside and pointed out that the piles were concrete and not wood. Some homecoming magpies started squawking in the macrocarpa and he told Angie that birdsong always reminded him of his happy childhood in the Wairarapa. He stood on the narrow, gravel road in the dusk and waved to her as she left.

Angie had been long enough in the business not to bring it home with her at night, and with a husband and three teenage children she had plenty to occupy her thoughts, yet she wondered about Cass Robbins — whether it would work out, whether he was as happy as he seemed, or if he was one of those dreamers about life in the country and the reality of it would be a bitter awakening. 'Well, he can certainly get away from it all down there,' said her husband. 'Jesus! Now that old Jamieson place was one I thought you'd never sell for sure. I've got to hand it to you.'

After lunch the next day, Angie took the papers down and a carton with corned beef sandwiches, some apples, a toilet roll, a tin of coffee and a plastic mug, an old scrubbing brush and some cleaning gear. Cass had rested his best trousers and tartan shirt and wore corduroys and a baggy blue jersey direct on his skin. She expected that if his enthusiasm had survived the night, then he would have made a start in the house, but he was giving the boxthorn a hiding with a slasher and saw borrowed from the Jamiesons. Short, pale and middle-aged, he wasn't an impressive man in appearance, but he plied the slasher with considerable strength and balance. He was thick-set without being fat and his chest stood out more than his stomach.

'You shouldn't have gone to all this trouble.' Cass put a towel on the mottled verandah edge for Angie to sit on so that they could share the sun and the view of the sea as he had the sandwiches. There they sat, Angie as tall and thin as a heron and Cass with his neck and hairy chest showing from the vee of the loose jersey. Some Romney sheep, seemingly unag-grieved at being denied the laundry for the first time, fossicked along the side of the building. 'One thing I don't need to buy is a lawn mower,' Cass said. The sheep themselves, and the verandah that had often been a camp for them, were aromatic with the oil-wool smell the hot sun releases. The sky above the macrocarpas was a pale, burnished blue; the loess at their roots a pale yellow; the sea darker and flowing in the gap Cass had cleared in the boxthorn. Apart from their own voices, the unhurried movement and cropping of the Romneys, the shingle sliding on the steep beach out of sight, there was no other noise at all. Angie was bound to agree that there were a lot worse places to be.

Cass paid the balance for the house in hundred-dollar notes. 'It's going to be my asset, though, isn't it,' he said stoutly. 'Could I ask for one more favour, that you give me a ride back to town? We can see the lawyer together if it suits you and then I can buy the things I need. It's urgent I get some wheels of my own and some bits of furniture and so on. I bet you could recommend the best second-hand places.' And so she could of course. She also had an inclination to ask him how he intended to make a living, how he was going to spend his time once the house was fixed and the boxthorn on the cliff was cleared to give him his sea horizon, but she didn't, because after all what business was it of hers and would she ever see him again anyway. 'Last night I had a dream about the pioneers who built this house,' said Cass. 'Fine people they were.'

Cass bought a second-hand farm bike and trailer and that was his sum total of transport. He picked up his furniture and pot and pans, bare essentials, at garage sales and second-hand shops; ferried them back to the old Jamieson place above the sea, bit by bit in the trailer behind the farm bike.

Old Gideon Jamieson maintained a traditional rural reserve for a few months, but when none of the Romneys went missing, he didn't find any odd plants among his shelter belts and the police didn't come with any enquiries, then he unbent a little and was a helpful enough neighbour. For his part, Cass Robbins wasn't selfish with his acre. The sheep wandered happily outside his windows to seek shade in the day and a wall at night, kept only from the verandah by a strip of netting nailed to the supports and from the laundry by the closed door.

Cass did some casual work for old Gideon Jamieson: help in the yards and the shearing shed, a bit of painting, potato picking. Through Gideon's laconic endorsement he began to get work from other local cockies and so the sound of his farm bike and the sight of his short, compact body became customary in the district. 'One thing,' old Gideon would say, 'he never whines, does he? You've got to give him that. Always the cheerful bugger.'

It came as a surprise to Angie Bruin when Cass rang her from a town phone box and wanted her and her husband to come out to his place. 'I owe you a meal,' he said, 'and I bet you'd like to have a look at how I've got the place and enjoy the view of the sea again. All that thorn's cleared, you know.' Angie had seen more ocean views than hot dinners, but she was interested to view the old place again, and very few clients had ever invited her back to a house she'd sold them. She insisted on bringing a salad, though, and a six pack for her husband, who felt the heat after a day in the woollen mills.

'What am I going to talk to him about?' Ross said dubiously.

The cottage hadn't undergone any transformation. Cass had replaced the missing weatherboards and given them an undercoat and taken off the rusted guttering that had been such an eyesore, but the place still looked what it was — an old wooden cottage in a paddock bare except for the macrocarpa. Inside was clean and tidy enough to suit a single guy, though Angie was appalled at the strange assortment of furniture and she could see he'd been keeping the farm bike in the laundry. Cass still thought the place was just Christmas, however, and took them round it and gestured at the sea view as if he owned a place in Kohimarama. 'Imagine how my asset's increasing,' he said. 'What do you reckon?'

'Well, certainly I don't think you've lost any of your twelve thousand dollars. On the other hand, being this far out of town isn't everybody's cup of tea.'

'It's quiet and no one to bother you,' said Ross, who had to put up with the noise of the woollen mills day after day. A beer in his hand, he found a comfortable canvas chair on Cass Robbins' sagging verandah and he sat there looking over the netting surround at the glitter of the sea out from the clay cliff.

'You know,' said Cass, 'overseas I reckon only a millionaire could afford this sort of privacy and this sort of view.'

'You could be right there,' said Ross, and though he winked at Angie, he could appreciate Cass's enthusiasm.

'For most people it's a question of job prospects rather than views of the ocean, though, isn't it?' said Angie. 'I mean, think of a family living out here. That's the problem.'

From his second-hand rock gas stove on top of the old coal range, Cass got a meal of sorts and they sat around the heavy, plain table, which had proved not to be totara after all. 'But all solid timber, absolutely throughout,' said Cass. 'Gideon Jamieson reckons it's been sitting right where it is since well before the First World War.'

'Old Gideon probably remembers when it arrived,' said Angie.

'What sort of work did you do in the North Island, Cass?' asked Ross. Angie was surprised how naturally he came out with it, while she had often wanted an opportunity for the same question. 'Palmerston North, was it?' continued her husband.

'Hamilton,' said Angie.

'I was a bright sign electrician,' said Cass. 'Twenty-five years in bright sign work and had a business employing three men.'

'Bright signs?' said Ross.

'Neon signs, you'd say, that sort of thing, though most of them these days aren't neon at all. Marching and flashing signs, colour alternates, running codes. I've done everything from major theatres to nudes above a massage parlour.'

'Jesus,' said Ross, 'and this place hasn't even got electricity. Now that's ironic, or poetic justice, or something.'

'I got so tied up with making a go of the business that it was my marriage which folded. When all that was over I had no business either. Then for a while I just did jobbing work. All in all I pretty much went off city life, and that's when you came in, Angie.'

'All that special knowledge,' she said. 'It seems such a waste really. There's always a call for a good electrician.'

Cass was serious, but not downcast, as he told them his reasons for coming south. He leant back in his ill-matched chair and watched the movement of his ocean. Far to the south, where the long beach was visible, the setting sun caught a roll of fine mist or sea spray, where the ocean met the land, and out of sight they could hear Gideon's tractor going home for the day and his dogs barking him in. 'The whole thing made me pull up and take stock,' said Cass. 'My marriage and my business gone, most of the complacent assumptions that stood for any real thought — gone. Your confidence suffers, you know. I could hardly choose between white and brown bread without my hands starting to shake.'

'A clean break was best then, I suppose,' said Ross. He hoped Cass wasn't going to get maudlin and embarrass him with a need for emotional support. 'Well, you've got a great little place here.'

'That's for sure, but it's not primarily a matter of a new place, is it? It's a new outlook yourself. That's what I've found. It seems to me now that happiness is the absence of pain, rather than something positive in its own right. Almost all of us in this country are better off in so many ways than ninety percent of the people in the world, but we never twig to it, do we? We're always worried by seeing someone who's doing just a bit better than us.'

'That's the motivation for capitalism, I suppose,' said Ross.

'All by yourself out here, though. You think that's the best way?' asked Angie. Two or three of the duller sheep still stood round by the laundry and one was giving a very human cough.

'I've never seen things so clearly. I've never before been able to make better personal judgements.'

'Personal judgements?' said Angie, and Ross popped the top of another beer.

'Think of it this way,' said Cass. 'All those people you meet who ask you what you do, and never a one that asks you why you do it.'

'I hadn't thought of it,' said Ross.

'You need to forget yourself a bit and be open to the existence of other things. The other day I saw a falcon hunting. How many people can say they've seen a falcon?'

It was dark by the time Cass saw them off, but warm on the headland road in the time between the sea breeze and the land one. Cass could taste the dust left in the air by the Bruins' car and see the soft Tilly light from the window of his cottage. The Romneys had a soft, dimmed luminosity in their movement. There was a bird calling below the cliff and the lights of Kakanui showed on the coast to the north. Cass stood on the headland to see over his night ocean and think for a while. He could feel the ash of the boxthorn fires beneath his sneakers.

Ross and Angie talked about him, of course, on their way home. 'What do you think he'll do then?' said Angie as they reached the town.

'He's licking his wounds, isn't he? Self-assessment can be a dangerous thing; maybe he'll become a bit of a weirdo out there. Who knows.'

'A bright signs expert, eh, and now he lives in a farm cottage and watches the sea.'

There's always work for a good electrician and Ross assumed that because Cass Robbins had run his own bright signs firm then he was no slug. As a day foreman, Ross had some initiative in things at the woollen mills and when various electrical jobs built up on their own staff, he had a word with the manager and then wrote a note to Cass saying there might be a few days' casual work if he wanted it. Ross was prepared to give a chance to any reasonable chap who was up against it. 'We'll see what he makes of it,' he told Angie.

He made a good deal of it, as things turned out. Cass came in every day for a fortnight on his farm bike and wearing his best tartan shirt. Even the maintenance engineer said quite openly that the little guy certainly knew his onions. 'Well, once you've sighted his qualifications then offer him a fulltime position,' said the manager.

On the day he started full time, Cass made a point of seeking Ross out and thanking him for putting him in the way of a job. Cass stopped in at the Bruins' after work with beer for Ross and a chardonnay for Angie. He had a new denim shirt and told them that the farm bike wouldn't be ideal for coming in and out each day in the winter. 'You're still happy out there, though?' asked Angie.

'Look, I found my real self in that place,' said Cass. 'After what happened to me up north I knew I had to get a grip on the things that really matter. There's too great a chance of losing yourself in a complicated existence. A good deal of what passes for necessary activity in everyday life is futile.'

'Tell that to the taxman,' said Ross.

Cass Robbins was senior electrician within three months and he started wearing an orange work coat with the company logo. He bought an almost new Honda Prelude, which he parked by the cottage and carefully covered from the frost. Ross told Angie he'd heard that Cass had started going out with Rebecca Levitt, who worked in accounts and whose husband had been accidentally shot while hunting wallaby in the Hunter Hills.

The next spring the company offered Cass Robbins promotion in Dunedin as maintenance manager. He came to see Angie about putting the old Jamieson place on the market. 'A nice enough little place,' he said, 'but I'm finding it a real nark to have no phone, or electricity. What with the shift callouts and everything I'll need to have something pretty central in Dunedin.'

'I know a couple of good people in real estate down there. I'll give you their names. Would you like a drink?'

'Thanks, but no. Time's money and as a matter of fact I've got someone waiting in the car.' Cass was wearing fashionable twill trousers and had begun a new look by combing his hair back from his forehead. 'I wanted you to have sole agency,' he said.

'You'll be looking for another place by the sea.'

'By the sea?'

'For your ocean view,' said Angie.

'Haven't much time to admire a view these days,' said Cass. 'A modern, low maintenance, all convenience place is what I'm after. As a matter of fact the firm's offering generous mortgage facilities, but don't tell your agent friends that.'

Angie rather expected that Cass would go on to say that he was going to be married. She hoped he might invite her to come out to the car and meet Rebecca Levitt, but he didn't. He shook hands almost formally and gave Angie his temporary Dunedin address. 'You know,' he said, 'I'm quite looking forward to the greater challenge of the city. Maybe Ross mentioned the scope of my responsibilities with the company?'

A few weeks later Angie Bruin had reason to be not far from the old Jamieson place and she turned off the main road and drove down to the coast. She wanted to have an up-to-date impression of Cass Robbins' cottage when she spoke of it to any possible buyers. It sat in the bare paddock on the headland above the sea; the high, half burnt out macrocarpas on the south side, the sheep with the run of the verandah and laundry again, the immensely powerful yet subdued sound of the swell and shingle up and down the steep beach. The paddocks had a tinge of green because of the season and the repaired weatherboards were still pink with undercoat. Otherwise it was much as it had been when Cass Robbins came to the place the summer before.

Angie Bruin looked from the empty cottage out across the gravel road and the headland. A new crop of boxthorn was already sprouting from the ash and stumps of Cass's onslaught, but for a time at least there was that complete and wind-raw view of sea and sky and the meeting of one blue with another which was the horizon.

LIVING AT THE BELLE MONDE

I NEED A lover; not just someone to lie in the bed with when it rains, or to stop the fridge banging when it switches off, but because my complexion is bad again. A roughness has developed on the skin between my lower lip and chin and my forehead and nose have a greasy sheen whatever cleansers or astringents I use. The women in my family have wonderful skin provided that they are bedded regularly. It isn't something we discuss often, but it's recognised all the same. I knew that Richard was having an affair when my sister Jane developed enlarged pores, and cousin Amelia, a PE instructor at the Police College, could talk all she liked about a vegetarian diet, but her life was in her face. Even without make-up she had a startling Revlon glow once she took up her posting.

It poses no great dilemma for me — needing a lover. There are neither moral nor practical obstacles to my achievement of the most satisfactory complexion. The world is full of men who are searching for someone to be with; their hangdog eyes drift across the rooms of parties and PTA meetings, glance from hotel windows and passing buses, accompany the items they pass you across the counter of Cheese Village, or Green World.

Don't think that I'm making any case for promiscuity. God knows, for us women there's rarely any advantage there. Patrick Benn gave me as much good complexion as I required and he was a very funny man; witty, I mean, in a fashion that only denigrated himself and he was good with his hands. Also he cleaned the bath without being asked. Why I ended it with Patrick was that he lived thirty miles away and I got sick of the formalities needed to work a relationship like that. Since Roddy Aspinall I haven't believed a modern woman wants to live with a man, but you shouldn't have to accommodate yourself to a timetable with a built-in delay factor. You should be able to pick up the phone and say, 'Hey, I've just poured two white wines here.' You should be able to open the window on a summer night and talk with your guy a while before he finishes walking the mastiff, or whatever.

I'd say I've got about a month before I have to start using an anti-sheen foundation and that slight rash comes up behind my ears. Long enough to consider if anyone in the Belle Monde Apartments themselves would make a suitable lover. I'm not putting any priority on that, but it would be an advantage when I was away on courses, sussing out the Australian season displays, or at my parents' in Nelson, if I could rely on someone close to keep an eye on my place.

Jason Bird is out for a start, although he's very clean, very athletic and has a tight bum. Whirly Bird we all call him at Belle Monde and sex is too important to him for comfort. A good complexion is one thing; being stuck with a man who can't think of anything else is a real bore. You want to talk about the article on proportional representation, you want to plan a trip to the Bay of Islands together and you can never get any sense out of him because he's still thinking of the grip he had on you half an hour ago, or nipping your knee with forefinger and thumb.

David Justice is a possibility. He hasn't been here very long, but the man has a marvellously well-modulated voice. He's a radio DJ, or somesuch. A lot of people don't realise how important a good voice is. You spend a lot of time with a man in the dark and his looks could be anything then, but his voice is just as important as ever; more perhaps. For myself I can be taken as easily with an educated voice as with forearm muscles, or even teeth and a slow smile. All those odd hours that he works though — the graveyard shift, or wake-up session. I mean I try not to get set in my ways, but I like a regular life. I don't like brunch and I don't like getting up in the dark. My career is significant and I need to be sharp to deal with the fashion buyers. I am something of a believer in regularity as opposed to routine, which is quite different again. Routine is the reason I finished with Stamford Myles. Sweet Jesus, the man cleared his bowels at seven fourteen every morning of his life.

Waka Sommers on the fifth floor fancies me and he's got that permanent suntan going for him. I've no doubt that he'd do wonders for a complexion; his wife Angela looks pretty satisfied that way. The thing is, though, with Waka that he's got too many friends and family; far too many people dropping by without a phone call, or a by your leave. It just doesn't work to have a lover with a wide and informal circle of acquaintances. Men new to the city, on promotion and suchlike, are the best prospect. Successful men, but with a little insecurity and something to prove, feeling a bit on the outside of things, make for suitable lovers. Waka reminds me too much of Solly Mahan, who would call to say he'd have to give it a miss because his club captain had come up from the Coromandel, or an old mate from the Territorials had fallen on hard times.

There's always Donald Macdonald, of course, but the name takes a good deal of getting over. Rather like living with a cartoon really and although he's got some nice dark suits and drives a Camry, I'd say he's a very hairy man. Within reason you've got to allow men to be hairy, but they can go to extremes, particularly the middle-aged ones. A hairy back, you see, is a very different prospect from a hairy chest and the parts that a man wears bare by friction on his legs rarely form an attractive pattern. My complexion was a talking point when I was with Andrew Plunneur, but in the mornings I was left alone with the dark, curled hair like watch springs on the sheets. And yet, to be fair, he had a better dress sense than any other man I've known. He had a particular flair for linens in earth colours and he could roll a sleeve to leave just one, smooth cuff on his forearm.

My friend Simone says that here at the Belle Monde Apartments is the last place that I should be looking for a lover, that it would be like taking up with someone at your work, but I don't see it. This is my home and so my home comforts should be here. A little closeness, some sharing of skills and outlooks, some emotional and physical transactions within set bounds of trust and privacy. Why should any of us in a modern age be coy about making the best life we can? Enough things work against you without creating restrictions of your own.

The thing to guard against in a man is dependence. You think that you have achieved an acknowledged equality of emotional support and then after a hard day yourself there's this guy taking hours of your evening to bitch about not being made a partner in the firm, or his fears of a tumour because he's twice felt dizzy after squash. That's the thing making me cautious about Ewan Price — dependence, I mean. I've always liked scholarly men, provided they don't stoop and have kept themselves in some shape, and Ewan on the seventh has a PhD from a British university and runs for fifty minutes four times a week. And he can meet your eye directly with all the goodwill and trust of a family dog. It's just that whenever I've talked to him I've detected something plaintive beneath the humour with which he describes an incident of his day, some tendency to unload that would probably be magnified by intimacy. Garrick Chesterfield is mayor of Napier, or Hastings, now, but he was that sort of man, always taking strength, always seeking reassurance that he would amount to something.

Well, there's time, I guess, but maybe not a month after all. I've hardly had a pimple since the sixth form, but yesterday my left eye was itchy a good deal of the time and last night I found that a spot was coming just under the arch of my eyebrow. After all, a woman has to look after herself.

Simone said there's this divorced dentist who's been looking at apartment 203.

THIS MAN'S ARMY

WHAT I REMEMBER about leaving for National Service is having my photo taken for the local paper, along with the five or six other guys who were also going to Waiouru. The photograph itself I never saw, but I remember standing on the platform with the wooden wall of the railway station behind us on which was hanging a row of empty buckets, God knows why. And this hugely pregnant girl who had come to see her husband off, and who discomforted the rest of us because of her condition. Maybe even before we were quite in the army we considered that she added a non-military element; maybe it was a misgiving as to which of us in the photograph would seem most likely to be responsible for her condition. I can't put a face to any of the other guys: we got split up in basic training. Just the grouping of us before the buckets I recall, and our disinclination to press towards the pregnant girl who was the centrepiece. She had a summer smock, large, white legs and straight, girl-next-door hair. Her meaty features quivered at the farewells, and I'll bet National Service was worse for her than any of us who left for the army that day.

On the train to Picton and on the ferry across the strait I could almost forget the destination, and the origin of my travel warrant, but at Wellington there were enough of us from that intake to fill a special bus to go north in the evening. A corporal with a clip-board, too, whose uniform was the unsought indication of things to come. I had a biro in the inside pocket of my sportscoat and body heat must have made it burst, for when I roused myself from lolling on the seat back and window I had a purple stain on the lining, my shirt, my chest. 'Now listen up, cocksuckers,' the corporal said, 'when you debus for Intake and Documentation I don't want nothing left on board. Nothing, right?' That stain went from my skin after a week or so, but much later when I collected my civvy gear to go home for the first time, there it was on my shirt and coat lining, and I heard that first corporal telling us cocksuckers to listen up.

Plain loneliness is what you feel most in National Service, for the first weeks anyway. After you make friends and realise that a good deal of all the hoopla is just show, then you move on to complex loneliness. You look forward to rec time playing table tennis, or sinking a few in the wet canteen, but at the centre of it all there's still loneliness that arises from not being in command of your own life, or among people of your own choice. Maybe loneliness isn't so much what I mean: futility perhaps.

Mail was brought to the barracks in the afternoons. When we got back from training, the letters would be lying on the right beds. They would lie at all angles, just as flipped onto the army blanket of perfect tension, and the bedrolls would look down on them. The blankets and sheets of the bedroll had to make perfect and alternate layers. Any crease at morning inspection meant a charge. When we came back from the butts, the gas hut, the confidence course, the lecture rooms, the bivvies, the first thing we looked for was mail. Guys read their letters in all sorts of ways and many places. The letters were part of our life on the outside, the only bits getting through to us. If I was first into the barrack room I always noticed the pale envelopes with their stamps, lying on the smooth grey of the army blankets. Some beds would have several; some beds never had any, no matter how many weeks passed.

At the end of each bed was a large wooden box for issue gear, and down the centre of the barrack room was a rifle rack for the Browning SLRs. The rifles had to be cleaned before mess parade in the evening, then the corporal for the day checked them in, drew a long chain through all the trigger guards down the rack and padlocked it.

The best letters I got were the few from Debra Eastcliff who was doing law at Canterbury. They weren't passionate letters because we'd been seeing each other for only a few weeks before the exams of the year before, and she lived in Nelson. Her life seemed to have so much more freedom than my own. Almost everything she talked about was familiar to me; almost everything around me as I read her letters, or replied, or thought about her, was incomprehensible to someone not living it. That particular sound of the chain through the trigger guards, the two guys who had started bumming in the showers, the MPs' Land Rover at three or four in the morning so that the barrack room was briefly lit with flashes through the windows. Miles Procter, who was cheerful all day, cried in his sleep at night. Benny Wesley tried to steal a live hand grenade to blow up his old school. There was a tin slide that you put under your brass coat buttons when you cleaned them that some guys could use as a bottle opener. Where else, I wonder, would this be considered a useful knack?

In certain circumstances you shut down some of your emotional responses, as a form of defence, in the same way that some animals slow their metabolism to get through winter. I could sit in the back of a truck coming back from exercises and for half an hour just watch the dust suck in under the canopy, stick to the sweat on the faces opposite and darken gradually as a make-up. The padre came into the barrack room one morning before parade, and our instructing NCOs discreetly, yet derisively, withdrew. He talked to a platoon of bland faces, and both he and we knew that none of us would go to see him.

Each barrack block looked much the same. All were wooden and one-storeyed and each had a letter on the end so that one could be proved distinct from another. Each block had its orderly room, its parade ground, its mess. In summer the heat shimmered across the parade grounds, and in winter the snow lay in the tussock slopes above the butts.

Debra Eastcliff had this vacation job ringing just about everyone in Nelson as part of a survey on newspaper reading habits. Every day she got offered dates from guys who liked the sound of her voice. I liked the sound of her voice very much myself — from recollection and the few calls that I made while other servicemen stood waiting. I liked the way she wrote, too: candidly, and with no reference to the excessive familiarity to which I was driven by my unnatural life.

Sergeant Neke was a regular army man. He regarded the responsibility for the basic training of our platoon as a form of penance, and so bore all the humiliation of it with sorrow rather than rage. The sarcasm and spurious intimidation were left to Lance Corporal Dellmer, who was also regular army, but limited enough to draw satisfaction from shouting at thirty people who had their own talents, yet were certainly ignorant concerning Corporal Dellmer's army. But don't imagine that he was a man of any real malice: all he required was our acceptance that there was no higher aspiration in life than to be a fighting man.

Sundays were designated non-training days, but we found that even recreation was compulsory. There was a choice of sports, but no alternative to participation. The monotony of softball on the brown summer grass I remember, and the cross-country winter runs that gave privacy at least. The combination of external chill and internal heat on those winter runs used to mottle my legs and shoulders brick red and white. We were convinced that the army authorities put kill-cock in our drink, but I think a policy of physical exertion was enough. Nevertheless, it was strange that the homely women who served in the canteen were transformed into beauties by the passage of time. Noeline had the best pair on her and consequently worked a very popular shift, but it was all a hopeless and muted lust.

There was a hot day when we sat in a dry creekbed while

Sergeant Neke explained to us the logic and formation of a dispersed infantry advance across open country. He had taken off his beret, and his straight hair was in quills because of the sweat, which also darkened his jungle greens in an arc that reached well down his ribs. There was a damp clay bank behind him, grey as pencil lead, and a mass of small, lilac butterflies swooped and quivered there. Nothing of Neke's instruction has remained, but there is the memory of him talking there and all the while the lilac butterflies a shifting aura behind him. It was a brief, random beauty and not one of us made mention of it.

Occasionally there were training films, with Corporal Dellmer quite pumped up with the novelty of such instructional aids, and Sergeant Neke providing a resigned introduction, his large, dark eyes glossy with despair. *Why Things Are Seen* we watched in a room inadequately blacked out, and with a platoon of B Company square bashing outside. The film's narrator told us all about shape, movement, colour and silhouette in a very English voice and in a very English landscape, while a light drizzle twisted in shrouds across the parade ground and clotted on the windows. Sergeant Neke left us after his introduction; the corporal stood at one of the windows, looked into the drifting rain and moved his lips exactly to make the drill commands his own. See the English hedgerow with a red triangle set among its amorphous green; see awkward Tutty a row in front with, behind his left ear, a mulberry birthmark that an army haircut doesn't conceal; see the B Company platoon fall in on its marker. The projector ran on with a clicking repetition that was a clichéd anachronism even then. We moved our shoulders, gaped like baboons, in some unconscious protest at the passing of our lives.

Our company did a five-day field exercise shortly before we completed basic training. Combat conditions, they said, and so we slogged around the hills with full gear, dug slitties, stood sentry, kept moving out at some Godforsaken hour of the night. The enemy were a group of officer cadets who had a fondness for extravagant camouflage, and lobbing thunder-flashes into our perimeter. As our section moved across this bush creek after midnight, Kyle MacDonald slumped down on the cool boulders and couldn't go on. We got his pack off and stood among the ferns of the bank listening to his forced breathing. The medic thought he'd had a heart attack, and at first light we carried him up to a tussock ridge and he went out by helicopter. We were impressed by something as solemn as a heart attack. It seemed the real thing among so much simulation. Our sympathy for Kyle MacDonald, and the unspoken regard for our own fortitude, were destroyed when we got back to Waiouru to find that he'd been diagnosed as having hyperventilated and was discharged after one night. After that we considered him a bit of a prick.

There were friends made, of course, whether of convenience, or necessity, we didn't stop to consider. Guy Wynn, who had a subversive humour that attracted me, and breath that repelled us all. Peter Evans who, because he was both lazy and powerful, had an easy disposition. 'She'll be jake,' he'd say of fatigues duty, or a charge for not being back in barracks. 'She'll be jake.' With all of that platoon I lived more closely than I ever did with my brothers — we were shackled together by the army squad mentality, by identical daily programmes, and an obligation of duty. We recognised it, and didn't blame one another for our predicament. Like porkers in a pen, we knew about enforced familiarity.

We had one big snowfall on Waiouru itself before I left. It started in the evening when we were coming back from the mess hall. In the dusk the snowflakes were almost invisible until they passed before the windows, doorways or large lights mounted on the street end of the barrack blocks. Like Lux flakes the snow passed almost horizontally before the light sources, yet I wasn't conscious of a wind. For a long time there was no sign that any snow ever touched the ground, but overnight it silently reached up along the sides of the barrack blocks as if to disguise their ugliness. When we formed up in the half-light of a winter morning, the tread pattern of our boots was minted over and over in the snow.

What I remember about leaving from National Service is just the green, covered trucks drawn up at the barracks to take us to the station. Northbound and southbound at different times, and the laughter and the relief and the pledges to keep in touch with mates that were never redeemed. And the things that had been invested with special power and significance, shrunk to objective appreciation. The empty rifle rack, and the beds revealed scarred and plain once the immaculate blankets had gone. A CSM's parade square cry become irrelevant, the cracked and dust-dappled windows of the wet canteen. 'Get out of here, you useless bastards,' said Corporal Dellmer, and stood smiling, flattered by our jeers of farewell.

DAY ONE

IN THE MID-SIXTIES I finished my thesis on extruded igneous dykes of Banks Peninsula and sat back to receive the plaudits and post-graduate study offers of the academic world. The academic world remained strangely mute and I accepted a job as assistant housemaster at a traditional boys' college. All the physical possessions that I owned in the world were crammed into my series E Morris and I drove up the day before the start of term one.

The great sycamore trees stirred like galleons on the expansive lawns beyond the stone gates and the side parking area by the boiler house was full of boarder parent cars. Those boys who already knew the school immediately abandoned their parents lest they be shamed by association with family. In threes and fours and anthropoidal amble they drifted back to old haunts. Only the third formers, bright as reef fish in their new uniforms, kept close to the adults as they wandered about to forestall farewell. The new mothers of the school maintained a despairing cheerfulness, smiling fiercely and commenting on the stained glass window in the chapel, and all the time hoping to see a familiar face. The fathers, whose minds had thankfully suppressed their own experience as new boys, patted shoulders with inarticulate support and murmured the bastard Latin of the school song.

I was a new boy again myself in a way and a little humbled to be seated by the secretary outside the head's study until he could see me. There was a box with a frosted glass front mounted by the door, which displayed COME IN,

WAIT or ENGAGED, at the direction of the person inside.

Ian Villier was the headmaster. I got a first glimpse of him as a father with an expensive tweed jacket was shown out, but Villier didn't want to meet my eye just then and turned back, closed the door, looked over my application and CV again perhaps. COME IN was then displayed in a shimmer of letters on the frosted glass. I did so, and walked a surprising stretch of opulent, heraldic carpet before I could reach the headmaster's desk. Villier had a great jutting face, with a nose large enough to saddle, and his grey hair was swept back directly from his face. His features were both exaggerated and impressive, like those of an aristocratic baboon. He had an expression as if he were about to be photographed, which he maintained over the several years that I knew him.

'A sound enough degree,' he said, while pointing emphatic-ally to a chair with a cloth seat of paisley pattern as if he wanted some comment on it, or from it. 'The profession is stuffed with geographers, however. Still, it could have been history. I could have had two firsts in history sitting in your place and one of them played for Manawatu.' I knew enough of the school to realise that any official reference to sport pertained to rugby. 'There's not a lot of advancement possible through the humanities, I'm afraid. I'd advise you to make the most of housemastering. A good housemaster now, there's progress in a career that way. Most of the principals I know proved themselves on the boarding side.'

He began each sentence with sufficient volume and clarity of enunciation to command the assembly hall and then, as if realising the talk was more personal, allowed his voice to drop away. It reminded me of Anzac days long ago. He wore an academic gown slightly greened with age and ran his fingers down the heavy, dark edges of it on his chest. He made a good deal of eye contact, tilting his head up so that the trajectory of his great nose altered and the large nostrils came level with my vision like the muzzles of a shotgun.

'You'll soon settle to it. Routine is the secret of efficiency. We have a full staff meeting early tomorrow.' The head passed over a folder containing my teaching timetable, a staff list, fire drill and a discount voucher from the local chicken nugget takeaway. His fingers rustled on the edges of his gown and he leant back in his chair, turning his eyes to watch the returning boarders in the grounds beyond his office. 'The team,' he said ringingly. 'The team is everything. Do your bit and it'll carry you along.' The inner door opened and the secretary mouthed a name at him and then withdrew. Villier spread his hands palms uppermost in mock exasperation at the need to end the meeting and I stood up to leave.

'Ontology,' boomed the head as we moved to the door. I could think of no reply. 'That's why I chose you. I rang the dean at the college and she said that you had it recorded as a major interest. I'm always drawn to a thinking man — and a man who appreciates the needs of a team, of course. Anyway, ontology swung it for you.' I had no idea what ontology was, had met the dean only twice, but I wasn't going to question the grounds of my appointment. Rather I took it as an omen of the sort of place that I had come to. Villier posed briefly in the doorway to farewell me; his great shoes of burnished oxblood leather shone like the hooves of a show horse. 'Ontology,' he said and tilted his head to suggest this would remain a secret between us, and to present his better profile to the camera.

Across the lower quad and furthest from the noise of traffic was the old hostel building known as the Gables, although they had been removed years before because of earthquake risk. The wooden building was dwarfed by modern, two-storeyed hostel blocks close to it, but still held the housemasters' study, matron's office, the sickbay, lost and found, and a display case of transfixed and mouldering native birds presented by the first dux of the school on his return thirty years later.

Already boys were coming and going at the Gables and they looked at me with a mixture of curiosity and derision as I went into the housemasters' study. Chink McMahon was duplicating dorm lists and not surprised by my arrival because the secretary had rung. Chink was head of hostel and got his name not from any oriental appearance, but because he resembled some general of the desert campaign who had the name. Chink had been there himself and after that time of trial seemed to find all of life trivial and fit only for grim burlesque. The fewer people about him who were returned soldiers, the greater his disregard for the present became. Beneath all was a bitterness that the epic world he had experienced was fading and that more and more of the Lilliputians around him had no understanding, no regard, for what had happened in the desert. Chink himself was far too proud to tell them and kept the flame alive by drinking whisky from a glass at the RSA and from a flask when he was off duty within the school grounds. It was said that his name was mentioned fifty-seven times in the battalion history.

'Seen the head then?' shouted Chink above the noise of the gestetner he was cranking. His wry grin showed the gap between his front teeth typical of his namesake. From time to time sheets stuck to the roller longer than they should, and shot high into the air. Chink snatched them down with the reflexes of a praying mantis while still cranking with the other hand. 'No need for a great deal of patter,' he said as he finished with the machine. He gestured to the long notice boards so festooned with ageing papers, many six deep to a pin, that they resembled soiled tutus. 'Duty rosters, bell routines, leave provisions, extension numbers, team lists, and so on. There when you need it. Learn the job by doing it, I always say.' He looked at me with his eyebrows up as if askance that one so young should be given even the least command.

'Oh,' and Chink took a couple of steps towards the quad window and patted a large, well-used book that had pride of place on a table there. 'Caning book. Caning book. Never forget it. See.' He flicked it open and with a pencil attached to the spine with twine, pointed out the headed columns that he had ruled in — date, name, strokes, reason, staff signature.

'Never forget it. The senior housemasters find it essential for their term reports.' I could see at a glance that the last boy had been punished for dumb insolence and imitating a hyena during prep.

Chink told me which house I was attached to and a few other administration things. There was no garage available, but Chink said that I could nose my car into the lean-to behind the boiler house where the figure targets were kept. 'No military service, I suppose?' asked Chink. I attempted to inject a degree of disappointment into my voice when replying that I'd missed out on National Service. 'Sport, though?' Chink knew that no one would be appointed to the college without some physical qualification and was barely mollified by my recital of considerable participation and notably less achievement.

When I was at the door again, about to leave in the direction of my house, Stanways, Chink made his one effort in pastoral guidance. 'Advice,' he said. I halted, wishing to show no disinclination to listen. 'Are you interested in advice?' asked Chink diffidently. I nodded.

Chink drew himself up and protected himself with an added formality of tone. 'Six things,' he said, 'in the school and in the hostel. Always be prepared, never permit insolence, never court popularity, cane severely and therefore rarely, never introduce a topic dear to your heart and never expect gratitude.'

I said that I would bear all of them in mind. Such precepts were far from those I had recently been introduced to at teachers' college, yet Chink's were easier to hold in the mind and experience was to prove them also more valuable.

Stanways was one of the new hostel blocks, built largely through the generosity of old boys who were determined that a new generation have things no easier than they themselves had found them. Change other than expansion was anathema to them, while demonstrative progress was even worse. Had it been possible, they would have insisted on the identical prescriptions, an equivalent number of wet Sundays and bullies, the very same teachers even, revitalised as caricatures generation after generation.

The housemaster of Stanways was John Roffery, known by the boys as Pecker because of his nodding head when stressed, which was ever the case. Pecker was in the second-storey fourth form dorm making copies of the wall graffiti in a scrapbook of low-quality paper. 'The little bastards keep telling me that it's already there from the year before, but now I'll have them, have the little bastards.' I had barely introduced myself before he had me counter-signing the sketches as a true record and then numbering the light bulb in each fourth former's cubicle with a green felt pen. Pecker couldn't have been more than thirty-five and had a soft, jellied face that quivered with high emotion because of the onset of another term. He taught French despite a temperament quite unsuited to the profession. Rage is the emotion in a teacher which most delights all students and once they recognise that it can be provoked, they'll go to any lengths to do so.

Pecker was not a fool and understood that he'd made the wrong choice of profession. He was a housemaster as well as a teacher at the college so that he could amass the greatest amount of money in the least time and then resign. 'A mussel farm in Queen Charlotte Sound,' he told me as we confiscated beer that incoming boarders had stashed in the lavatory cisterns. 'You go out in the boat with a few select companions,' he said, 'and no one else can come near you all day.' Some weeks later I was with Pecker in the Collar and Tie Bar and, when a visitor asked his job, he replied that he demeaned himself for a living. Pecker could see his own situation even if unable to rectify it immediately.

Pecker went into the third form dorm and rounded up several red-eyed, small boys to help me bring in my gear. After I had parked the Morris among a mass of Hun target flats like protest placards, and as the laden new boys and I trekked back to Stanways, I could see in the growing dusk and at the periphery of vision, skulking figures drift towards the car. The third formers piled my stuff outside my room and, despite the agony of their homesickness and the brief time we had been together, it later proved that they had got off with six bottles of Australian shiraz, my running shoes, a flashing works lamp, all my love letters from Molly Parmenter and several male-oriented magazines.

The room was well appointed and quite new, with a view over the fives courts and the ramps behind the kitchens where the pig drums were rumbled out each morning. Unfortunately during the vacation a starling had blundered in somehow and shat on almost all the furniture before dying at last behind the wall heater. 'Just heap your stuff in for the moment,' said Pecker, 'and I'll take you down to the house prefects' room so that you can get to know a face or two.' Four or five of them were there, all uncouthly large and hairy and with knuckled hands that seemed to gravitate naturally to the crotch — their own in the first instance, at least — or to the destruction of what furniture hadn't already been unravelled. Pecker rattled through their names and said it was important, as a housemaster, to carry the prefects with you — vital in fact. An exhausting task judging by the size of them.

The head of house had just got in and still wore his school blazer with his achievements scrolled beneath the crest like campaign medals. 'We shall find a name for you, sir,' he said to me kindly, 'but it may take a few weeks' observation.'

'Maybe prickface,' I heard another say as Pecker and I went back down the corridor.

As it was the boarders' in day, the meal was a good deal later than usual and the lights were needed in the dining room by the time nearly three hundred boys were seated and Chink led in the staff. There were just six of us that first night: Chink, Pecker, a large marshmallow who was the nurse, Jetarse Munns who was head of Chivers, and Neville Gillespie who was, like myself, new to the school.

Our table was a little raised, presumably to allow masters

to exercise a supervisory function as they ate. It was rather like having a meal on a crowded railway platform; no awareness of individual speakers, but a disconcerting general roar of voices and occasional surges to the kitchen slides. From time to time Chink stood up from his meal, showed his gapped teeth like an old lion, and paced down a few aisles.

'Dining room supervision begins for one of you tomorrow,' Pecker told Neville and me. During the rice pudding course Jetarse Munns suddenly sprang into the throng and dragged from the room a mid-sized boy with a continuous eyebrow. 'Marriage collapsed last year,' said Pecker. He tapped his forehead. 'I give him a term, that's all.' I presumed that the description applied to Jetarse rather than the boy.

'I don't believe I caught your name,' said the nurse to Neville and, after being given it, turned and asked the same question of me. She had the softest flesh I have ever seen, palely luminous and so unresisting to gravitational forces that when she rested her arm on the table it spread out like cake mixture. 'Treat me as a confidante,' she said.

'Notices,' roared Chink and the noise in the dining hall gradually fell to a menacing rumble while Chink sucked his teeth and seemed to be contemplating a bayonet charge. Pecker motioned to us and we quietly filed away while Chink read the list of outstanding detentions from the year before. As we passed into the quad, Jetarse was there in the shadows still haranguing the mid-sized boy with the never-ending eyebrow. The boy's body language suggested to me exactly the term dumb insolence that I had read in the caning book, though Jetarse was contributing the animal noises.

Neville and I grouped together for support, as is always the way of newcomers in a unknown environment. We had little in common apart from our profession and our predicament, but it was weeks before our mutual antipathy developed. For that first night we were the best of friends and sat in his room, which was starlingless, drinking vodka and lime as the school whirled around us. Neville was a five foot five mathematician with a penchant for savage sarcasm and a complete tolerance to alcohol. We assured each other that we were born teachers. We got drunk by the window open to the summer night, ignoring the strange cries and jostling shadows of an educational Serengeti. We watched the moon and stars, and a line of glowing, red dots closer to the horizon that were the cigarettes of seniors sitting on the back field.

Even very drunk, I retained an odd, ambivalent reaction to the new world in which I found myself — part exhilaration and part apprehension. I had commenced a career.

Minutes

OF THE SEVENTY-NINTH ordinary meeting of the Management Committee of the Colenso Squash Club held in the changing room, Colenso Squash Club, evening 15th August.

PRESENT: Kevin Fortescue (Chair), Misses Mavis and Ruth Oliphant (in front of the heater), Toby Jardine (as close to the heater as the Misses Oliphant would allow him). Alex Smyth and Paul Essens were still showering when the meeting commenced, passed briefly through the meeting in towels, but were afterwards in attendance.

APOLOGIES: Were received from Ollie Oliphant (hospital; probably a vasectomy, but the Misses Oliphant would neither confirm nor deny) and Sarah McEldowney. Mr Jardine made the point that Miss McEldowney's letter was not so much an apology as a protest at what she alleged were unconstitutional rulings at previous meetings concerning whether the Ladies' Plate final should have been played with a yellow or white spot ball.

MINUTES: Were taken as read (Chair, Jardine) because no one could understand Sarah McEldowney's writing, but in matters arising it was moved Chair and seconded Jardine that the yellow spot be confirmed as the official ball in any club championships, or local tournaments. Motion carried with abstentions Smyth and Essens as they came from getting changed on the court too late to hear the preceding discussion.

The Chair expressed the meeting's appreciation of Mr Jardine acting as Secretary in the absence of Miss McEldowney.

CORRESPONDENCE: The Acting Secretary was in receipt of

three correspondences. A letter from the New Zealand Squash Association Grading Panel confirming that Club President Kevin Fortescue had been confirmed as an official E grade player and two letters concerning payment of $297 for the replastering of the court front. The first letter was a final demand from Hanning Plastering Ltd; the second from their lawyer, R.A. Pacity. It was moved Chair, seconded Jardine, that the accounts rendered be tabled for consideration by the AGM and the incoming Committee. Carried. It was moved Jardine, and carried without show of hands, that Mr Fortescue (Chair) be congratulated on his confirmed E grade national grading. The Chair thanked the meeting for its expression of wishes, spoke for some time on his various ranking games throughout the season and said that he saw the grading really as a sign of the overall vigour of the Club rather than a personal distinction.

FINANCES: The Acting Secretary (acting as Secretary-Treasurer) reported that the Club's No. 1 account (day to day) was overdrawn by $92 and that the No. 2 account (maintenance and reserves) held $53. The Misses Oliphant asked the acting Secretary-Treasurer through the Chair for a list of members who had not yet paid their subscriptions and were informed that a list was being compiled for the forthcoming AGM. It was proposed and seconded (the Misses Oliphant) that no member be permitted to take part in Club or Tournament play who was not a member of said Club. Mr Fortescue (Chair) said that the constitution already contained such provision. Mr Smyth asked the Misses Oliphant if they had never played with any member other than a financial one and went unanswered. The Misses Oliphant then raised the question as to why certain Club members, who could be named, continued to play during the present season, but were not current financial members. Mr Smyth said that he thought there was general opinion among members that they had the current financial year in which to pay the subscription for that year. Mr Essens (defeated 3–2 in the pre-meeting game by Mr Smyth and with a thigh bruise developing as a result of ball strike) disagreed strongly with Mr Smyth. The Misses Oliphant also disagreed.

Mr Essens then reminded the Chair that there was a motion before the meeting and that unless it could be shown that the constitution already bore the substance of that motion, then the motion should be put without further delay. Mr Fortescue (Chair) replied that as he had been one of the founder members who drafted the constitution he thought he should be reasonably familiar with its contents, although he did not have a copy to hand at that point in time. He ruled the motion out of order on the grounds that it was already covered in intention by provisions of the constitution and that if it wasn't, then it was still out of order because any motions of a constitutional nature had to be given prior notice of twenty-one days.

There being no further discussion on subscriptions, it was moved (Chair), seconded (Jardine) and carried that the $53 in the No. 2 account be transferred to the No. 1 account and that the attention of the AGM and incoming Management Committee be drawn to the serious state of the Club finances.

GENERAL BUSINESS: The lack of changing facilities for women was raised by the Misses Oliphant. Miss Mavis Oliphant said that the only night the changing room was available exclusively for women was the ladies' night on Fridays, the choice of which continued to be a grievance to women members, the meeting would be well aware, she said. On other occasions women members were forced to come already changed to the court, or change in their vehicles, and the shower was virtually out for them. Miss Ruth Oliphant said that even making bookings could be embarrassing, because although the booking sheet was supposed to be on the nail behind the front door, men kept taking it into the changing room to sign and leaving it there.

Mr Smyth said that either of the Misses Oliphant were welcome to come and use the changing room, or shower, when he was there and that he had been for some time an admirer of their ball skills and general athleticism when their backs were to the wall. The Misses Oliphant said through the Chair that there was no call for that sort of talk and the Chair said yes, Alex, there was no call for that sort of talk even if such sentiments were widely held.

Mr Jardine pointed out to the meeting that despite the general discussion on facilities for women members and banter arising from it, there was in fact no motion as such before the meeting. It was then moved and seconded (the Misses Oliphant) and carried without further discussion that the Committee recommend to the incoming Management Committee that it look urgently at the question of adequate and separate changing facilities for women members of the Club.

It was moved from the Chair (seconded Jardine) that the Honours Board be updated in terms of the inscription of Club championship winners. In speaking to his motion, Mr Fortescue said that when all was said and done the object of the organisation was to promote the sport of squash and that the inculcation and record of a competitive spirit was vital in that regard. The Misses Oliphant said they wondered if the President's attitude would be the same if he wasn't Club Champion. There followed unusually free and general discussion on the point, during which Mr Essens said that he was bound to say that he was continually disappointed by the stress placed by some of the Club and administration on winning, rather than the fellowship aspects which were surely the primary objective after all. The Misses Oliphant said hear, hear many times. Mr Smyth considered it was no use hiding your head in the sands and that the world is a competitive environment in which people had to put themselves on the line. He himself, he said, blamed a lot of the soppy attitudes about at present on the schools and welfare handouts. Mr Essens considered the discussion to be straying from the point.

The Chair recognised its own right of reply and said that views had been fairly canvassed and that it seemed quite clear to him that the Honours Board should be kept up to date as the foundation of burgeoning Club tradition. The motion was read once more by the Acting Secretary, was then put and lost 3–2. The Chair said sometimes he wondered why he bothered putting in the time and effort and would the Misses Oliphant quit fiddling with the heater and give their attention to Committee matters.

The Chair then said that if there was no further business, he would declare the meeting closed as he and Mr Jardine were to have a game following the meeting. The Misses Oliphant said that if the Chair looked at the booking sheet he would see that they (the Misses Oliphant) had the court for half-past. Mr Fortescue (Chair) said that he was bound to feel disappointed when established convention was ignored and that his travelling fourteen ks to preside at meeting of the Committee deserved some consideration. Mr Smyth wondered if the Misses Oliphant would prefer to play alternative doubles, but they refused.

Mr Essens wished the minutes to record that he would be unavailable for renomination to the Management Committee at the AGM, because he was no longer in harmony with the philosophic direction of Committee policies. The Misses Oliphant said they too were considering being unavailable.

Mr Fortescue as Chair said he wished to thank members of the Committee for their attendance throughout the year, but that he felt obliged to say in his forthcoming report to the AGM that there had been some Club members willing to accept Committee status, yet unwilling to assume the associated responsibilities. The Chair considered that this outgoing Committee should in fact make some recommendations to the AGM regarding the selection of Management Committee members for the forthcoming year and was about to word a motion to that effect, when Mr Jardine pointed out that with the departure of the Misses Oliphant to get changed in the carpark and that of Mr Smyth to ensure they were undisturbed while doing so, the Committee no longer had a quorum.

The meeting was therefore closed by the Chair at 8.33 p.m.

GOODBYE, STANLEY TAN

WE DIDN'T SEE the Raffles Hotel; it was closed for renovations. Isn't that always the way and now if ever the trip comes up in conversation with other people, they expect us to have been to Raffles. We saw the merlion at the harbour, though, and the useless gun emplacements on Sentosa Island. We climbed to Fort Canning on the site of the ancient royal palace. We had our photo taken with a black snake at the cable-car terminal and in the Tiger Balm Gardens and in the Orchid Gardens and with pigmy hippos only a fence away. We have a photo emphasising my bulk as I board a bum boat, a photo of my wife boarding the bum boat, a photo of a woman from Tuttle, North Dakota, who for an hour was our best friend in the world, disembarking from a bum boat. We have photos of our hotel bed covered with a day's purchases from plazas twenty storeys high. We have photos in which we can identify nothing, not even ourselves, and for which there seems no earthly or unearthly reason. These photographs tend to cause disagreement as to whether they even belong to the Singapore album, or whether they are of Hong Kong, or Penang, or Bangkok. As if there were any real connection between the settings and ourselves.

But you know all of that. It is part of collective tourist folklore, so let me give you three things that come from a working visit, when I was twenty-seven and had a larger appetite for experience and a smaller perception of its whereabouts, than my own country suited. Flotillas of scooters and motorbikes at the very start of the day, with riders wearing their jackets back to front as a windbreak; lizards on the walls where the first sun strikes; Thais, muffled like gangsters, spraying weeds and verges and, unmuffled, doing many of the other menial jobs. From that time I have only one photo. Dog-eared and monochrome, it shows me with Stanley Tan outside the illegal pig abattoir in which we worked. Strangely enough, it was my farming background which provided for me in that close pressed city. That more intimate knowledge of Singapore is like a dream now and provides no link with the present place. For some months I lived closely with Stanley Tan as a friend, but even then we knew that it was the fortuitous friendship of circumstance and not something that could survive once we left the squeals of the abattoir and the concrete room by the old harbour where we slept with the continual noise and smell of the city through the metal bars of the door. There is a sense of free fall in the relationships of youth that is lost in a later regard for security.

The woman from Tuttle, North Dakota, is a different story. An hour on an Asian bum boat seems to have cemented our lives together. She has since sent postcards from Nepal, Denmark, Egypt, Timor and Tuttle, North Dakota. She is planning a trip to New Zealand with her husband largely on our unsuspecting praise of the country. Her husband, she told my wife, is six foot three and was legal counsel to the previous Governor of North Dakota.

My wife and I stayed at a hotel in Orchard Road that had an atrium designed by the Pharaohs and a labyrinth of soft, air-conditioned corridors. I slept more poorly there than I had years before in the barred, concrete room by the estuarine harbour. My wife likes hotels, but I lay listening through much of the night to the shouts from the streets. It was as if gangs still fought there, which, Stanley Tan said, was the regular thing before Lee took over.

So safe a city did he make it that Stanley and I, my wife and I, years apart, could wander late at night and feel quite at ease. My wife is a perceptive traveller, whereas I am merely a bewildered one. She pointed out to me that although people drove on the left in Singapore, they tended to walk on the right. Nobody whistles as they go about their business, she said, and she was right. I guess that it's some cultural thing between Singaporeans and ourselves.

Orchard Road was like a drying room into which a community had been herded. The cries began with intensity, but were rendered languid by the hot, moist air as they rose towards our hotel room. When we had finished work, Stanley Tan sometimes took a shower in the flush room where the gutted pigs were given a final hose down and their bristles shaved if the buyers preferred them that way. The naked pigs were similar in colour to the naked Stanley, but carried more fat. If he jostled them as he held the hose with one hand and washed with the other, the carcasses would sway coyly away, then back again. Occasionally I showered there myself; it was cooling, but I disliked the feel of blood clots and fat between my feet and the concrete floor. If he showered at the abattoir, Stanley usually took a head he could buy cheaply and exchanged it for the favours of a very short, smiling mother of two who had a calligraphy stall in the direction of our room.

My wife said that I should attempt to find the places I was accustomed to from those far off months in Singapore. Long hours and little money had reduced my view of the city. After more than twenty years how was I to find the site of an illegal pig abattoir smaller than a New Zealand family home, the barred apartment cell Stanley Tan and I shared, the parasol shop that twice a day served fried rice and vegetable ends among the umbrellas to a few regulars who worked close at hand? The owner of the abattoir saw no reason for breaks of longer than twenty minutes. I could still find my way to Raffles, of course, although my wife and I couldn't go in. Twice I had been there before. Once with a Canadian girl whom I met lost by the parasol shop; once to have a gin sling with Eddie Gilmore who supervised my thesis. There were the ceiling fans and a good deal of dark wood. There was also an air of self-conscious history. Eddie Gilmore was to give a plenary address at the three-day conference, but knew he wasn't well. 'Would that I were in the abattoir with you,' he said with feeling. 'Killing pigs and young again, or better still that I were here and young again.'

Our American friend from Tuttle told my wife and me on the bum boat that of all the places she had visited, and she seemed well through the places of the world, Singapore was the cleanest and the most orderly. She said that they had the sense to teach everyone English in Singapore and so put them in the ballgame with everyone else. Certainly it's comforting to have foreign people speak your language in their country. The friend from Tuttle, North Dakota said that she found it easier to understand the Singaporeans than she did us, though we also were in the same ballgame, I guess.

One morning of lurid skies when Stanley and I arrived for work, the old wooden door was still closed and the cobbled pen at the back empty of porkers. Mr Ng stood with a police officer by the wooden door, but what was going on had nothing to do with the abattoir being illegal: in the whole incident that didn't arise. The police in Singapore were busy people with strict priorities. Two people had fallen, or been pushed, from the top of the old building that had the parasol shop on its ground floor. It had happened in the darkness, but the bodies still lay uncovered, though watched by another policeman with folded arms. Mr Ng was impatient with the time taken by police procedure; he wanted to truck in his pigs, but could hardly do so under the very noses of the authorities.

Gold is very special to the Chinese and my wife had heard of a manufacturing jeweller in Bukit Timah Road who had lovely stuff, and all twenty-two carat or better. We went there in a taxi and, sure enough, the bracelet chains and necklaces were superb, but my wife wasn't the only one to have heard of them and there were whole busloads of people, from all over the world it seemed to me, crowded into a small showroom.

Our friend from Tuttle, North Dakota, seemed the only tourist in Singapore at the time who wasn't there.

After a while I went out and sat on the parapet above the carpark on the shady side. I sweated quietly there and watched an employee from the pottery next door working a pug mill for reconstituted clay. I wished my wife good fortune in finding just the gold chain that she wanted within her budget and I had a sudden foresight that thereafter, whenever she wore it, whenever it was remarked on, I would again be on that parapet in the hot shade, watching the boy working the pug mill. The clay made a glistening cream right up to his elbows. Several times he looked up and smiled; once he raised an arm richly gloved in clay. I felt a whim to explain to him that years before I had lived in the city, worked with Stanley Tan killing and gutting pigs, eaten in the parasol shop, covered the cheerful woman calligrapher with some considerable goodwill myself while her younger child watched with religious solemnity, been taken by the police to see if I could identify the bodies in the street.

Stanley Tan and I had been regulars for the cheap meals at the parasol shop and it was thought that we might recognise the dead men, but we didn't. One man was quite plump and much of his chest and stomach was showing from a shirt completely open at the front. There was no sign of injury, but his body was an odd purple-grey that I recall unpleasantly well. Mr Ng was quite sure that they were gamblers who had brought death on themselves and told the police so.

As we went by taxi to the airport my wife and I talked of what we had done in Singapore, so that we could reach agreement on the things to be considered high points and the incidents of disappointment and bad service that we would retain as criticism. So much experience in between had to be discarded as transient to make room for the next destination. As we talked I half recognised the area through which we moved. Stanley Tan and I had driven out towards Changi sometimes to collect pigs, years before the new airport was built there. We had travelled in an old Bedford truck and usually at night. There had been fish farms down Tampines Road then and the moon and few artificial lights would flick and scud from the heavy surface of one pond after another.

Stanley Tan had a smile that was all in the eyes and in the crinkles around them, while his mouth stayed the same. As we came back past the fish farm pools one night, the crate sides of the Bedford tight with pigs from the small holdings, he told me very dirty jokes that I've forgotten and talked as well about the tigers which his grandfather could remember in the area. 'Forget the lions,' said Stanley. 'Singapore was tiger country and the Chinese owners of the pepper and gambier plantations had no end of trouble getting coolie workers because of the attacks. You, now, has your family given up anyone to the tigers?'

I began to tell my wife about the tigers and the Tans, but the heat, the noise of the many aircraft overhead and our provincial anxiety to do everything right at the airport distracted us and so there wasn't much pleasure in the telling, or the listening. A kind attendant in the flight lounge, though, took a photo of us both. We are standing close together, both in affection and in accordance with subject grouping, and we have smiles fit for a new destination.

CLIVO SUDAMUS IN INO

*S IR N OEL AND Lady Hallibat, Your Worship the mayor,
distinguished guests, members of the board, parents, staff, friends
and students of the school. It is with pleasure that I present to you at
the prizegiving tonight the ninety-seventh annual report of our
school and eleventh since I became principal. In each of these eleven
reports I have been able to be progressively more positive in my
outlook and more convinced by practical achievement that the
objectives of our charter are indeed being realised. Indeed I am
somewhat bewildered as to where one should start to enumerate the
worthwhile things of the past year.*

All down the long field end of the school was a row of
sycamores: huge and fresh with new leaves for summer and
with the trunks healing the names and hieroglyphics carved
there. In autumn the third formers put pins through two of the
winged seeds, fixed them to straws and ran through the
grounds with the straws aloft and the propellers whirling. In
winter the drizzle dripped from the branches on to those loyal
few watching the house rugby, or the larger number watching
the girls' hockey. That odd kid, Pearlman, used one of the
sycamores by the bikesheds as a refuge and even ate his lunch
there, hunched like a sick chook and never looking down, or
answering, when he was shouted at. 'Hey, dorkbrain, you
pulling yourself up there, or what?'

There was this boy from Fiji, but not a Fijian, who had
ringworm so everyone gave him a hard time and a wide berth.
Children are medieval in their attitude to disease, believing
absolutely that it comes from some guilt or deficiency on the

part of the sufferer. Mrs Maslin got Polly to write to the boy from Fiji on behalf of the class when he was away having treatment. Polly, who read her letter to the class before sending it, used the phrase 'quick recovery and return'. She had a broad, smooth face and freckles on her neck and arms; at that time you wouldn't have thought that, by the sixth form, she would have the best tits in the school. Despite Polly's copper-plate letter the ringworm guy didn't come back to class. Someone said that he had died of it all over his body, but it turned out that Reuben Fourgier's father was teaching him at the Tech School. Mrs Maslin said it was to give him a brand new start.

In curricular matters, also, the year has seen advances of far-reaching consequence. For too long that substantial proportion of our seventh form which doesn't find the Bursary exams a realistic goal has nevertheless been obliged to mimic an academic programme, albeit in a watered-down form. This year, largely through the work of a senior studies review committee chaired by Mrs Buchanan, there has been available a fully independent and free-standing system of lifestyle options including such subjects as snorkelling safety, personal hygiene and the supervision of under twos.

It was in the old cadets' prefab by the cricket pavilion that Bruce Hilton used to do Heather Posswillow fourth period on a Thursday when he had a study and she was excused PE. It went on for almost a term and then Bruce went back to the farm because his father had an accident and Heather never let anyone else touch her. Bruce said that she never made a sound, but used to stroke his hair and let her tears slide on to the dusty floor. Trevor Belleknowles claimed the old prefab after that. He told Gobbo that he thought that there should be a place set aside for intellectual pursuits and that he intended to set up a sixth form poetry and debating society. A non-institutional venue was needed, said Trevor, and a committee of participating students only. Gobbo was almost beside himself with joy; as HOD English he saw it as one of those groups set up by precocious, literary boys in English public schools. He imagined a flattering mention for himself in the school magazine, perhaps even a quiet approbation from the principal. He had the caretaker take out most of the old Hun figure targets and put a padlock on the door. Trevor Belleknowles was given a key.

Confucius would have been proud of the importance Trevor placed on ritual. At the very first meeting Trevor carved the words 'plaisir d'amour' on the spot where he was adamant Heather Posswillow had been regularly laid and he said that on no account was anyone to sit there, or anything be placed there. His first act of poetic leadership was to declare 'Posswillow' an esoteric synonym for great joy and success. It was a Posswillow, for instance, when Laurie Schoone was selected in the under eighteen reps; a Posswillow when Trevor himself was first equal with Debbie Naylor in the senior speech cup. The topic was 'That Youth is More Than a Preparation for Adulthood'.

As well as Trevor and Laurie Schoone there were others who came with some regularity — Dave Hiakai, Peter Mulholland, Garrick Browne, Vince Kidson-Clarke and Carlos Valera. Debbie Naylor, and Bridget Judkin with the birthmark, came a few times, but it didn't really work out. They were better at poetry and debating than any of the others, but sexual tension is bad for intellectual concentration and besides, the dean of sixth form girls demanded visiting rights. In a large co-ed school privacy is an even more valuable commodity than the opportunity for contact with the other sex. Trevor and the rest found that having a mixed group created too much unhealthy interest among staff and students who had no real commitment to the life of the mind. The Posswillow group were very generous in the amount of time they allowed in their lives for sex, but the meetings in the old target shed were not part of it.

While it may be true perhaps that, in a narrow statistical profile, the results of the school's representative teams differ from some other years, staff concerned are adamant that the level of participation and the physical and character benefits remain fully as high as at any other time. Of individual highlights I have only time to read briefly from the coach's report on the under fourteen girls' softball team and mention the latest national triumphs of Sarah Innes.

Well away from the main entrance to the school were two rows of rather apologetic prefabs that had been brought in as a temporary measure forty years before and survived to see off some of the permanent buildings. They had new concrete ramp approaches and pipe retainers in case some pupil in a wheelchair should find it necessary to take a class there. Even with new ramps the prefabs and the activities they housed were low in the pecking order. There were the counsellors' rooms, a home room for the special fifth form known as potato palace, departmental resource rooms, the two rooms for the new horticulture course, with a dangerous chemicals igloo close behind them. The oldest prefab was fittingly the home of Museum and Archives — there was a name board above the door.

Museum and Archives was the brain child of Dr Mark Chester, who had two years as a teacher of history and social studies before being diagnosed as clinically depressed and becoming a voluntary patient at Happy Glades. After he left no one bothered about the pin board displays of old school photographs, the uniform collection, the 1911 school reports on Violet Maude Anderson donated by her family. Starlings got in and shat on 4L's papier mâché relief map of the local region and the campaign medals of a former deputy principal. Miss Proctor had such a success with *Jesus Christ Superstar* that she was allowed to store the scenery flats in Museum and Archives and begin claiming the room with the spider's silk of drama. So empires wax and wane.

The computer suites, on the other hand, were at the front of the school and very much on the circuit when dignitaries were taken around the school by Bomber, or the senior mistress. The showpiece was Room 10 Com with 24 EMG 486DX Slimlines on display and a commercial laser printer named TITAN at ease on the back bench. So much gleaming and obedient technology, so much nett worth and investment. How their keeper, Skunk Wilkins, wished he could spend all his time alone with them and barricade the room against the little bastards who had no reverence at all.

Yet wasn't there something still to be discovered about those flickering screens. Dave Hiakai was coming back from athletics practice one afternoon when he found Miss Prentice blacked out by the door to her gym office where she'd been putting the sports programme on disk. Completely out the monk, he said, and making a snoring sound. He put his track suit top under her head, went for help and the next week had to go up on stage at school assembly to be congratulated by Bomber. Trevor Belleknowles reckoned that because of that Dave was a shoo-in for head boy the next year.

There used to be this school gala once a year to raise funds for some special project and each class was expected to come up with a money winner of its own. Most of the stalls were on the playing fields down by the sycamores, and for days beforehand the only work that mattered, or was accomplished, was for the gala. It became the excuse for everything except drunkenness and pregnancy, and teachers were played off endlessly one against the other. There had to be a selection committee, of course, otherwise every class would just set up a dunking seat for staff and prefects. Some teachers hated the commercialism and showed it, some just hated it, some found in it an opportunity for achievement or status denied them in the usual run of things. Hippo McCullers could paint a parent's portrait in sixty seconds, although despised for the rest of the year as the worst teacher of economics in the school and the heaviest sweater. The principal suffered the day with steely cheerfulness, being dunked to cataclysmic applause on the hour, every hour, as he had agreed. The shouts of 'bombs away' became extended to 'Bomber away'.

The school has remained fully and competently staffed. The considerable turnover I take to be a reflection of the eagerness with which other schools seek the services of teachers who have proved themselves here. It is with special sadness, however, that I remind you of the sudden resignation of Mr Grimsby. Mr Grimsby was hoping to reach the round thirty years of service next year but the term two explosion in the new lab deprived us of his services. To our friend and colleague Lyall Grimsby we say, get well soon, the lab is always waiting for you.

The school cafeteria, with its heavy wooden shutters, was a single-storey, weatherboard extension of the science block. At least once a term it was broken into and the shutters were tattooed by the remains of old padlock plates. The place was robbed blind every day from within as well, the student cafeteria assistants being notoriously well fed and corrupt. They were regarded with both contempt and envy: contempt for the obsequious sacrifice of their breaks and lunchtimes, envy for the clutch of jelly babies their pockets always held and the pies they guzzled. The nominal adult suzerain was Snoz Bailey, a six foot three retired postal worker with lenses in his glasses so thick that his eyes loomed into blurred view like tropical fish in a round bowl. Snoz would peer helplessly over everyone's heads and intone 'Keep in line. Keep in line, that's the way', while the contemptuous plunder went on around him.

One day in August, just before the end of term, there was this hell of a hail storm, which dinted cars belonging to the staff. The hailstones blocked the gutterings and the water flowed down the inside walls of the Home Ec rooms. It must have got into the wiring and Jenny Lyttles, who was the brighter one of twins, was electrocuted. Carlos Valera's sister said Jenny went to turn a heater on and there was just a cracking sound and Jenny going back with a sort of cough.

One year, the gala funds were used to create a senior common room by renovating the old boiler house. Aluminium 'greenhouse' extensions were created and sixty felt and corduroy bean bags provided as modern seating on the polished wooden floor. The seventh form invented a game called Crappo and within four weeks had torn the bean bags to shreds and done seventeen hundred dollars worth of damage to the light fittings. Brenda Neumann invented Crappo, but Bomber blamed the boys exclusively and banned them from the common room, leaving the girls to sunbathe in the extensions with their skirts pulled up.

Brenda Neumann was an immensely strong girl who didn't play any sport, but liked to fight. She had a go at Vince Kidson-Clarke for what she said was staring and split his lip, but finally Eddie Rines settled her hash after a senior dance. It was difficult to know whether to regard him as a hero or a villain, but Brenda didn't go looking for fights with seventh form males after that. Probably Eddie wouldn't have waded into her if he hadn't had several brandies in the carpark. Brenda was a very odd person, but everyone thought she took it well considering; she stopped the blood with her gown and went quietly home without any parents, or staff, even realising what had happened.

The new art teacher was called Tits Wilson for two points in her favour and also to distinguish her from Flat Wilson who was a biologist. Tits Wilson had the idea of painting a mural on the blank end of the new boiler house. It was part of what she termed socialising the environment and she won the support of the senior mistress, despite the opposition of Hippo McCullers who was peeved that he had neither thought of the idea himself, nor been invited to help. The seventh form practical art class seemed to get right behind the project and came up with a Bruegelesque design for a scene of the school grounds at lunchtime. The mural was immensely popular when finished and only gradually did the staff realise that many of the figures in the middle distance had an element of caricature. There they were for those in the know — Skunk, Bomber, Hippo and Gobbo, Tits and Flat Wilson, Hermit Muldrew, Squeaky Klein, Babyface, Hotshot, Gazoo, Zambesi Joe and Mightymouse — fixed immutably on the boiler house wall in shorts, or tartan skirts.

No report on the school's activities would be complete without mention of the tremendous input and contribution made by parents and friends. This assistance is forthcoming in a formal way through the Activity Supervision Society headed this year by Mr Ted Blaines and the Gala and Fund-raising Committee chaired by Ms Pamela Hobbes-Furness. Parental interest is also obvious by the number of impromptu visits that I and the administrative team receive and while we are grateful for this direct access to parental opinion I do take the opportunity to remind you of the procedure for making appointments as set out in Newsletter Number 13 of September this year.

The geography of the school had all the socio-political characteristics of a city. There was a central business area — a downtown — and places of lingering decay; there were upwardly mobile zones and ghettos and shunting yards where authority rarely went. The school pool in winter was a gangsterland of fear, power, alternative allegiance and revenge. A theatre of cruelty and a stamping ground of club-footed ego. Hidden by high walls, the baths lay well away from the main school traffic ways; the changing room locks were only apparently secure and so within was litter of plastic bags that stank of glue, of butts with more complex aromas, of rats ends of food, of clothes discarded, of starlings bludgeoned to death. It was a point of honour with Rainbow Johnson and his friends never to use the lavatories, but to shit beside them on the floor. Occasionally there were gladiatorial fights on the concrete, bayed about by a quick crowd; more often, Rainbow and his mates slipped furtively within and set up sentries so that various transactions and carnal investigations would go undisturbed. It was a small, fierce, mutant kingdom that others were happy to forget.

Summer was a different story. The PE teachers motivated their swimming classes with the example of Sarah Innes and during lunchtimes and after school kids honey-potted from the high board and churned the water in games of polo. Sarah Innes was a prodigy so glittering that she was beyond the envy of her own generation. Because of her dawn practices with her coach at the civic pool, she never started classes until ten and from each national, or pan-Pacific, tournament she would return with medals to display from the stage of the assembly hall while Bomber smiled proprietarily and stepped back. She addressed the junior staff as equals and thought the whole world amiable because it was so — to her.

Between the two old labs in the Underwood Block was a little room called the prep cubby; never a place in which homework was done, but once a chemical storage and demonstration preparation area. The senior master, who was noted for his sense of ironic euphemism, set up an envoy centre there: two pupils each day rostered from the school roll to act as messengers for the school administration. Maybe someone had to run over and get Cordelia Jarvis from Hippo's 5c economics because her brother was murdered for a few dollars while backpacking in Brazil; maybe someone had to find the caretaker because of flooding in the loos; maybe Flat Wilson had to be summoned to Bomber's office because of a parent there claiming victimisation.

Most students liked the novelty of being envoys in the old prep room. When not in motion they were expected to work, but they didn't. They rummaged in the old sets of biology texts and the *National Geographics*, they squirted water from the oddly slender and arched taps above the old science sinks, they talked and as they talked carved 'Wanker' and 'Chaos Rules OK' into the dark stained bench. Friendships, feuds, limericks and romances were begun there. Essie Fairburn, who later became a member of parliament, met her husband in the prep room. She fell in love with his brown forearms and dark eyebrows as he slept amid the stacks of biology texts and she ran all the messages for two hours so that he wouldn't be disturbed. Garrick Browne, on his day as envoy, made the decision to try for a career in professional tennis. It struck him as he was coming back from taking a change of staff meeting time around the prefabs and saw Sarah Innes arrive at school in a taxi and stroll towards the senior common room. Two years later he won a sports scholarship to Nebraska and no one ever heard of him again.

Jake Revell was unfortunate enough to be both good at schoolwork and useless at games. This made him unimportant among the boys and because he wasn't sexy he was unimportant among the girls. He had one virtue, however, which established his right to an existence — he could hold his breath longer than anyone else in the school. It wasn't just that he held it longer, but much, much longer. While Jake was at school, holding your breath under water became an unofficial event at the swimming sports just before lunch, and after all the other contestants had burst to the surface, ugly Jake remained beneath holding on to a grille cover and with his image strangely refracted and twisting. Even Sarah Innes couldn't take him on at breath holding. Maybe after he left school he lost even that opportunity of making any name for himself and had to be content with being a dentist, or an accountant.

Our roll this year, I am pleased to say, has been maintained on a par with the last two, but this has been achieved only with the most vigorous and entrepreneurial action and at some cost to our budget for class activities and minor maintenance. I am especially grateful to those parents who boarded the Guatemalan students during their brief stay with us and exceedingly disappointed with the inflexibility of immigration authorities which resulted in the loss of those same students.

Bridget Judkin, who went to the debating and poetry society for a while, was best friends with Rae Hurinui and Katherine O'Houlihan and they used to sit together on the fire escapes at the back of the drama theatrette and listen to pop music, even though transistors weren't allowed. If they saw Brenda Neumann coming they would get up slowly and wander off talking, as if they were going anyway and not giving up a prime spot because they feared familiarity almost as much as confrontation. Bridget Judkin was famous for a scornful wit she had developed as a result of the birthmark on her neck, but Brenda Neumann was impervious to either scorn or wit; bone on bone was the only form of contention she knew.

It was Katherine O'Houlihan who was going with Ninja Michaels, halfback for the firsts, but she dumped him when he had some sort of seizure during the theatresports final and vomited on the school stage. You never knew when it might happen again, she said, and maybe it was contagious. Katherine had an almost photographic memory for formulae and definitions — her mark in School Cert chemistry was 97 — but her dream was to be a rock singer. In her first year at university she married a bald-headed triathlete from Cairns who had come over for the Coast to Coast.

There was a kind of foyer where you had to wait if you were sent for by Bomber, or Pongo the deputy principal, or either of the SMs. Rainbow Johnson spent most of his school days there, picking his nose, scratching his crotch, sneering at anyone who passed, and taking as much wear out of the mushroom carpet as he could. There were two cherry red leather chairs there for adults: students were supposed to use the tubular class ones. It was an old joke to leave any new kids sitting on red leather as they waited outside the offices. The blood would come up in Pongo's face to match the colour of the chairs. On the foyer walls were photos of ebullient ex-pupils who had gone on to fame and groups of staff who stared out of the greyness of history with the bitter futility of performing bears.

Between the great sycamores and the boundary was a sloping bank which, in late summer, gave both shade and a view of the main playing field. The seniors possessed it in the breaks, loose groups and straggles, the occasional huddle; combinations of utter lassitude and sudden, convulsive energy. Ninja challenged others to a sprint quite free of fits, lovely Polly Lee sat to talk to Reuben Fourgier, Eddie Rines and Dave Hiakai and Peter Mulholland argued about the best university, Heather Posswillow lay dreaming, Jake sat holding his breath, Bridget Judkin said something outrageous and made Essie and Debbie laugh. Trevor Belleknowles shared with Carlos his omened conviction that he would either die early, or become a great courtroom lawyer. The sycamores undulated in the breeze and the third formers spiked the seed heads to make propellers and ran whirling and shouting, never realising what lay before them.

Gathered here together as an educational community — which most of us, I hope, think of more as a family — we have another opportunity to dedicate ourselves to the tolerance, co-operation, pursuit of excellence and consideration for the needs and feelings of others which have characterised the school's life during the past year and which exemplify the school motto that students have striven for over so many years — Clivo Sudamus in Ino. That concludes my report and now I invite you to join in singing the school song, United Set We Forth.

FLUTE AND CHANCE

RABBER WAS, LIKE ourselves, something of a smart-arse and lived, though not by choice, in an all-male flat on the steepest street in the world. He was beginning that year a PhD thesis on nasal wind instruments in traditional Pacific communities and most days he carefully descended the steepest street in the world in crêpe-soled shoes and walked down North East Valley and through the gardens into Castle Street. That was his most direct route to the anthropology department at the university. Rabber liked to see the ducks in the park and the rose gardens out in summer. He was rather dapper, with a cloth cap and a briefcase. In the department he shared a small room on the south side with three other post-graduate students. They had a phone and their own extension number.

After a tough day, Rabber decided to amuse himself with non sequiturs on his way home. He had spent several hours reading catalogue printouts from the Pacific collections at two Australian museums and had failed to turn up even one Melanesian single-stop resonance conch nose flute. He needed a diversion. The departmental secretary saw him on his way from the south side. All agreed that she was a lovely woman and unjustly afflicted with a broken marriage and a son who would never make anything of himself. 'Oh, Rabber, there's a note from computers.' Rabber pirouetted in the corridor, his briefcase extended. He swayed his head back towards the entrance to her office.

'Leap year is a propitious time for alpine cheeses,' he said.

On the bank past the staff club a group of Japanese

clustered to take photos of the clock tower on the other side of the stream. Rabber climbed a modest stone wall and gestured to them with exaggerated familiarity. Several, including the interpreter, came towards him. They were bowed down with cameras. 'Pardon?' said the interpreter, though Rabber had said nothing.

'Who rescues the tiger from the pit?' whispered Rabber.

In Castle Street, Rabber came across a student from his stage one tutorial group. 'Hi,' he said. She was a large girl from the Rai Valley near Blenheim. Everything about her was smooth and copious except the short spikes of her hair — 'Hi,' she said — and her conversation.

'Prorogation is rarely an easy constitutional option,' Rabber told her. He looked into her face and raised his eyebrows as a sign he expected a response. She shrugged the backpack uneasily, lifted her smooth face to the sky in a simulation of thought. From that pose she was able to take several steps backwards, turn with her face still full to the sky and escape without meeting Rabber's eye. He had a recollection of the sides of the Rai Valley clothed with pig fern and he imagined his student standing there, her smooth bulk rising from the green and brown of the fern and her eyes fixed on the blue heavens.

Rabber crossed the footbridge and began his walk through the gardens. There were great trees bearing name tags on their chests and lowly, but more colourful, beds of annuals welling up from the lawns. But Rabber knew better than to leave the path because the grass was mined with duck shit.

Two men by the hothouses were putting up netting to keep the ducks from an assault on flowers already bruised purple. One man was pale and old, with all the weight of him seemingly slumped to the swollen, grey gardening boots he wore. The other man was young and had his overalls folded down to his waist so that his square, brown chest was in the sun. Rabber examined the netting of the roll. 'In the Devonian period,' he said, 'the brachiopod was a prevalent mollusc.'

Both men stopped work as Rabber spoke. A conversation was preferable to hammering the waratahs and attaching the netting. 'Nothing that the Hubble telescope descried was conclusive proof that after the big bang the galaxies condensed from the outside in, or the inside out,' Rabber told them.

'Well, hell, you got me there, mate, I must say,' said the young man.

Rabber left the gardens by the main gates and entered the supermarket, which was among the shops at the mouth of North East Valley. There were one or two things he needed for the flat. The checkout girl had a very long, sinuous neck, and a very small, even-featured head. She looked like a white swan in a company smock. 'Have a good day,' she said.

'Despite its name, the arum lily isn't a true lily. Not in strict botanical terms it's not. The floozie of the funeral parlours is really *Zantedeschia*,' said Rabber.

'Eh?'

'The secret of humour is irrationality. That's why sex is so amusing,' said Rabber. The white swan arched her neck away.

The supermarket bag was a handy counterpoise to his briefcase, and Rabber strolled up the North East Valley. He had only another two or three years of research into the place of nasal wind instruments in traditional Pacific societies and then the world would be his oyster.

Ahead, Rabber saw some sort of stooping misfit in a long coat of blue cloth despite the sun, and heels scuffed away. As he drew level with the man, Rabber was aware of a smell compounded of soot, sweat, steam, silverside sandwiches and leather. 'The Jesuits were founded in 1534 by St Ignatius,' said Rabber blithely. 'Not a lot of people know that, or care.'

'Precisely,' said the misfit eagerly, turning his face to see and be seen. Rabber had half expected a dingy beard, but the man's tight, narrow face had the gun-metal shine that is imparted only by a cut-throat razor. 'Precisely.'

'A Barsac though, eh?' murmured Rabber. 'A child of the true and noble rot.'

'My words exactly,' said the misfit. He put his left hand into an inside pocket, produced and unfolded a cut-throat razor, rested the blade below Rabber's jawline. No doubt it was the razor that had given him such a smooth complexion himself. With his other hand he assumed a fond grip on Rabber's arm not far above the briefcase.

'Whoa. Now hang on,' said Rabber, but the misfit kept them both walking up the North East Valley.

'The darkest blood flows back to the heart,' the misfit said. 'You and I talk the same language, amigo.'

Rabber and the misfit were exactly in step: Rabber made sure of it for that way the blade had the least pressure at his throat. The North East Valley seemed remarkably quiet. There were just two uniformed schoolgirls who passed engrossed in their own shrieking conversation. Rabber made a quick prayer in which he gave God carte blanche over his life in return for its continuation.

'Lucifer doesn't need an arsehole. Can you work that one out?' said the misfit. He guided them round a left turn and down two blocks to where the houses ended at the Lindsay Stream and a hill thick with trees rose beyond it. Across a small bridge a dirt track led to a wooden farmhouse high above. 'No kingfisher here today,' said the misfit. 'Ah, what burning colour has old *Alcedinidae*.'

'Now look here,' said Rabber weakly. The misfit jostled him down the bank and motioned beneath the bridge with the cut-throat razor. 'I've nothing against you,' said Rabber. The motion was repeated more insistently, closer to his face. Rabber waded beneath the planks and stooped there, still holding the briefcase and the supermarket bag. The misfit hunkered down on the grass alongside, undoing all the buttons of his long, blue coat so that he wasn't constricted. He had no shirt underneath, just a tight, leather jerkin, and the hair of his chest showed between the buttons. Rabber began to shiver, though the water wasn't inordinately cold.

'I saw a pig stuck under there once,' said the misfit. 'In the flood and all jammed in with branches and that. It had started to swell.' He leant forward and tugged gently at the shopping bag until Rabber released his grip. The misfit held the ivory handle of the cut-throat razor in his mouth while he looked through Rabber's purchases. He put a tin of marmalade and a packet of Oddfellow mints in the pocket of his coat; the five other things he guided into the stream. He took the razor from his mouth. 'You would have hated my Aunt Rosie,' he said. 'The bitch gave me fruit for Christmas presents.'

The misfit leant forward again and patiently prodded Rabber with the cut-throat until they had exchanged the empty plastic shopping bag for the briefcase. Rabber had sunk somewhat in the slush beneath the small bridge. The water was up to his groin, and his head free of the underside of the wooden planks stained with asphalt from above. The misfit let all of Rabber's papers float away, but he was delighted with the two-stop West Irian nose flute that Rabber's thesis supervisor had lent him two days before. Still on his haunches, the misfit held the flute aloft and said, 'See with this sceptre I absolve you.' He then turned the razor very close to Rabber's face so that, even beneath the bridge, Rabber could see the white glint of the blade. 'Bow your head,' the misfit said and he cut Rabber vertically on both cheeks. Rabber hunched, pulling his chin down to protect his throat. The cuts were very thin and the blood came almost unwillingly.

The misfit stood up and buttoned his coat. He folded the razor and put it away. 'Justice is a privilege,' he said. Not for a moment was the nose flute a mystery to him; it was almost as if he had reclaimed something of his own. He put the flute to his tight, clean-shaven, gun-metal face and walked back to the North Road, playing a few exploratory notes. Rabber came cautiously from under the bridge and put his head above the bank to make sure that the misfit was really on his way. The two cuts on his cheeks were narrow, but brilliant in the last of the sun, glistening as did his tears. The misfit didn't look back.

THE BIRTHDAY BOY

THE WOODEN HOUSE on the corner had been built for a successful grocer, long dead and with no later generations remaining. The big house had all the chapters of a slow decline and was eventually divided into three flats so that the place became a mixture of cheap, ad hoc alterations and solid, original carpentry. Gazz and Vicky had four rooms at the front of the house; three were self-contained, but to reach their bathroom they crossed the communal hall with its central strip of raddled carpet, flanking floorboards of mahogany stain, and the dim, green-yellow glow from the front door leadlights.

Gazz was sleeping in the mid-morning. A pink sheet was held across the window with drawing pins. The corner nearest to the bed was often used by Gazz as a napkin. He didn't snore, but lay very quietly with a damp patch by his mouth and the scar showing in the hairs of his left eyebrow. There was a tartan rug over the wall side of him. The other side was naked apart from his blue underpants. A thin, hairy leg, an arm with no tattoos, a soft stomach, one nipple in the straggling hair of his chest. Gazz was thirty-seven years old that very day, but he'd forgotten it and no one else would jog his memory with a celebration.

His eyes opened quite suddenly; nothing else changed as a result. Gazz lay just the same except that he took in what he could see of the room. There was someone knocking on the front door, but Gazz was neither interested, nor alarmed. He knew there would never be any good news, that any of his few acquaintances would come again, that Vicky had her own key. It would be the landlord, or a man about starting your life anew with Christ, or a kid selling chocolate eggs out of season.

When Gazz sat up, his clothes were to hand where he had left them on the floor. It took him forty seconds to put them on and to run his fingers through his hair. He then stood by the side of the window, pulled the sheet back a little with one hand, picked his nose with the other. The twitch was almost up to the window sill; the chestnut that the grocer had imagined one day shading his entrance was a broad stump; a large japonica, though, made a blaze of pink. None of these things was of the slightest interest to Gazz.

Vicky came up the path. Her head was like a pear, heavy cheeks and chin towards the bottom of it. A fine, big, white arse, though, when he could get the clothes off it. Their eyes met without message as she passed.

'So you're up at last,' said Vicky.

'Yeah.'

'No joy with dorkface down there. He won't give any credit.'

'Shit.'

'I had to use more rent money.'

'Shit.' Gazz screwed his face right up for a moment as if he had a belly pain. He made a hissing sound through his teeth. 'Shit, another week behind. Any fags?' Vicky offered him the packet she had already opened.

'Maybe if you went back to Gabites Plywood and told them that you're not sick any more. You're just so slack.'

'Someone was hammering on the bloody door before. That prick for the rent, I reckon.'

Gazz went from the bedroom, across the hall to the bathroom. Further down the hall, Turtle was about to go into his door.

'Morning, Gazz.'

'Yeah.'

Gazz left the bathroom door open so that if he spoke up,

Vicky and he could keep talking. He washed his face with his fingers and cold water, brushed his teeth without paste.

'Hey, don't you use my bloody brush,' said Vicky.

'Eh?' said Gazz, as he did just that.

'Do you want to eat soon?' she called.

'What time is it?'

'After eleven.'

'I don't mind.'

'What?'

'I don't care.'

'Eh?'

Gazz turned the water off with a sudden wrench. 'I don't bloody care,' he shouted.

'Well, fuck you too.'

Gazz stood in the hall for a time after he left the bathroom. He listened, then moved through the diminishing green-yellow light towards the back of the house where Turtle and the Tierneys had their flats. He listened at Turtle's door, then the Tierneys'. The Tierneys had external access to their larger flat through the back door, but sometimes they left their hall door unlocked and Gazz could get down on some fags, a few dollars, or a bit of booze. Enough to be useful without stirring up the Tierneys too much. He listened and decided they were at work. He tried the handle. 'Shit.'

He went back into the bedroom and took his electric shaver from the water-stained and lifting walnut veneer of the duchess. He could hear Vicky in the kitchen, so he had a quick flick around the room in search of her cigarettes. 'Shit.' Gazz left the bedroom, eternally darkened by the pink sheet, and went through into the kitchen, which was half an original room with a particle board partition between it and the Tierneys' kitchen. Less plumbing and electrics that way. Gazz stood behind Vicky to shave; he could see a sufficient reflection of his face in that part of the microwave front not covered with insulating tape. Vicky was heating a spring roll. He stretched the thumb and fingers of his left hand apart so that he could get a grip of her backside through the leather skirt. It seemed a long time since he had last had that big arse.

'Bugger off.'

'Come on, Vick. Just a quick one.' Gazz put his other hand, with the razor still buzzing, around her waist and pulled her back.

'No,' she said. 'I've had a shower and I'm not going to work this afternoon all smelly.'

'Aw, come on, Vick.'

'Bugger off.' Taking his hand from her waist, she took her spring roll from the microwave, sat down at the laminated table by the window and cleared some space for her plate. Gazz was left with his reflection and his shaver.

'I might have one of those,' he said later. She told him to make sure that there was one left for her at night. 'So how long you going to be?' he asked.

'I've got three hours' cleaning at the Richmond. Maybe four at the most, Tracey says.'

'Where's that?'

'By the hospital, Tracey says. Used to be called Aspern, Aspen, something.'

'So you'll be back pretty early.'

'Yeah, I guess so,' said Vicky. 'What about you?'

'I might see if the guys in the mart want a hand. Humping stuff off the trucks.'

Vicky was idly looking at the newspapers in front of her, but then it was as if she remembered some decision that applied immediately. 'Yeah,' she said and put down her fork to concentrate. Her face was made up for the day: blue eye shadow, heavy powder over her orange peel complexion. Her gloss lipstick was worn away by eating, except at the corners of her mouth. 'Yeah. It's getting pretty shitty around here without even the rent money,' she said. 'It's not on, really.'

'All right,' said Gazz.

'You reckoned you were happy to pay the rent and share all the other stuff — food and that. You were dead keen then.'

'So I've been short. Jesus, no need to make a thing about it.'

'It's just getting all shitty, that's all I'm saying.'

Tracey leant on the horn when Vicky was touching up her face and Gazz looked out of the window to check. 'It's that Tracey,' he said. Vicky took her clutch purse and went down the hall, through the leadlighted front door, down the concrete path that was tilted to the side among the weeds because of subsidence over the many years since the grocer's death. The noon sun glinted on the chrome buckles of her leather skirt and her solid leg muscles showed as she went warily over the camber. Gazz watched her from the top of the path by the door; Tracey watched her from the car.

'See you then,' said Gazz as she went further away.

'Haven't you ditched that loser yet?' said Tracey as she came closer. 'Has he got a feather on the end of it, or bloody something?' It was the direct humour that Vicky liked about working with Tracey.

'Don't tempt me,' she said. 'I've just been giving him a bloody razz-up.'

Gazz stayed outside in the sun while he finished the last cigarette Vicky had given him. He took in the smoke with a very long breath and then allowed it to ease out. He looked over the rank lawn, the chestnut stump, the coral of the japonica, the section of fence that had come down. 'Well, shit,' he said mildly to himself. The smoke drifted with his breath as he spoke.

When he went inside, Gazz continued down the hall to Turtle's. Turtle had been quite a successful commercial artist until he developed arthritis. With the loss of his one talent he went quickly downhill, but Gazz found that he always seemed to have a few dollars stashed away.

'It's me. Gazz,' he said after knocking. He could hear soft noises. 'Hey, Turtle.' The noises became even softer. 'Open the bloody door, Turt. I know you're in there.'

'What is it?' Turtle's voice came from so close, just behind the door. He must have been standing right there with his face to the wood.

'Let us in,' said Gazz. 'I've got to go to town soon — to work.' Turtle didn't answer, but Gazz could hear him unhooking the safety lock.

Turtle didn't have a hell of a lot going for him once he couldn't draw. He was into his sixties, small, fat, a very slow mover and with a few freckles so big on his pasty face that they were like birthmarks. He once told Gazz that he'd spent a fortune on gold injections. Turtle tried to make up for his delay in opening the door by swaying, smiling, offering coffee.

'Nah,' said Gazz. 'The thing is, see, I need a few bucks to tide me over until the eagle shits.'

'I saw Vicky going off somewhere.' Turtle looked at the vinyl furniture in his living room. It was a tidy room, but not a clean one. He knew that neither changing the subject, nor avoiding Gazz's eyes, would save his money.

'She's got a few hours' work on.' Gazz knew that Turtle was soft on Vicky, that he talked to her when he had a chance, that he would wait with his door ajar for her to walk across the hall in knickers and a top. It was pathetic, wasn't it.

'Aw, come on, Turtle. You won't miss a twenty for a day or two. You can come
in later for a drink. I'm late as it is.'

Turtle went through to his bedroom and drew the door behind him. Gazz listened to the slow, soft noises there, imagining Turtle getting the money. Turtle was pretty much a creep, but he had his uses. When Turtle came back he held the twenty out as if he were surprised to discover it and could think of no better use for it than subsidising Gazz. 'Hey, I hope I can help out a friend,' said Turtle, with his voice jollied up.

'Good on you,' said Gazz. 'Well, things to do.'

Gazz walked in the sun for fifteen minutes to reach the Norfolk Hotel, but he thought of nothing around him as he walked, remembered nothing of it, assumed it the same as all the other times he had walked there to save drinking money. He had no curiosity concerning people who walked or drove by, no expectation of recognition. He wore soiled, white sports shoes that were copies of a good brand and a hip-length grey jacket with a black plastic cat hanging from the zip. He spat occasionally, without any shame to make him look around before doing so.

Gazz was known to the barman in the Oakleaves Bar of the Norfolk. Not that the barman could remember Gazz's name, but he knew the combination of grey jacket and the scar over Gazz's left eye. 'How you going?' he asked.

'Getting by,' said Gazz.

'That's the ticket.'

'Yeah.'

'Keeping you busy?'

'So, so,' said Gazz.

He took his jug to a blue-topped stool by one of the windows that had a striped awning outside. He passed Norman Rouse, who had worked with him for several weeks on the Parks and Reserves gardening staff. Neither appreciated the other sufficiently to give up his solitude. Gazz settled down to spend his afternoon the best way he knew how. He took a mouthful of his bitter, letting it flush into his cheeks and eddy in his mouth. He looked around the bar to see if anyone had left the day's paper on a stool or table.

Two hours later Gazz stood at the back door of the Norfolk after coming from the lavatory. He enjoyed the sun on his face. He gave a long yawn without raising a hand to his mouth and so his slightly yellow side teeth and the dark line of fillings on his lower back ones were plain. He adjusted his trousers at the crotch, moving his cock to the left as he preferred.

A tall man in a brown suit was leaving his Camry in the carpark. When he put the keys into his coat pocket the tag still hung outside so that when he pulled the coat at the front and jerked his shoulders for comfort before walking away the keys flipped from his pocket to the ground. Gazz saw the quick glint of them, but he made no sound, or movement. His yawn continued to close. He stood by the door and watched the tall man walk through the archway and into Gordon Street.

When the carpark had been quiet for a full minute, Gazz walked over to the Camry, picked up the keys and let himself in. He drove slowly into Gordon Street and then Marsden Road. From there he drove to the old cemetery and parked inside the gates long enough to check the back seat and the boot — only two packets of photocopy paper and a cake mixer with a repair ticket from Nimrod Electrics. Gazz headed into Riverside until he reached the panelbeating shop at the far end of the service lane behind the bakery. He parked the car behind a Telstar that had suffered a nasty frontal.

Gazz walked across the oil-stained gravel to the main building and looked at the two men working there. He didn't know them and they didn't know him, so he went around the side of the building to a tin, tilt-door garage that served as an office. Bernie Thompson was sorting through files in a carton that had once held twenty-four 190 gram packets of Nacho Style Corn Chips. It took Bernie a while to remember Gazz, but then he smiled and said, 'Gazz. How's things, Gazz?'

'I've got a Camry I don't need.'

Bernie became very matter of fact, very business-like. He pushed the Nacho carton aside and came out with Gazz and they walked over behind the Ford to look at the car. Bernie assessed it for a full thirty seconds, then he said, 'Nice car.'

'It's yours for five.'

'Come off it, Gazz.'

'Four on the fucken knocker, or I'm off,' said Gazz. 'You know that's fair.'

'It's a nice car,' said Bernie. 'One thing is, we got to get it away pronto and then I'll bring the money. You know I don't have four thou here.'

'Yeah, okay,' said Gazz. He gave Bernie the keys and then went and sat in the garage office. He had no curiosity about Bernie's business; just sat quietly on the office chair and heard the considerable noise that Bernie's two men were making in the panel shop. Bernie Thompson was back in twenty minutes so Gazz took his envelope of money, walked out of the service lane and began looking for a taxi rank. It was well under an hour since he had left the hotel carpark. 'Well bugger me,' he said as he walked. 'How about that.' A little imagination started up in him as happened in the few times he scored. Money provided options in his life.

When Vicky returned from the Richmond — opened the front door, entered the green-yellow world of that long hall — she could hear Gazz and Turtle laughing. Turtle's laugh was infectious, eager and appeasing at the same time. Gazz's laugh was harsh, short, almost as if he were jeering at himself and all else beside. Both of them had been into the hard stuff. Gazz had an impressive collection on the living room table, including two bottles of gin, which was Vicky's favourite. 'What's all this then?' she said.

'I came across this guy at the mart who owed me a few hundred,' said Gazz. 'I'd just about given up on it.'

Vicky hadn't much enjoyed four hours of cleaning rooms at the Richmond. She was in the mood for welcome news and relaxation. She let Turtle pour her a really stiff one as an opener before she went through and changed her shoes. She had cleared the letter box and still carried the bundle in her hand. She dealt the pieces quickly like cards on to the duchess. Supermarket coupons, householder circulars, pre-paid donation envelopes from Corso and the blind, a flyer concerning the Mad Mitch Show in the RSA Hall, a civic explanation of the new refuse scheme, a photocopied slip to let them know that Partietime home caterers was under new management. 'Jesus.'

'What?' said Gazz from the other room.

'Just once. Just once I'd like to get a friggin personal letter. Just once a bloody letter asking how I was and that. Is that so much?'

'Turtle'll write you a letter. Won't you Turt?'

'Sure, if you like.' For a small, soft guy, Turtle could put away a fair bit. Maybe he calculated it the only way he was likely to recoup the money that Gazz chiselled out of him. Vicky, too, drank as if there were a pot of gold at the end of it, but Gazz was steady, persistent, as though it were just the best way he could find to pass the time. By summer nightfall the three of them were kicking up a fair din. Turtle was attempting a falsetto for 'Bridge Over Troubled Water' when the Tierneys banged on the kitchen partition. Gazz went through and beat on the wall with a pan, yelled 'Shut your fucken hole' seven times. There was no more trouble after that.

Turtle became quite talkative. He kept drinking although he was soon brimful of it: his eyes swam, his lips gleamed wetly, as did his pale face with its great, blotched freckles. Vicky encouraged him to describe some of the odd-ball characters he'd come across in the boarding houses. A woman who had an imaginary husband and did both voices, even arguments. A retired gold miner who was caught having sex with a pony. Vicky straddled the sofa arm and shrieked. Gazz wondered how Turtle could remember it all, but his reaction was not admiration, only derision. What was the point of anything once it was done with? Turtle's shirt ends had come out the way they usually did; something to do with his belly. They hung outside the green corduroys that he wore even in summer.

Gazz interrupted their laughter. 'Hey, Turtle. I'd say it's about time for a feed.'

'Sure. You're right.' Turtle was reminded not to get above himself.

'That outfit closes at ten, that's all. You don't mind getting some greasies, do you?'

'Right,' said Turtle. 'May I have your order, madam?'

'Why don't you bloody go?' Vicky asked Gazz.

'I don't mind, but Turtle's got a bike. Haven't you, mate? You want to see Turt on that bike. Fucken hell. He's up and down like a whore's drawers.'

Turtle gave an appreciative and lengthy laugh and tried to tuck his shirt in. He wiped his damp face with his hands as he worked out with the others what to buy, then he went into the hall and down to his own room.

'Give him some money,' said Vicky.

'He's into my grog, isn't he?'

'Stop being a tight-arse and give him the money. He shouldn't pay for us.'

'Yeah, okay,' said Gazz. He had a particular reason for wanting Vicky friendly while Turtle was away. He walked down to Turtle's hall door. Turtle had assumed that he was alone and so hadn't fully closed the bedroom door. From the hall doorway, looking across the living room, Gazz could see all of the bedhead and chest of drawers and Turtle wasn't in sight. The soft noise of Turtle retrieving money came from the other end of the room. Gazz stepped back into the hall and didn't show himself until Turtle was on the way out. He walked with Turtle to the front door, stood on the darkening verandah while Turtle unlocked the chain from his wheel. 'No need to rip your guts getting back,' said Gazz. 'Know what I mean?' Turtle wheeled his bike away on the concrete path. Gazz couldn't make out his expression in the dark.

Vicky wasn't all that ready to fall in with Gazz's plans, even though she kept the gin bottle busy and allowed Gazz to have his hand between her broad thighs in a companionable sort of way. Gazz tried to push her back on the sofa. 'Get off,' she said languidly.

'Aw, come on, Vick.'

'We can have it in bed later on, for Christ's sake.'

'Aw, come on.'

'Turtle will be back in a minute.'

'So what,' said Gazz. He wished that he'd never invited Turtle anyway. He was just an old sod. No use at all.

'Yeah, you'd get a buzz out of that, wouldn't you? Turtle coming back and seeing us. Well, forget it. Did you give him some money?'

'Yeah,' said Gazz. He made the most of feeling her up and drew her head onto his shoulder with the other hand, but he felt irritation not tenderness. And Vicky had used some sort of hair spray that was unpleasant on his cheek and left a smell that reminded him of the floral air freshener in the staff cafeteria at Gabites Plywood.

'We'll be able to pay some of the back rent, won't we?' said Vicky.

'I suppose so,' said Gazz.

Turtle was something of a gentleman and made a noise coming in the door and down the hall. He looked sillier than usual, with his corduroys tucked into very short, white socks. 'My hero,' said Vicky and she went into the kitchen to fetch plates and tomato sauce.

'Good one,' said Gazz. He noticed that Turtle put his keys on the mantelpiece of the walled-up fireplace before sorting the food. Gazz handed the second gin bottle to Turtle. 'Get some of this down you while it lasts,' he said.

It was Vicky's habit to become girlish when drunk, giggling and pretending to be shocked by behaviour that she'd exceeded for years. Not that there was anything to shock her about Gazz and Turtle. Gazz drank slowly, saying less and less; Turtle was the reverse on both counts. Vicky and Turtle had a butting contest on the sofa. After the first bout or two, Turtle caught Gazz's eye before starting again, but Gazz gave no sign that he cared. 'Playing silly buggers,' he said. The scar above his eye seemed accentuated by the drinking and he tipped his head right back to blow smoke at the single light bulb. Turtle began to sing 'Lili Marlene'. He said his father had been an artillery colonel in the war. Vicky joined in, her voice high, penetrating and unmusical.

Vicky was the first to fall asleep and Turtle pretended to be, because he wanted to stay there on the sofa with his face pushed close to her chest. Gazz went quietly into their bedroom and packed the best of his stuff into the large duffle bag he used instead of a case. When he came out again he could tell that Turtle was really asleep, because his head had rolled out from Vicky's breast a little and his breathing was wheezy. His worn, but oddly boyish face had a sweat of drunkenness on it and his shirt was rucked up to expose the tunnel of his belly button in the roll of his stomach. Vicky slept with a fatuous but good-humoured smile on the large pear of her face. Gazz could stare at their unprotected faces, which seemed in relaxation to be lumpish, functionally organic — like a head of cauliflower, or a canker on the bole of a cherry tree. 'Completely out the monk,' said Gazz softly to himself and he made a noise in his nose that sounded like a succession of sniffs, but was a reduced laugh.

Gazz took Turtle's keys from the mantelpiece and closed the door behind himself as he went into the hall. The light there was no longer green-yellow, but almost grey from the one small bulb at the Tierneys' end. Gazz unlocked Turtle's door and went through to the bedroom. It was drab, but tidy, with just one large Toulouse Lautrec poster as a sign of any other life that Turtle may have had. Gazz knew which end to search, even though it appeared unlikely. There was only a two-bar cabinet heater and Gazz soon found the envelope hidden in the back. He counted at least seven hundred dollars. 'Cunning old bugger,' said Gazz. His tone was half admiration, half contempt. He added Turtle's notes to his own and was so intrigued by the bulk he had in the wallet that he squeezed it several times to feel the wad expand again within the leather. 'Shit,' he said.

On his way to the front door, Gazz didn't check on Turtle and Vicky. He put his duffle bag on his left shoulder and walked carefully down the subsided concrete path past the stump of the grocer's chestnut tree and the japonica blooms that were colourless in the night. He made no pause at the gateway; he marked his departure in no way whatsoever, not even a glance up at the house. He walked steadily away along the dark, quiet street. What reason was there to look back? There were just the two lights showing. The white light from the room where Vicky and Turtle were sleeping and the pink light through the sheet pinned over the bedroom window.

A LATE RUN

'SPRUIKER?' CALLED THE attendant. No one moved, or replied, and the man looked at the slip of paper again. His lips shaped the name to check pronunciation. 'Spruiker?' he said more coarsely.

Reece Spruiker had been watching through the foyer window as a southerly came up. There'd be a fair blow and cold rain as the front moved through. 'That's me,' he said. It was no longer of any real concern to him what the weather did.

'Well, come on, come on.' The attendant took Spruiker's two suitcases that showed cardboard through the wear on their cheap mottled surfaces. He carried them to the mini-van and slid the door open for them and the old man who followed.

'Now, Mr Spruiker,' said the attendant loudly. 'I'll put you on at the depot, right, and your daughter will meet you in Dunedin. Right? Don't wander off at any stop in between except for a quick piss.'

'I know all that.'

'Then why have you been in the bin?'

The attendant didn't find a park close to the depot and had to carry both cases a fair way. 'Jesus,' he said. 'What you got in here? You murdered somebody or something?'

'Not lately,' said Spruiker.

The attendant didn't feel any need to wait around until the bus left. 'Remember you stay put until Dunedin,' he said and leant forward for the next few words. 'Watch yourself, you old prick,' he said.

'Soft bugger,' replied Spruiker. He waited to make sure that his suitcases were loaded, then climbed into the bus and took a seat as far back as possible.

Some faces are as if carved from soap — sanitised, opaque, all of a part. Others are wonderfully physical, animalistic even, with veins, sprouting hair, blemishes, folds and stains, gleams of linings and liquids and the stench of life. Spruiker's head would look at home on the body of a goat. He watched a woman board who must have been barely forty. She had excellent tits, but instead of taking pride in them her expression was one of discontent.

As the bus journeyed south into the evening, Reece Spruiker watched the farmland and assessed the crops and stock without being aware that he did it. An old man is mainly conditioning. Only the thistles were green in the dry, autumn paddocks. Eventually he could see no more than his own reflection in the dark window. He had been accustomed to sit on the step of his hut at Erewhon in the evenings with a beer and his dog, watching the shadows close in on the Rangitata headwaters, but a new owner can't be expected to inherit goodwill towards an old shepherd who's well past it. Spruiker saw no reason for self-pity in that, or in the fact that, out of five children, only his eldest daughter could be bothered with him. He hadn't gone out of his way for them and expected nothing in return. You had to be prepared to take in life what you dished out.

June and Keith were waiting for him and took him home to the small, weatherboard cottage by the old Caversham shops.

'Is any other stuff coming down?' asked June.

'I sold the dogs,' he said.

'Just two cases then,' said Keith, 'and June was wondering where we'd put a load of stuff. Jesus! Good on you.' Keith put the cases in the small, south-facing room. It had a high ceiling and a built-in dark varnished wardrobe with leadlight glass in the door to the hat compartment. Tricky, bubbled paper gave the walls a strange sinuosity.

'A pretty flash place,' said Spruiker, and meant it. He could even catch sight of trees on the hill above the motorway.

'You can't be knocking about by yourself at your age, Dad. You can't do for yourself for ever.' June didn't mention the memory problems he had, the hospital assessment. Spruiker had forgotten all about it.

He wasn't any great trouble, both June and Keith were quick to say that. She did grit her teeth when she heard him spitting phlegm into the basin and she had to raid his room to get clothes for the wash. He was good at preparing vegetables, doing shopping for her, taking in the washing by four during the winter when she was still at work. Mostly he walked, often down to the various grounds to watch sports teams practising — any sport. Also he liked television; mainly sport again, but also films that often had women's legs and breasts bared for him.

Apart from money for a beer in the evening, he gave his modest universal super to June. In his own odd, selfish way he was a proud man and, faced with the realisation that he might live a good while longer and not be able to maintain his independence, he wondered if he might end up being a nuisance to the only one of his children who didn't treat him with the same cheerful disregard with which he had treated them. Maybe his physical toughness would rebound on him in the end, if the mental side went first. There were special homes, he knew, which charged hundreds a week.

'Dad's always gone his own way. You know that,' Alec had said. 'Tough as old rope.'

'He never interfered; that was the good thing,' Margie had said.

'The bad thing was that he never cared.'

'He wouldn't thank you for doing anything for him. Not a bit of it,' Nigel had said. 'Old people set in their ways are best left alone. I read this article on it somewhere.'

'I've got commitments closer to home, that's for sure,' Louise had said.

But June reckoned that, with nowhere to go and being seventy, her Dad needed some help, at least until the latest memory problem sorted itself out. Keith was very fond of his own parents. He could see that June needed to make something of an effort.

'I'm fine. I'm fine,' said Spruiker. 'Jesus, I've looked after myself all my life just about.'

Of the five children, June had the fewest resources to assist her father. Nigel was actually rich, but was cautious about admitting it. June worked in a bakery and Keith did part time in the Civic Information Centre, after suffering a breakdown while teaching.

Quite often Keith had time to sit with his father-in-law during the day and watch television, or endeavour to keep up with him as he walked about the city. Keith held no grudge that Spruiker hadn't bothered to give June and him a wedding present years before, though his own parents were very different. He rather enjoyed the old guy's earthy directness, his contempt for his fellows, his emotional reticence.

In the spring a veterans' athletic series from America was shown on afternoon television. Wrinkled people with necks full of tendons, taking themselves seriously in a whole range of events. Some of them were has-beens who couldn't give up gracefully; some were never-beens who found that they could foot it at the end of their lives. Spruiker laughed until his eyes watered at such people making goats of themselves; rejoicing in twilight victories and medal ceremonies; confiding in the interviewers as to their training programmes; sporting their monogrammed gear and warm-up exercises. 'What a load of wankers,' he told Keith. 'A bunch of bloody nellies.'

He stopped laughing when Keith pointed out to him the size of the crowds there to watch and the size of the cash purses. 'It's a fad thing in America at present,' said Keith. 'Something to do with their determination to empower the old and enhance their sociological profile. And money's no problem over there, you know.'

'How much did that old coot get for winning the hurdles?' asked Spruiker.

'Fifteen thousand dollars US. Nearer thirty in our money.'

'Eh!' said Spruiker incredulously.

'Nearly thirty thousand dollars. And that's a regional meet.'

'Jesus George! What about that spindly, hatchet-faced bint who won the long women's race?'

'I think it said not all that much less.'

Spruiker watched the series with less contempt after that. He was amazed that there was a market for all those old people aping the athletics of excellence. He asked Keith to keep a record of the winning fifteen hundred metres times.

'Why, do you think you'll have a go?'

'Don't you tell any bugger.' Spruiker was quite sensitive to ridicule, although he didn't show it.

'There's no money in veterans' athletics here anyway,' said Keith.

'Never you mind.'

On a September Sunday morning when the sun was bright, but without heat, old Spruiker asked Keith to go with him down to the Caversham Oval. 'Don't say anything to any bugger, not even June. I'm not going to be made a laughing stock. Has your watch got a second hand?' Spruiker carried a cheap and new pair of tennis shoes in a supermarket bag. 'I haven't the skills for the specialist events,' he told Keith, 'but I reckon I can run as fast as those old bastards there on the television.'

'I think you underestimate them.'

'I was mustering until just a few years ago,' said Spruiker. 'I've never smoked. I've had years and years of high-country air, not like those poor city buggers. And I haven't talked, shagged, boozed, or molly-coddled myself into weakness.'

There wasn't anyone else at the Oval and that suited Spruiker just fine. He put on the tennis shoes and tucked his trouser cuffs into his grey socks. He took off his green woollen jersey to reveal a grey workshirt with a blue stain at the pocket where a biro had burst. He spat on the ground where the track was marked and lifted his arms rather awkwardly a few times as a suggestion of limbering up exercises. He was of only average height and he was thin, ugly and seventy years old. He had lines so deep running from both sides of his nose and down past his mouth that his face seemed to have been put together in segments. Years of sun had created a blossom of small cancers on his weathered skin. 'Say go when you're ready,' he told Keith, who tried not to smile. 'Four times around. That's what you said?'

'That's right.'

'Okay then,' said Spruiker.

'Get set, go,' said Keith. He made a show for the old guy by looking keenly at the watch. Spruiker kept his arms low while he ran and his shoulders turned from side to side in what seemed to Keith a poor action. Spruiker's knees didn't come up far either, but he had a surprisingly long stride. He ran round the Caversham Oval four times without any apparent variation in pace, or action, and when he'd finished he'd come within nine seconds of the man from Wabash, Indiana, who had won fifteen thousand dollars at the regional veterans' meet at Tulsa.

'Jesus,' said Keith. 'Jesus, Reece, you did just fine. But maybe I made some cock-up with the watch.'

'No,' said Spruiker. 'As soon as I saw those old pricks on the telly I knew I'd do almost as well. All my life I've had good wind. For years and years I was the top beat musterer on every station I worked on. I reckon there's an opportunity to take some easy money from those soft American buggers who've got so much of it they'll spend it watching geriatrics rupturing themselves.'

'It's not a bad idea, I suppose.'

'It's got to be done in the next year or two, though,' said Spruiker. He put his jersey on again, replaced the tennis shoes in the plastic bag. Keith waited in the cool sun. A tall woman with imperiously piled grey hair was walking a King Charles spaniel that was sorely in need of exercise. A young guy, cutting across the Oval, had stopped to comb his hair, using the club house window as a mirror. Keith knew that Spruiker was most comfortable when coming out with things in his own way and his own time.

'The first reason,' said Spruiker, 'is that I'm seventy. I'll be among the youngest in the seventy to seventy-five age group. That's a real plus, I reckon. You can go down hill bloody quick at my age. The other thing is that the old grey matter is getting a bit dicey. I could be making chicken noises to myself in the corner any time now.'

Keith and Spruiker talked a good deal about the first point on their way home. The other thing was never mentioned between them again.

'Maybe,' said Keith to June that night, for, as a good husband he told his wife everything in secret, 'maybe your Dad's really on to something.'

'One way and another he's been running all his life,' she said.

Keith, who considered that his teaching experience fitted him for both tasks, became coach and manager. As coach he insisted that Spruiker buy some first-rate running shoes; as manager he corresponded with the United States Pan Veterans' Athletics Association and boned up on all the rules and requirements. He began to read a good many books about motivation and metabolism and budget travel, which increased his confidence, but had no other benefit.

Spruiker ran three afternoons a week — around the Oval if it was free, or into the hill suburbs. June pretended to know nothing about it; Keith paced him on the bike if it was road work. 'There's no hills on those athletic tracks,' he said.

'Hills are good for your wind,' said Spruiker. And he enjoyed seeing his son-in-law suffer a bit.

The television series was long over, but Keith was getting all the meet times sent out to him. He even built up files on the most consistent fifteen hundred metre winners and the nature of the different venues. 'Yours is a glamour event,' he told the old guy. 'Top prizes for it.'

Within three months Spruiker was recording times that would have put him in the money if he were running in the States. Keith had spent a lot of time talking to him also about tactics and motivation. 'Visualise yourself passing Dan Swarfest of Shadow Man Falls, Montana; visualise yourself breasting the tape,' he told his father-in-law. Spruiker never bothered to answer. He did agree, however, that he should have the best steak twice a week, and his legs massaged regularly by Mrs Drummhagen who lived next door and used to be a district nurse.

Keith and Spruiker had a meeting after a tea of curried sausages one night. Spruiker said that it was time to go to the States and take some money from the Americans. June pretended to be surprised by the project, but she and Keith had already decided that it was worth while backing the old guy to have a go. What else did he have? June said. It would take all of Spruiker's small savings and the bulk of June's and Keith's. 'I'll win enough to set us up nicely, to more than pay my way in the family, but I don't want anyone getting wind of it. You understand. If anyone asks, it's just a holiday.' Spruiker never overcame a certain self-consciousness, almost shame, about the whole thing. A lot of silly old people flogging themselves in games, taking their laughable performances seriously.

Keith and Spruiker flew to Los Angeles on a Big Top from Christchurch. Spruiker first ran at a qualifying race at the Wachumpba spring festival in Fresno. His first prize barely covered expenses, but enabled him to enter the Pan Veteran indoor event at Sac City, Iowa. He came fourth in the final because he was elbowed in the face at the final turn, but it was a lesson learned. He was never less than third in the thirteen regional meets he competed in after that. He won at Savannah, Lubback, Seattle, St Cloud, Saratoga Springs and Troy in Alabama and was a close second to Dan Swarfest in the national final of the United States Pan Veterans' Athletics fifteen hundred metres at Glameen Park, Chicago. He received 40,000 dollars and a citation and his name was entered on a copper plaque above the members' cocktail bar at Glameen Park, between that of Dan Swarfest and Wesley Boist Smith, who was third.

Keith was amazed and grateful and interested in all around him. He wanted Spruiker to take it easier, to see something of the country and the people while they had the opportunity, but his father-in-law saw it all as a vast sham that might collapse at any minute. Spruiker insisted they stay in modest motels and the only friend he made was a seventy-six-year-old ex-miner from West Virginia who was doing all right in the hammer throw. They used to watch blue movies and drink Hills pinball beer together after the meets.

One week after Glameen Park, in unit nineteen of the Saddle Sore Motels on the east side of Beaumont, Texas, Reece Spruiker told Keith that it was time to get out, time for a reckoning.

'One of my legs is going,' said Spruiker, 'and I'm fed up with the people. I reckon I've done my dash.' From the motel window they could see a group of young hoods trashing cars in the park of the El Pecho Diner and Bar. The neons were starting to brighten in the dusk. 'What have we got clear?' he asked Keith. 'What can we get back home with?'

Keith got out the laptop that he had purchased from their winnings for managerial purposes. 'In the vicinity of one two five New Zealand,' he said.

'What vicinity? How much clear when we're back home?'

'I'd say 126,000 dollars,' said Keith.

'Half for June and half for me,' said Spruiker. Keith assumed charitably that June and himself were seen as indivisible. 'And I don't want any bugger to know more than he needs to.'

In Caversham Spruiker slipped back into his pre-athletic role as if all the rest had never happened. He was happier, though, because he was certain that he wasn't beholden to any bugger, that he wasn't a drag on his daughter. Nothing that the rest of the family could bitch about. He let Keith keep his last pair of expensive running shoes in case his son-in-law developed talent in old age himself. Spruiker reduced his exercise to walking again, watched a lot of television, drank rather more beer — all the same sort of things as before. But he decided that he needed to keep on with the massages from Mrs Drummhagen and just occasionally came out with a turn of phrase which betrayed his American career and friendship with the West Virginian. Like when he told the plumber that the new bath was as smooth as a prom queen's thigh.

If anyone ever bothered to ask him what was the best thing he'd managed in his life, he always recalled the time he and Buck had won the Canterbury Huntaway Championship at the Windwhistle dog trials. That dog could walk on water, he said.

COMING HOME
IN THE DARK

Windswept to a bowl of peerless blue, the sky arched above it all; not oppressive on the landscape, but rather an insistent suction that offered to remove everything into the endless, spun abstraction. The lake had a chop on its milk green opaqueness. The mountains of black and white rose up ahead. There was a fixed intensity in the delineation of shapes and colours; no compromise, no merging.

'We'll see Cook again soon, I think,' said Hoaggie.

'It's the boys' first time up here,' said Jill.

'So it is, and it should be a view today that they'll remember. I hope that all their lives they can think back to this trip — their first sight of Mount Cook.'

'I wish we were going to ski, though,' said Mark.

At the head of Lake Pukaki was the flat outwash of the glaciers and the cold, braided streams milky with rock flour. Hoaggie noticed how the sun caught and glittered from surfaces and turns of the water as he drove. For a selfish moment he was without family, and felt a pack on his back, boots on his feet, and heard the skirl of the wind on the rock faces.

Jill was telling the boys what the Hermitage was like, based on somewhat hazy recollection of a visit well before she and Hoaggie had shifted to Auckland. Her sons were more interested in the outside opportunities of the place. 'Well, make sure you don't lose anything today. We can't come back. Check your stuff.' She didn't believe in having the twins dressed the same. She said the modern thinking was to encourage a natural growth of separate identity. Both the boys wore linen shorts, but Mark had a jersey and light, suede boots, while Gordon had a ribbed, blue jacket and sneakers. Gordon had more to say, but Mark was more stubborn.

They passed Bush Creek and Hoaggie recalled for his wife a climb that he and Tony Bede made to the saddle from there. He experienced as he talked a quick reprise of the euphoria of youth, but had no words to articulate it. They passed Fred's Creek and saw a Mercedes abandoned on its side in a ditch of stones.

'Look at that. Yeah, wipeout,' enthused Gordon. He and Mark scrabbled to see more from the back window as they went on.

'Someone overdid it there,' said Hoaggie.

'And can't have had any help for miles,' said Jill.

'You remember when Bruce Trueno broke down on the Desert Road last Christmas and when he came back with the tow-truck he found the wheels stolen.'

The outwash was mainly an expanse of shingle, but those parts not recently swept by the channels had rough pasture and matagouri, briar, clumped lichens. Beef cattle were feeding by the road. There was oddity in the sight, because of the close proximity, although distinct by altitude, of ice and snow and screes. The inside of the car was more comfortable still: the sun warmed it and the breeze was excluded.

'Moira wants to nominate me as the Regional Arts Council rep on the Grants Board,' said Jill.

'Who better if you've got the time. Go for it.' Hoaggie was always gratified when his wife proved her competence in her own right. Successful himself, he felt no threat from the achievement of others. He realised also, that because of his own focus on work, his wife had given up much of her own time to the family. 'They would be lucky to have someone of your ability,' he said in all sincerity.

'Flatterer.' She rested her hand on his arm. 'You won't say that if you're left to cope when I'm away.'

They came up the final slope to the head of the alpine valley beyond the lake's expanse. Scenery has little intrinsic appeal to the young, but even the twins, accustomed only to the landscape of the North Island, gazed quietly for a few moments at the sheer valley sides, and the towering bulk of Cook and Tasman among their barely less impressive fellows. Then Gordon elbowed his brother. 'Now those suckers are big,' he said.

'I had a talk with Athol Wells at Rotary a while back,' said Hoaggie. 'Did I tell you that?'

'Athol Wells?'

'He's the deputy principal at Westpark. You must remember; I said that maybe he'd have an angle on a school for the boys.'

'I don't want them to go to a boarding school. You know that.'

'Well, neither do I personally. It's what's best for them in the long run though, isn't it?'

'What better environment can you have than your own family?'

'Roddie Sinclair says he's going to Wanganui Collegiate,' put in Gordon.

'Spastic,' said his brother. Hoaggie had almost forgotten that they were in the back. He dropped the subject.

Hoaggie turned off the Hermitage road and on to the track that led them to the area where camping was allowed. He was pleased to see almost as few amenities, as few small climbing tents, as he remembered.

When the family stood on a knoll not far from the car, prepared for their walk up the Hooker Valley towards the glacier, they could see over the way they had come and the end of the road. Hoaggie noted that the Hermitage had been developed a good deal, but even so the view was almost entirely unspoiled. He hadn't been to Cook for more than fourteen years and he refreshed himself with all the defiant angles and peaks, the low alpine vegetation, the mutual touch of bright sun and sweet, cold breeze.

'Come on, come on,' shouted Gordon, and as if it were a consequence almost immediately there was the shivering rumble of an avalanche on Mount Cook, although not on the faces they could see.

'Let's hope no one's under that lot,' said Hoaggie.

'No one would be climbing where that's likely to happen, would they?' asked Jill.

'Sometimes I guess it's just luck.'

The four of them started on the walking track to the Hooker, which wound through the tussock and thorns of the old, heaped moraines. They were out of the breeze from the snowfields for a while and it was pleasantly warm. Jill put her hand on Hoaggie's collar. She ran her nails up and down the back of his neck as they walked behind the twins. 'Maybe you're right,' she said. 'About the secondary school thing.'

'Maybe not,' said Hoaggie. 'What the hell. We can work it out among us all. It's about giving them the right start, isn't it?'

Mark had found a stick, discarded by a previous walker. He flourished it proudly, and Gordon began questing on both sides of the track as they went on, searching for a stick that would restore his equality. They could hear the sound of the swift stream from the little lake at the glacier's snout and the track began to wind over heaped greywacke shingle and boulders.

Below them two other people were climbing up to join the track. The man in the lead was thin and pale; he shrugged his shoulders as he walked. The man behind was immensely solid, the features of his full face seeming indented like those of a snowman. He wore a denim jacket so tight that it pulled his arms back, accentuating the bulge of chest and stomach. Neither of them was old, but men nevertheless, not boys. The big man behind was singing a song from *Phantom of the Opera*, but only the tune was an identification; the words had been replaced by ta and la. The one in front wore a denim top as well, but of a much darker blue against which light stitching stood out. The stoop of his thin shoulders made the sides of the jacket hang below his waist, while the back rode up showing the grubby white of his T-shirt.

Having ta-laed himself to the end of the music of the night as he reached the path ahead of Hoaggie and his family, the big man followed his friend with a gait grown suddenly shambling without a melody. Neither man looked back; neither waved.

Gordon sniggered and was joined by Mark. 'Don't be rude,' said Jill.

'What a geek,' said Gordon, doing a quick, chesty imitation of the man's walk. It was true they seemed unlikely nature lovers.

'It takes all sorts,' said Jill.

The two men were soon lost in the turns of the track through the moraine and when the family reached the swingbridge there was no sign of them. Hoaggie was happy to share the surroundings with no one but his wife and children: he had deliberately planned on being there before the school holidays began and in that had been very loyally supported by Gordon and Mark. Such feelings of exclusivity were selfish, Hoaggie knew, but part of his response to beauty.

There was the small lake among the shingle and boulders at the glacier's end. Etched icebergs floated there, freed from the rocks that covered the ice flow. Some of them had seams of dirt, or stones, some had the flat tints of very old milk. Other ice showed in the banks where the overlay of shingle kept it from the sun. Impressive though it was, Hoaggie knew it to be only the remnant of the ice-age days and he pointed out the ledges and striations hundreds of feet up the valley sides where the great rivers of ice had been thousands of years before. 'Hey, yeah,' said Gordon. 'Next time, Mark and I'll climb up there and roll stuff down.'

They walked for an hour up the Hooker and then sat for a

while before beginning a return. In the clarity of the mountain air the soaring ridges and coruscating sweeps of snow were deceptively near at hand, and even the stunted olearia, hebe and cottonwood where they rested seemed to have a special sharpness of form. Just occasionally they were caught by the edge of a passing breeze and drew their shoulders in for warmth.

On the way back, shortly before the carpark, Hoaggie took a snap of his wife and the twins just below a cairn that commemorated the death of mountaineers many years before. As he lined it up through the viewfinder he had a sudden sense of image within image, of time within time: the shot as it would be with all the others in the album, the wider freeze frame, transient, but stronger just for that instant, showing the four of them together there at the foot of the mountains with the grasses and flowers, the spiked matagouri and the sheen of the great snow slopes in the distance. Hoaggie had no god to pray to, but he offered a sort of prayer nevertheless, which was part gratitude for what he had, and part plea for continuance.

'Take another one and let me hold the stick in it,' called Gordon.

The brown grasses were ungrazed and high as Hoaggie's knee. Where the moraine was exposed the grey stones bore badges of lichens — green, yellow, silver and silver-blue. Some puffed out a little from the rock like the frilled head of a lizard; others were so fine, so delicate, they seemed more like fossils within the rock than anything that grew on its surface. The small white and pink flowers glistened on the humped bushes among the stones, and flies, quick and colourful, were in a euphoria of pollination.

As the family went on to their car and the grassy clearing where camping was allowed, the sounds from the Hermitage carried clearly to them, but subdued in that great natural space. No wind at all in the low clearing, and just a toss of cloud at Cook's summit to show the westerly at work.

The boys wanted to eat at once, but Jill didn't wish to have their picnic near the tents and within sight of the small toilet block. 'There's always red sleeping bags and socks out to air,' she said. 'Always someone with an empty, unpleasant laugh.'

So Hoaggie drove back down the valley just a short distance, and took the turn-off to the Blue Lakes and ventured into the tussock grass along its side. There was a bridge not much further on, and on the high side of that a cluster of alpine beech as a feature in the treeless area around them. Hoaggie nosed the Volvo between two matagouri bushes so that the boot was ideally placed to service a grassy area behind it. Jill took out the tartan rugs and told the twins to sort out a good place without stones. The long, dry stalks held up the rugs at first, but Gordon and Mark rolled over and over on them to crush them flat.

'I hope you checked for any stuff under there,' said Hoaggie.

'You mean poop,' said Gordon delightedly.

'Anything,' said Hoaggie.

'But especially crap,' said Gordon.

'Crap,' repeated Mark.

'That's enough,' said Hoaggie.

Hoaggie and Jill ate on the rugs there, propped on their elbows like Romans, and looking down because of the late-afternoon sun. The boys grappled and snorted through their food, pursued grasshoppers, collected chrysalids, scratched themselves, claimed to see skinks beneath the stones they lifted. Eventually they, too, lay on the rugs, talking in their own close language.

Hoaggie relaxed on his back, his hand across his face as a shield from the sun. He could smell chlorine from the swim a day ago, and the sultanas from the muffin he'd held, and also a scent from the hair on his wrists that had something of tobacco although he didn't smoke.

He was wondering if it was time to consider buying a bach in the Coromandel, and thinking of the joy the twins would have there, when they stopped arguing with each other and in the pause he heard Jill say, 'Hoaggie.' Her voice wasn't loud, but had an odd formality. He took his hand away and squinted up into the sun. Two men were standing close to them, among the briars. The same men that the boys had laughed at on the track.

The big man put on a silly smile when he realised the family were watching, as if he wanted to appear friendly, but had never checked the expression to ensure that it accorded with his intention. He cracked his knuckles and looked at the food on the rugs. The other man was more interested in the twins. He took several long steps to bring himself up to them, and as they sat up he pushed them down again with his foot. Mark still had something of a smile, as though he thought the men might turn out to be part of a joke his father was playing on them, and he didn't want to be too easily taken in. 'Oh, my God,' said Jill. She put her hands to her face. Hoaggie stood up, clumsy after lying in the sun all that time.

'Okay, Tub,' said the thin man in the darker denims, and Tub reached Hoaggie at the same time as Jill stood up to help. Neither Hoaggie nor his wife knew much about hurting people, but Tub did. He ignored Jill, who was tugging at him, and concentrated on pushing Hoaggie back onto the boot of the car and then abruptly breaking his right forearm on the curve of the metal. He slammed it a second time, which caused a great deal more pain, and Hoaggie slumped down by the car. The dry grass rustled as he slid into it, and he crushed a spray of tiny white flowers.

Jill was left pulling at Tub and yet trying to back off at the same time. Tub's large hand encompassed her wrist as a precaution against the latter inclination winning out.

'Mandrake?' he said, in a voice both surprisingly high-pitched and equable.

'Enough of this shit,' said Mandrake. He had a sawn-off .22 and he held it to Gordon's head. 'Now that you know we're the bad guys, no one else needs to get hurt, okay. You there, Dad, you give these kids the message just to lie still.'

'It's okay,' said Hoaggie. 'It's all right, boys. Just lie still.'

'There you go then,' said Mandrake. 'Easy as fucking pie.'

Hoaggie was still slumped in the grass with his back to the side of the car. With the pressure of his hand, Tub made Jill sit down again beside the twins. Only Tub and Mandrake were standing. Tub started eating sultana muffins and neenish tarts from one of Jill's oblong, green containers. Mandrake looked off among the grass and stunted bushes towards the road. 'Just a little, old family picnic here, folks,' he said loudly, and then grinning, and almost at a shout, 'Nothing to see here.' There was no response. The sun was all brilliance in the high, clear air. Mandrake shifted his grip on the rifle so that it hung more comfortably.

A long way off the height of a bus showed itself on the way to the Hermitage, and a pair of paradise duck gave their tuneless call from the flats at the head of the lake. The olearia had fresh and fragrant flowers that glowed like coral amid the leaves and the burnished thorns of matagouri. Cicadas, briefly subdued by the flurry about the car, came back as a chorus. Above everything was the great, sharp angle of Cook with a nightcap of cloud streaming from its peak.

Mandrake jiggled his foot playfully on Gordon's back. 'This is some place,' he said. 'What a strange thing bloody privacy is. We could be a world apart here, yet radio waves are going right through us this very instant, aren't they? Full of ski reports and talkbacks and government promises and music from Memphis, Tennessee. We hear nothing of it at all, though, and they've no idea we're even alive. Things can be so close, yet have no point of contact.'

'My husband's hurt,' said Jill. 'I need to help him.'

'Tub's just broken his arm,' said Mandrake, 'so he doesn't think he's a fucking hero. Take his jacket there and wrap it tightly round his arm. That way it won't jar.'

'He needs a doctor,' she said.

'You play the doctor then,' said Mandrake. 'Go on then. Tub will help you.'

Tub took hold of Jill by her hair in a matter of fact way and forced her around to Hoaggie at the side of the car. Her face looked very young because of the skin being pulled upwards. With his free hand, Tub kept a grip on the muffin box. Jill wrapped the jacket around Hoaggie's broken arm, and while attention was on that, Mandrake shot Mark and Gordon. Mark died almost immediately, with only a bubbling sound and the shaking of his suede boots, but Gordon struggled to get up from beneath Mandrake's foot and called out piercingly, 'Look at this. Look at this,' until he was shot several times. He arched powerfully in his death, and his face had one last primitive, instinctual expression before it relaxed.

The shots were not loud, but sufficient to quiet the cicadas briefly again and startle goldfinches, which fled in an alternating series of violent wing-bursts and dipping glides. The sun flashed on the bright feathers of their head-dress. A patch of tussock fluffed up suddenly in a gust of wind, as an animal's fur rises for an instant in alarm.

Jill was held back by her hair as she tried to reach her sons, calling loudly. Hoaggie tried to move towards them too, but Mandrake stepped to the car and put the short barrel of the .22 into Hoaggie's left eyesocket to push him back. The crudely sawn muzzle made a cut beneath Hoaggie's eyebrow and blood ran, diluted with tears, as a pink wash on his cheek.

'Enough of this shit,' said Mandrake. 'Get into the car. Open the door, Tub, and get them into the car.' When both of them were in the back seat, holding to each other for some comfort, Mandrake reloaded the small magazine of the rifle. 'Go out towards the road and look around,' he told Tub. 'See if anybody's about. Make sure everything's okay.'

'I'm still hungry,' said Tub calmly.

'Better still,' said Mandrake, 'wrap the kids in a rug first and find a place for them somewhere. There's tons of stuff you can eat here when you come back. We won't be leaving until it's pretty much dark.' Tub wrapped the boys in a rug of red tartan and took them away through the high grass and low bushes. He experimented to find the most comfortable carrying position as he went.

'It's actually better for them this way,' said Mandrake at the window. 'Nothing drawn out at all. You know what kids are; as time went on they'd be getting in our way more and more. Jesus yes. Were they twins?' Jill and Hoaggie didn't answer. They hardly heard what he said. 'I reckon they were. I reckon they were twins,' Mandrake said. He checked the fuel gauge at the dash of the Volvo. From the picnic things he took up a wedge of egg and bacon pie and ate it carefully, lifting his lips at each bite so that his teeth were visible.

Mandrake leant on the car in the sunlight while he ate and looked in at Jill and Hoaggie from time to time as if he quite fancied a yarn while they all waited for Tub to come back. 'I don't suppose there's any booze,' he said, partly to himself. He yawned in the sun and ran his free hand over his face as he watched Tub return alone.

The big man settled down very deliberately among the picnic food and began to eat. As he ate one thing, he fossicked for others, saying 'yes' to himself at the most welcome discoveries. He was scrupulous to replace the lids of each container when he'd had enough, in case the bright, darting flies might join the feast.

Jill tried to concentrate on what she had left to love.

'How do you feel, Hoaggie?' she said. He just gazed at her wet face.

'What did she call you?' said Mandrake. 'Speak up.'

'Hoaggie,' he said.

'A special name, is it? Something intimate between husband and wife? Hoaggie, Poaggie, Boaggie.'

'It's short for Hoaganraad. That's my name — Hoaganraad.'

'I like it,' said Mandrake, lifting his head, and his lip to show his upper teeth, in a posture of contemplation and assessment. 'It's friendly and fucking informal. Hoaggie, yes.' His face lifted to the sun again and he shaped the word several times more. 'Wasn't there a Hoagy Carmichael?' he said.

'You may be right,' said Hoaggie. A conversation so unreal was more a blessing than the reverse.

'I am right, old son. A musician, wasn't he? What did he play?' He stooped in to look at Jill. 'Come on, I'm sure you're a bright woman.'

'The trumpet?' she said.

'You may be right,' said Mandrake. 'What do you think, Tub? Is Hoaggie a name that takes your fancy?'

'Sounds like shit to me.' Tub lay on his back amid the picnic things with his arms and legs spread like a starfish. He had a stalk of grass in his mouth and he switched it back and forth with his tongue, or puffed his cheeks and made a succession of small, poofing sounds that caused the stem to tremble. Maybe the poofing sounds had something in them of the music of the night.

'And what sort of a name is Mandrake?' asked Hoaggie. All he wanted was an opportunity to show his contempt. What he saw, though, even as they spoke, was Tub carrying away his sons in the tartan picnic rug.

'I'm a bloody magician, aren't I. It doesn't take all that much with the people I spend my time with.' Mandrake's contempt was equal to Hoaggie's and the object much the same.

'How's your philosophy, old son?' he asked Hoaggie.

'It's not my line,' said Hoaggie. The tears, pink on one side of his face, shone on his skin. He thought of the twins: their affection and abilities, all the opportunities that had been before them. He wondered who would ever find them. He thought of them lying all alone in the coming night.

'The big fucking mistake, Hoaggie, is to imagine that evil and beauty are antithetical. Don't you think? That's where people go wrong despite one experience after another. There's no natural affinity, but no mutual exclusion either. Don't you think, Hoaggie? Anyway, I've pretty much thought that one out to my own satisfaction.'

'What you did to Mark and Gordon. What you did,' cried

Jill. She looked away from him, through the window on the other side, where the thorns of the matagouri and the alpine briar made a lattice against the sky. While mentioning her sons she had thought for a moment that the deaths were contestable, that what had happened could be overturned, then her head and shoulders sagged down.

'There's nothing you could've done,' said Mandrake. 'Nothing to be done now. Just one thing impinging on another as the philosophers tell us. The whole thing is bad luck on your part: just a matter of timing. It's like going out driving, and hitting two, or even three, birds when it hasn't happened for bloody ages, and when you get back and have a look, there they are, packed tight into the grille by the impact.'

'I wish we hadn't come. I wish we hadn't come. I wish we hadn't come.' Her voice was muffled by the seat back, but rising almost to hysteria.

'Shut it,' shouted Mandrake, but almost immediately he was reasonable again. His hand steadied her shoulder through the open window. 'It's best for us all if we do things quietly. A fucking uproar gets nobody anywhere. You've no reason to blame yourself for anything. Take it easy. Bad luck is really just bringing forward what's bound to happen.'

The sun was going down over Cook; different shadows were at play over the rock buttresses, screes and snowfields of the mountains. With the dropping of the sun came an obvious dropping of temperature. The sound of the river became more distinct; the briar and matagouri bushes took on a tinge of purple; the cicadas ceased their song. Tub stood up and tried to pull the sides of his jacket together so that more of his front would be covered. Mandrake still leant on the side of the car. He held the rifle loosely, and partly disguised by the line of his leg. Hoaggie and Jill sat silently in the back seat. Hoaggie cradled his broken arm with the good one and his wife's sobs had subsided to a wide-mouthed, heavy breathing.

'Let's piss off,' said Tub.

'In just a bit,' said Mandrake. 'Better that no one gets a clear look at us on the road.'

'It's got cold.'

'Yeah, but tonight we won't have to be out in it. That's the difference,' said Mandrake. Tub nodded to that. 'I think we should check on the playmates,' said Mandrake, 'to take care of stuff that might get lost.'

'Bloody right,' said Tub.

Mandrake already had the keys; he took Hoaggie's wallet and Jill's handbag with just a motion of the .22 and gave both to Tub, who went through them with the single-minded curiosity occasioned by the unfamiliar. All the money, Tub put in his trouser pocket; something of a struggle because of the tautness of his belly and backside against the cloth. He gave the credit cards to Mandrake, who was saying how he was looking forward to getting back into the city — not the fucking sticks he said. An urgency seized him and he broke off, opened the car door and put the rifle to the back of Jill's head. 'It occurs to me, old son,' he said to Hoaggie, 'that you're just the sort of yuppie bastard to have a cellphone, and just silly enough to keep it hidden.'

'I haven't. We're on holiday, for God's sake. There's nothing at all.' Mandrake looked carefully at him, at the same time lifting the short barrel of the .22 through Jill's fair hair, which parted noiselessly, brushing the metal and falling into place again with its own smooth weight.

'No, of course you haven't,' said Mandrake. 'Silly fucking me, eh. You know, I'm prone to an odd, paranoid notion that people are out to get me. Funny that.' He closed the door again and stood in the last of the light, laughing. Hoaggie and Jill could see only the contrast stitched denim jacket, but they could hear the laugh which was subdued, like that of a panting dog. Tub joined in for a time on a higher and less controlled note.

Mandrake decided that he would do the driving. He had Jill come into the front seat beside him, and Tub sit with

Hoaggie in the back. 'This is a class car,' he said as he nosed from the grasses on to the road. The flat outwash before the lake was becoming an indiscriminate mix of dark evening shades, and only Mount Cook and its fellows were still sharp against a westward edge of sky, ember lit by the sun. 'Tub and I recently had an unfortunate experience with a Mercedes,' he said. 'It was a great car, too, but I don't think we quite had time to get used to it. Eh, Tub?'

'Bummer,' said Tub. He confined Hoaggie to a small portion of the Volvo's generous squab as he settled down to rest. His obvious feeling that neither Hoaggie nor Jill could pose any threat whatsoever increased Hoaggie's sense of helplessness.

For a time, as they drove in the gathering darkness with the steep hills on one side and the leaden expanse of glacier-fed lake on the other, Mandrake quizzed his captives about their lives for information that might be helpful to him. He was disappointed to find they had no home in the South Island. Soon, though, he indulged his fondness for speculative, even intellectual talk. 'You wouldn't know it, but I'm a bugger for the reading. I reckon I would have done all right at university had things been different,' he said, 'but sooner or later the point of every lesson that you can be told about occurs in the course of your life anyway. It's the capacity to see to the core of things, to put aside that fucking self-deceit, that's the important thing. Don't you think?'

'You're a murderer, a senseless bastard,' said Hoaggie. The great, dimly seen platter of Tub's sleeping face was close to his shoulder and the man's breathing had become an adenoidal whine.

'You are a murderer,' said Jill distantly and she wept for the proof of it. Mandrake drove on beside Pukaki, which was assuming a pale luminosity as the mountains around it retreated into darkness.

'As to a bastard,' he said. 'You're right there in any way you like.'

'You're not right in the head,' said Hoaggie. 'Who kills people for the sake of it?'

'I'm on the outside, Hoaggie. Don't you fucking get it? I'm on the outside of this whole thing that the rest of you have got going. Nothing connects me with it except bringing it down. That's all an outsider has, you see. What the books call a negative capability.'

'You'll get caught.'

'Wonderful, Hoaggie, but what's that to me now? Don't you see? I've always been caught, so there's no difference. I'm teaching a few people, and you're one of them, that I'm determined to have all the things I can't claim within your rules. Get it? You never asked me to any dinner party, old son, yet here I am with my hand warmed by your wife's thighs and my heart by this philosophic discussion. Boredom and truth, they're the two things that have done for me. I tend to break down if my life's too flat. Yes, Hoaggie, boredom's a killer and so is truth.'

Mandrake's long, mulish face came alive when he talked, and he was his own best listener. 'I reckon truth is the worst affliction that anyone can have. Most people are shielded by stupidity, convention, or privilege, but I wasn't lucky enough. By the time I was fourteen I was on my own and could see what a fucking, rat-arsed world we've got here and entirely rigged against pricks like me. Everything comes to nothing, Hoaggie, soon enough. Nothing that anyone does ever matters.'

'None of that's an excuse for the things you do. It's pointless, it's horrifying.'

'You know sometimes I horrify myself. Can you believe that?' Mandrake gave his panting laugh. 'But the more you get into it the more you need the kicks. You get so far down the line that there's no way back even if you wanted it. You're fucked one way or another.'

Jill was stiff and quiet, her head turned away from Mandrake and against the glass of the window. Hoaggie wept for a while, the sound of that conjoining within the car with the noise made by sleeping Tub. Hoaggie attempted to adjust the coat twisted as a support for his fractured arm. The Volvo swept on past the lake towards the Tekapo road. 'Did I tell you that Tub and I spent last night in the open?' said Mandrake. 'Well, near enough. Jesus, it got cold. You wouldn't think it at this time of the year so much, but I suppose it's the height and being so far inland.'

They met only one or two other cars in the night. The Volvo headed back towards Tekapo through the desolate Mackenzie country. The lights on full swept the thin avenue of seal before them or, on the bends, caught the barren undulation of the landscape beyond, with not enough vegetation to hide the rabbits that moved there. Just the fierce spaniards made profiles and a few, small pines wind-sown across the stony ground. In the dark felt of the sky hung a gibbous moon and the bright barbs of stars.

Mandrake took his free hand from Jill's leg and marvelled at it all. 'Look how there's light on some of the peaks,' he said. 'White on white until they glow. I wonder if any bastard climbs there at night, do you think. Jesus. I remember, oh years ago, when I spent a few weeks in the Hokianga and some nights, after we'd had a fair bit of shit, we'd row this old dinghy out and just sit and talk and watch the lights of Rawene down the harbour. We'd smoke and lie back, rocked by the swell. It always seems to me that the sky is closer when you're out on the water.'

Jill had begun weeping and to Mandrake it made her less attractive: it also distracted him from his conversation. 'Quit all the blubbing,' he said. 'It gets on my nerves.' But she was past the point of caring even for the things that Mandrake could do.

'Leave her alone,' said Hoaggie.

'All this fucking snivelling,' said Mandrake. 'What's the point.'

They came down past the few shops and the hotel at Tekapo. A brief oasis of lights in the night and the lake like a pale carpet spread into the mountains. Tub woke and said that he wanted to get some booze, but Mandrake said maybe at the next pub, Burke's Pass. 'Jesus,' he said to Jill, 'haven't I been telling you to shut up?' On a long, climbing straight with not a house for miles, he pulled abruptly to the side of the road, cut the lights and, leaving the driver's seat, went round the front of the Volvo and pulled Jill from her place. He held her among the low lupins as a shearer holds a sheep, steadied in a crouch with one hand and a knee. Her crying altered not at all in intensity; without resistance she held any position into which he forced her. Hoaggie managed to get his door open before Tub reacted.

Mandrake shot Jill twice beneath the ear and then Hoaggie once in the flesh of his upper leg. 'Get that prick back inside,' he told Tub, and he rolled Jill through the soft, rustling lupins into the grassed ditch flanking the road. She lay there very low, very relaxed, almost as if she was pressing herself into the scented earth. The noise of her weeping had been with them for so long that the silence which succeeded it was a noticeable release. Mandrake walked back to the driver's side and had a stretch there, his long arms reaching up as if for a hold among the stars. Tub quietly held Hoaggie in the back seat; nothing seemed to disturb the equanimity of the big man's life.

'That's a whole lot better,' said Mandrake. He made himself comfortable in the car and placed the .22 carefully at his feet again. He shrugged his shoulders in the denim jacket as he had done on the track to the Hooker Glacier when Hoaggie had first seen him, and then began driving again up the lonely road through the tussock to the pass. 'Women have a tendency to whine, don't you think, Hoaggie? And besides, I've been quite considerate. The worst thing for you would be to go first, imagining me at play on your wife. Aren't I right?'

'Bugger you,' cried Hoaggie. What else could Mandrake threaten him with once Jill and the boys were dead. 'You're nothing — nothing at all,' he said in a voice that had become almost a whisper again.

'The odd fucking thing is that I can't get it up these days! Your wife's okay for looks. I took to her voice and the way her hair was done, but I can't get it up any more. Some sort of punishment I suppose, Hoaggie, and you'll be pleased to hear that. Yet I can still sleep like a baby.' Mandrake bounced his head on his chest and gave his panting laugh.

'You're nothing,' said Hoaggie harshly. He rocked a bit. 'Jesus,' he said. With his good hand he tried to hold his handkerchief to the wound in his thigh.

'Come on, Hoaggie,' said Mandrake. 'Be a man. No one dies from a fucking .22 in the leg. Most likely you'll hardly even bleed.' At the crest of the pass the lights for a moment pointed up to nothingness and then the car dipped over the highest place and the beam caught again the sealed road, the median white dashes, the treeless hills above.

'Does it look any different out there, Hoaggie, than when you came up? I often think that's the thing, how little connection there is. Indifference, Hoaggie, that's all there is in nature. In a community, a family too I suppose, people can babble on to conceal it, but when you're on your own, when you come down to it, then it stares you in the face if you've any brains at all. No wonder so many people get pissed, or turn to religion.'

'Your apple barrel meditations are rubbish,' said Hoaggie. 'You've killed people for no reason, no reason at all.'

'Well, you're an educated man, Hoaggie. I'm just a fucking bum trying to get some share of the action and make sense of things. But I reckon that I have reasons: it's just that for you they're not good enough.'

'You could've had the money, the car, without hurting any of us.'

'But that's not it, Hoaggie. I want you to see me, to take me seriously. Get it? From time to time I need intelligent conversation. I will have attention paid to me, see?' Mandrake struck the wheel in his vehemence.

Before the Burke's Pass Hotel and the three or four other

buildings, isolated a little higher on the slope, there is a graveyard with wooden gates and a line of oak trees facing the road. Consecrated ground no bigger than three or four urban house sections. Mandrake pulled into the dirt track of the entrance and stopped there. He cut the lights and told Hoaggie that they were going to take a breather. 'Tub will give you a hand,' he said solicitously. 'What with your arm and leg the way they are.'

It seemed very dark at first, as if there was nothing present but themselves, and then, as Hoaggie's eyes adjusted to the absence of the headlights, his surroundings gradually came up before him. First the sky as a sheen with hump-backed moon and a scatter of stars, then the dark but individual masses of the oak trees and the pines on the other boundaries, with a glimmer among them in one quarter from the hotel.

It was a lawn cemetery or, rather, a rough pasture one, with the older monuments at the higher end catching enough light to show the symmetry of their shapes. Mandrake walked in further from the road and Tub took a good deal of Hoaggie's weight as they followed. 'Jesus, what a life you have,' Hoaggie said to him, but Tub just turned his great, flat snowman's face to him and said nothing. Hoaggie felt and heard dry acorns beneath his shoes as he went through the gateway and the night breeze drew through the trees of the cemetery with an easy sigh.

'I could stay here all night talking, just about,' said Mandrake. 'I love the night. It's the other side of the coin, isn't it? People think that it's just some sort of pit that separates one day from another, but there are sights and sounds and smells that exist only then: there's animals and all sorts that have their whole life when most of us are sleeping. It's an alternative, Hoaggie, isn't it, and that's always a good thing. I always feel uneasy when there's only one choice, one way of looking at things.'

Tub had drawn off towards the trees and was having a piss, which cascaded long and loud into the rank grass. It reminded

Mandrake that time was passing. 'The thing is,' he told Hoaggie, 'that Tub's keen to get down to the pub and that's fair enough. He doesn't ask much. He's a fucking natural man and doesn't pretend to love his fellows, but he's very loyal.'

Hoaggie sat down on the cold, concrete bed of one of the graves. His arm ached, his leg ached, but the real anguish was that of loss. It occurred to him, quite without irony, that he would like to read the inscription on the headstone, so he would know his companion for the night. He could see the graves more clearly then, and realised that the night was their natural time — cold and quiet and peaceful. No matter what Mandrake, Tub and Hoaggie could do there, the place was one of serenity. The trees, the old stones, the wrought iron surrounds of some of the oldest plots, caught the more subtle light of the night. Hoaggie was amazed by the coherent detail that formed about him.

Mandrake looked at the shadowed graves with interest. 'Everyone living must be considered an optimist, for they've had the alternative of suicide after all,' he said. 'Hold on to your philosophy, old son. That's the bloody thing to do,' and he lifted the hand which held the sawn off .22 and began the gasping that was his laugh.